THE QUEEN *of the* LEGAL TENDER SALOON

THE
QUEEN *of the*
LEGAL TENDER
SALOON

by EILEEN CLARKE

Greycliff Publishing Company
Helena, Montana

Cover design and painting by Biff Karlyn Studios, Helena, Montana

WHY DON'T YOU LOVE ME, by Hank Williams
© 1950 (Renewed) Acuff-Rose Music, Inc., and Hiriam Music
All Rights Reserved   Used by Permission
WARNER BROS. PUBLICATIONS U.S. INC., Miami, FL 33014

This book is a work of fiction. Names, characters, places, and incidents either are
products of the author's imagination or are used fictiously. Any resemblance to
actual events or locales or persons, living or dead, is entirely coincidental.

04 03 02 01 00 99 98   10 9 8 7 6 5 4 3 2 1

LIBRARY OF CONGRESS PUBLISHER'S CATALOGING-IN-PUBLICATION DATA

Clarke, Eileen
    The Queen of the Legal Tender Saloon / by Eileen Clarke.
        p.   cm.
    ISBN 0-9626663-5-1 (alk. paper)
    I. Title.
    PS35553.L318Q44   1997
    813'.54—dc21
                                                                97-4031
                                                                CIP

For W.H.R.

THE QUEEN *of the* LEGAL TENDER SALOON

ONE

I GREW UP in New York City. Which is not to say I'm one of those street-wise, gum-snapping, pushy broads most tourists remember. My mother's always saying I'm "sweet" like any mother from Iowa would say of her younger daughter, but from my mother's lips it sounds like a handicap, like, "You're blind, but I still love you" or "I don't know how you'll get along with only one leg." Maybe in some ways she's right.

She says I let people use me, like my father did. He was a tall man, handsome, with a large jaw like John Wayne in *The Quiet Man*. I think he always tried to look like that because it was the look of his generation. Just as my mother, especially when she still worked for the phone company out of high school, tried to look like Maureen O'Hara. Those were their dream people.

In one of those old movies his hero ice-skated, or maybe it was what my father thought rich people did—skating in tuxedos around little cafe tables in Switzerland. Anyway, he liked to take his girls, my sister and me, skating on Saturday afternoon. Sometimes he took us to Wollman Memorial Rink in Central Park, and sometimes down on the bumpy natural ice of the Bronx River—to remind us that life was real.

When I was eight and Katherine eleven, he paid for lessons at Rockefeller Center at $10 a half hour—a week's rent in our apartment then—so we could keep up with him. My mother made us matching skating outfits: short, black velvet whirly-skirts with red, black and white dizzy checks for lining, white long sleeve blouses and black velvet bolero jackets. The last lesson, Mom borrowed a movie camera and came down to see us skate graceful circles beneath the golden statue of Atlas. It's still painful for me to watch in my mind's eye: a gawky chicken of a child stuttering around the ice. Katherine looked better, but I knew our father was proud of both of us.

He took us to the Saint Patty's Day Parades, holding us on his shoulders so we could see and buying us hamburgers at the lunch counter on Columbus Circle when the parade was over because that was where he always ate lunch when he worked in the Coliseum, which was more and more as we grew up. In those days, the Coliseum was brand new, built in the early Fifties for the big trade shows, with truck-sized elevators and carpet rolls that could have covered the Grand Canyon. The earliest I remember, my father was one of the men who hung velveteen material in carefully pleated folds around the exhibitor's booths. Red, green, and gold. Then he went to work as a salesman, selling floor space to exhibitors. His office was in the basement of the Coliseum.

My sister and I could come and go as we pleased because we were Mike Holloran's daughters and everybody knew Mike Holloran. New York was different then. An over-protected Irish

Catholic girl could walk almost anywhere alone and be safe. It was a city of immigrant children, people who'd grown up during the Depression and World War II and believed that God was a beneficent being who always rewarded hard and good work.

Mike Holloran had few regrets. One of them was me. Not the person I was—he always had faith that I would still grow up—but that I hadn't finished college. I went one year, and then announced one Sunday afternoon after church, as he sat down to his mug of tea with milk, and peanut butter toast, that I was looking for gainful employment. He saw to it that I found a job in the basement of the Coliseum with his company. In some ways, his regret was mixed with the knowledge that I would be closer for a bit longer, driving to work together every morning and taking lunch at the same lunch counter every day—not growing so much older and smarter than his eighth grade education. That was something he could live with for a time. But then there was the regret he filed away in his top dresser drawer. No college degree I ever earned could have taken that away.

In the top right drawer of his dresser, a shallow drawer designed for keeping small, unimportant flat things, like playing cards and tie-tacks, was a small white envelope in which he kept everything he owned of his father.

There were Grandpa's discharge papers from His Majesty King Edward VII, after the Boer War; homestead papers from a place called Philbrook, Montana, which I could never find on a map; a postcard, "Miles City, Montana, Bucking Horse Sale, 1909," full of cowboys and horses—feet in the air, bodies flying to the ground, twisted and crossed like pickup-sticks—and no message on the back. Grandpa had obviously bought it for himself and carried it back on the train from Montana to New York, as much in love with cowboys as I would be two lifetimes later.

The fourth piece, it was always fourth in the pile, and I made four my lucky number because of it, was a picture postcard of Grandpa in his cowboy clothes: chaps, vest, and white, long-sleeved shirt, like Marshal Dillon or those cowboys in the Bucking Horse postcard, except this was my grandfather. His name appeared in pencil in the space provided below the photo, the lettering almost completely worn off unless you cared enough to hold it at a 45-degree angle to the window: Michael Joseph Holloran. My father's strong chin, my sister Katherine's wide, dark-lashed eyes and that unruly mop of hair that only I inherited. That unruly mop was my mother's nemesis. Every morning before school, as I wiggled under the tugging and pulling, she would tell me that someday when I was a young lady dressing for my prom, I would be grateful that we had taken the time to train my hair properly.

Grandpa had obviously not had the advantages of such careful schooling. His hair took off from his neatly honed part like a jet plane flying into the wild blue yonder. Stacked neatly behind him lay his saddle, his lariat and fringed jacket, with his cowboy hat on top, set down for just the few minutes it would take to snap the photo.

The first time I saw that photo I was five, old enough to write my name, and the first thing I did was sign up for a win-the-pony contest, arguing with my mother that we had plenty of room to keep a pony in our three-room apartment. They were grown small just to fit three-room apartments.

I used to imagine Grandpa sleeping on the ground inside a circle of cow ponies; he could get up and ride any one of them, anytime, anywhere, and not have to obey the Parkchester policemen yelling at us to keep off the grass. He could lie down on the prairie any time he wanted and watch shooting stars without the buildings and streetlights erasing them all. I'd imagine that Grandpa came to our apartment and camped on the living room floor with me to watch "Fury" and "My Friend Flicka" Saturday mornings when my father was working thirty-six hours straight putting in a show at the Coliseum and hadn't come home yet.

While I invented memories, my father only believed in truth. First his mother had died. Then Grandpa died of cancer, leaving Dad and his three sisters to St. Mary's orphanage. He remembered the nuns thought he wasn't bright enough to put through high school and turned him out at fourteen in the middle of the Depression. Each time I asked to look at Grandpa's picture, my father would tell me about his first job, the only job he could get: lookout, he said, for a bunch of lousy-mickrumrunners. He believed that was all one word, all one dirty type of man.

He wouldn't look at Grandpa's cowboy postcard when he took it out of his dresser drawer for me. He'd turn his back and look out our third-floor window, waiting for me to be done, say it was work that made life good, not wandering around gawking, spending your money on phony nonsense. His hands would roll through the change in his pockets like gears turning in a clock.

"When the first Irish came over," he would tell me, "there were still salmon spawning in the Hudson. More jobs than people to work them. A fella could make a living. By the time the old man got done traveling the world, it was all picked over. All used up. He shoulda come sooner, seen what was happening. Then he shoulda stuck. Took care of himself. Worked at one thing instead of gallivanting around. You shouldn't have to work as hard as your aunts did, Evelyn." Auwnts. That was the way he always pronounced it. "It was hard on them," he'd tell me. "Took away their beauty before their time. His fooling."

So Michael Holloran, son, stuck. He worked hard, bought the house on Long Island before he was fifty, saved for his girls' education and on April 10, 1976, died on the floor of the Coliseum, two hours short of the show's opening. One hundred percent his show now: his accounts, his exhibitors, his labor problems. In his suit and tie and his professionally laundered Brooks Brother's shirt. He'd been on his feet eighteen hours trying to beat the deadline, which he thought was okay because he was still thirty-seven hours short of his non-sleep record. No sweat. Except he was suddenly sixty-nine years old. April, 1976.

That was four years after I'd started working for the company and two months before I quit, because hard as the funeral was and as many promises as they made at the company to keep me on, there was a peculiar silence around my desk. No one told a joke around me. No one talked about the work going on on the floors above our heads. The boss took me to lunch once a week and told me stories about my father. What a wonderful man he was, how hard he'd worked to make the company go. There would never be another Mike Holloran. What had once seemed like a perfectly good job, one I could grow with, maybe even become a sales rep, now seemed like a black hole. Mom was only half right. It wasn't that I was letting them use me up. They weren't using me at all. Mike's poor daughter. A nice Catholic Charity wrapped up with pretty pink ribbons of sympathy and support.

One night Mother and I were home alone watching the eleven o'clock news. Dad had always watched for the sports, mother and I for news. None of us ever stayed tuned for the weather. Mother stood up, about to turn it off as the weather maps came on the screen.

"Are you okay?" I asked.

"Sure," she said. "I'm fine."

"I mean about Dad," I said. "I mean, I've been thinking of finding a new job. I've always wanted to go out west."

"Getting bitten by a horse and a terminal case of poison ivy wasn't enough?" she asked.

"That was a stupid nine-year-old at summer camp."

She looked at me. "How are you going to get there?"

"I'll buy a car."

"If your father were alive, he'd buy you an airline ticket."

I thought about that. He would have insisted on the airline ticket. And he would have insisted that someone responsible, him or Mom, maybe Katherine, come out and make sure I got settled properly. With him, there was the wrong way and his way. He planned his own funeral. Six single-spaced typed pages of instructions, down to the container they'd put his ashes in for Mom to take home, sealed in an envelope, in the company safe.

"I want to see where I'm going," I said finally. "You know. Not just the airports, but all the stuff that goes in between. I'd like to take my time at it. There's no place for me in the company anymore."

She knew that. "I'm not surprised, the way they took advantage of your father. The fights they used to have. I wonder, now, if that contributed." She fiddled with the TV knobs, adjusting the color. "When will you leave?"

"I gave notice today. A couple of weeks. But I'll wait— find something else—if you need me to stay."

She shook her head, and sat down on the couch next to me. For a few minutes we both stared at the satellite photos of the Midwest and eastern seaboard—the real West, my cowboy West, still somewhere *out there* sliding off the end of the earth. We watched the clouds move in great thousand-mile jerks across the screen. It was the only light in the living room and threw red and blue shadows across the breakfront and the family photos clustered on the end table. Katherine and me at First Communion. Katherine and me graduating from high school. Katherine graduating from college. Katherine in front of her classroom teaching math. Mom and Dad had gone to her first parent visitation day and were the only parents to take photos. And the drapes behind all of it, that took seven years to have made because Mom wanted purple—bright purple— and Dad had finally settled for orange. Which led to the custom-made orange and red matching love seats. They'd spent their whole lives working hard as hell for a three-bedroom tract house in Franklin Square, Long Island, with a cyclone fence around the yard, a sheltering elm tree and a two-foot-square corner of dirt Mom called her truck garden.

We leaned against each other, holding each other up, and she rubbed my back slowly, quietly. Then she stood up and turned off the TV.

"Call me every night you're on the road."

I nodded.

"Life's too short to live it for someone else, Evelyn."

"You're sure?"

"I'm not exactly helpless," she said and pushed my bangs off my face.

I called home every night, and every night almost said I was turning back the next day. All I saw was flat farmland and burly men in plaid shirts and baseball caps driving their big tractors around and around their neatly fenced fields. Neat little white houses erupting straight out of the flat ground, with neat little beige-haired children and doughy, beige wives riding lawn mowers over perfectly square lawns around perfectly square houses. And all the roads at T square to each other, going absolutely east/west or absolutely north/south. A safe little box of manicured civilization for a thousand miles.

Then I crossed the Missouri River. The neat picket fences

disappeared and were replaced by rusty barbed wire, strung between fence posts that alternated between freshly peeled posts and twisted stumps. Men smiled more. They still wore baseball caps, but instead of chemical fertilizer logos or bank emblems, they proclaimed the virtues of King Rope and Too-Broke Cattle Company. Men became lanky, long Gary Coopers and gap-toothed Slim Pickenses.

Then the fourth day I stopped for lunch out of the picnic cooler Mom had packed with New York cold cuts and good Jewish rye. There was no escaping the wind outside the car. Inside, the prairie sun baked you in five minutes despite the thermometer's alleged fifty-five degrees. I compromised, leaning against the hood of the VW with my face to the wind and sun both, and ate my sandwich. As I scanned the horizon, tiny white pyramids danced in the turquoise sky. I stopped chewing, stood up on the front bumper and tried to shield my eyes from the wind. They were mountains. Brilliant, white-capped mountains. Mirage made them dance. Mirage and 400 more miles of flat, open prairie. It took me another day to be in the middle of those mountains, but once there, I began to look for a place to stop.

That night I called Mom from Missoula, Montana, and told her I had stopped. I'd taken a motel on the east edge of town at dusk, after driving past Missoula once on the interstate, driving into the pine-covered foothills and dirt roads on the other side of town. I pulled off at the next exit, turned around and in ten minutes drove back to the edge of town closest to New York.

"It's a nice place, Mom," I told her. "It has streets, and houses with doors, and everything."

"Okay," she said, but there were enormous doubts in her voice. Doubts that could stand up and be seen 2,300 miles away. I had a few of them myself.

TWO

I SUPPOSE if you drove a hundred miles north of New York City you'd find a town like Missoula. Look for a place that says it has 25,000 people that's more than a hundred miles from the next town of 25,000 people. Then start looking for clean rivers. None of that musty foam or styrofoam quickstop coffee cups floating in the backwaters. Clean. With deer in their red summer coats walking undisturbed across the gravel bar to sip water, and mountains rising 6,000 feet higher than the tallest building. Missoula started out as a trading post: the confluence of five major valleys opening onto a vast, fertile river bottom. The interstate sliced through one of these valleys, ran through the north edge of town and disappeared completely behind a cloud of paper mill smoke. Another valley headed south, home to a string of bedroom communities—

Lolo, Florence, Stevensville, Victor, Hamilton and Grantsdale. If you sat at any stoplight long enough to collect yourself, you would look south to the star of the Bitterroot Mountains, Lolo Peak, 9,075 feet, snow-capped, purple mountain majesty. It was more than twenty miles away, but it towered over the town.

The main industry was logging and logging trucks ruled the road. Whether in town or exploring the valleys surrounding Missoula, I was never far from this symbol of prosperity or my windshield entirely safe from the red-handled screwdrivers all truckers stabbed into the last longest log of their load to hold the red DANGER flag.

I spent two days exploring neighborhoods, then the third day found an apartment south of the river in the oldest residential part of town. It was a huge bungalow-style house from the thirties that had been broken into three apartments, one for each floor. Mine was the top floor, what must have been a ballroom originally, with triple-hinged windows facing all four points of the compass, that opened, folded, opened and folded, until the walls were nothing but trees, sky and air.

The ad in the paper said to knock at the house next door. The landlord I'd expected was a landlady who couldn't find the keys. She was quite fat and, as if she wasn't aware of that, wore a shapeless housedress as she ate a donut with a large dollop of red jelly on the top, which she propped on the tips of her upraised fingers as delicately as a Jamaican woman carrying a gallon jug on her head. She kept rummaging through the same green plastic Tupperware bowl full of keys and little toys, then finally remembered she had left the door unlocked after defrosting the fridge.

I rented it. Luckily it came with a little bit of furniture the previous tenant had left behind. Now all I needed was a job. I woke up bright and early, a Tuesday it was, and started a serious job search.

I interviewed as attendant in two nursing homes, beginning

bookkeeper at the particle board plant and cocktail waitress at the local college beer hangout. These were all minimum wage jobs: no health insurance, no sick days, no frills. In fact, the beer hall owner required that you come to work at the beginning of your shift and sit, unpaid, till you were needed, if at all. He also required a uniform (which I'd pay for) too short to cover my underwear if I reached across to wipe peanut shells off the table. But he didn't require experience, and I learned right away there weren't too many places that hired young girls to answer the phone for Daddy and do a little bad typing.

By Friday evening, I'd started feeling sorry for myself. I was sitting on the front porch steps of my new apartment throwing bits of the flaking concrete walk into the grass and trying to figure the minimum amount of cash I'd need to make it back home, when my landlady walked out on her porch. She had a drumstick ice cream cone in one hand, eating it as fast as she could before it melted and dripped down her arm, which it was doing anyway. Every fourth lick on the cone, she took one long lick up her arm to catch the drips. She called across the driveway.

"You looking for a job, ain't you honey?" she asked.

"Yes." It was still real bright out, despite being 9:30, and I shielded my eyes to watch her cross the cement drive.

"I been to my dentist today. He's looking for a girl." She took another long lick of melted chocolate off her forearm, holding the cone up high to keep it from melting faster I guess. "He keeps hiring these young girls and they keep running off and getting married. So this last one, he hires a married lady and her husband just got a law degree, Vickie, and they're going back to Great Falls to live closer to their families. You want the job, I'll go call him for you."

She pouched out her belly to hang her arm up higher, like a pregnant Statue of Liberty. Except this woman was well past childbearing years, unless she wanted to have a mongoloid baby, and she already had at least four kids. I'd only been there a week and counted that many already.

"I don't have any experience," I said.

"Oh what's the big deal? All you do is ask him what he wants and then go find it and give it to him. Solve both our problems. He gets help; I get my rent." She turned around without waiting for me to answer and went inside. In a couple of minutes she was back out on the step, holding the cone far out away from her skirt (which she'd already dripped on) and stretching like a giraffe to lick the ice cream two inches down inside the cone. "He's coming by to take a look at you after Bible study. Tonight," she said and disappeared inside.

And that was about all he did to me: take a look. After Bible study, about 10:30. But he didn't ask any questions about experience or anything, and when I asked him if he minded I'd never worked in a dental office, he said he preferred it. He said, "It just makes it easier, because then I don't have to unteach you bad habits. Besides I can tell from just one look—nice teeth, no nicotine stain, no smoke odor, you don't smoke. And you look honest. An honest day's work for an honest day's pay. That's all I ask."

He wandered around my underfurnished apartment, looking out the windows into the back yard, the dirt alley behind the house and the junk-filled yard of my landlady next door. All this time he was talking. "Make your bed every morning, whether you expect company or not, that's a sign of moral strength, discipline. That's good qualities for a dental assistant. Discipline and loyalty. Walls need a little something though."

He almost had to bend over to go through the doorways he was so tall. But it was mostly legs—legs and cowboy boots and cowboy hat. I apologized for the empty walls, not explaining that I didn't have much more than a month's rent left in savings, much less decorating money.

"No need, no need. I like a person's got a sense of their own style. Bide your time. Don't put just anything up on the wall to say you've got something. Wait for the right stuff. I'm that way, too. Saved antique horse tack for years to hang in this new office. Kid comes in and nails it all up with galvanized nails. I said, 'What's wrong with you: I have rusty nails here. You don't hang up rusty tack with shiny new nails.' Can't teach 'em if they don't know. Get my drift?"

"Well, it's not really that," I said.

"Well listen, I don't have time to talk about wall hangings. I think this'll work out. Bad timing for Vick to leave right now, just when we're moving to a bigger place. Can't use you, though," he said, looking out the window at a couple walking down the alley. "Not till we get into the new office. Won't have room. But that's only two weeks, if you can wait till then. I'll pay you three dollars an hour, and there'll be lots of hours with summer vacation and all the school kids coming in for checkups."

He walked around some more, pacing—the man never really came to a full stop—pulling a sandwich out of his pocket and eating on it for a while as he looked out the front window, then in motion again, ending up at the door as if by accident. "Two weeks from today," he said, putting the sandwich back in his pocket. "We'll work out all the details then, kid," he said, bending his knees and combing his blond curly hair while he looked into my door jamb as if there was a mirror there. Then he disappeared out the door. After he left, I walked over to the door jamb and looked for the mirror. There was none. Then I wondered if I really had a job or if the doctor was just saying nice things to make me feel better. But he called me three times and dropped by once more to make sure

I hadn't changed my mind—just sticking his head in the door that second time with a motorcycle helmet still on his head—and finally, without ever seeing his office, I decided he must be for real and I stopped searching the papers for jobs and relaxed.

Knowing that I had a job waiting for me to pay the bills, I felt doubly lucky. Doubly blessed. It was the Bucking Horse Sale and Rodeo Weekend and I had money coming in. I took out fifty dollars from savings and packed up the little, yellow Volkswagon. Miles City, let er rip. Two lifetimes later; two lifetimes my grandfather had never known.

To begin with, I fell in love forty-seven times—forty-six of those with sorrel and black horses, all long-legged and all topped by little kids in brightly colored satin riding outfits. Then there was a parade with horses; the rodeo with horses; the sale of rodeo bucking horses. And everywhere, people just sitting on horses: drinking a soda or going to the Dairy Queen on horses as if they were common as bicycles. I had my picture taken at a studio specializing in cowboy replicas with dance hall and schoolmarm outfits for the women and piles of ancient horse tack set up in the background. That was for the men's photos. Like my grandfather's photo. I was dizzy with cowboys; sorrels and bays danced in my head. And it was over in a second. Monday morning I went to the 600 Cafe for a bite to eat—to make the weekend last just a little longer and to settle me down—before heading back to Missoula.

A circle of men arrived just before me and had set up shop in the back of the cafe. There were fifteen or twenty of them, sitting in the corner booth, in the booths on either side, and in a great confusion of loose chairs taken from other tables. They were sitting astride the chairs like cowboys, but they were bikers. Motorcyclists. And in the center, one man held everyone's attention, including mine. A thin man with dark brown eyes and short black hair—uncombed and wild looking—that he ran his fingers through mindlessly, till I could feel the silkiness of his dark hair on my fingertips.

He looked up. I looked away.

I was fourteen, the summer before entering Theodore Roosevelt High School and my friend Lynn introduced me to Richie. He was seventeen, male and polite. He showed me slides of his family's vacation at the Grand Canyon. And he had that same soft black, uncombed hair, and the lean look my father must have recognized from his CCC days. (We have pictures of *him* at seventeen, digging holes, not nearly as deep as the hungry anger in his eyes. Anything. Anything to feed the gut-gnawing ambition, to get away from the tough Micks he didn't want to be. The same look.) And Richie had a motorcycle. Dad heard that coming up the driveway and forbid me to see him.

It was my job to tell him. And I would have, the first time I saw him—in the staircase in front of the principal's office my first day in high school—but he kissed me. No brotherly peck on the cheek. No shy fourteen-year-old boy hoping clumsily to cop a feel. He touched my shoulders gently, drawing me just two millimeters closer, and softly touched my lips with his. At fourteen I was innocent—a tomboy still—a dull-headed reader of eighteenth-century British novels who missed all the sexual innuendo and prurient imagery, but loved the romance and the heroes. I leaned into him like a question and he enveloped me. I was breathless, not caring if I got caught. Then he stepped away.

"I want to keep seeing you," he said.

I snuck out for a while—a month, maybe two—meeting him at football games and polite middle-class bowling alleys. But at seventeen, he wanted no more of kids' games and little girls who wanted to kiss and kiss till they couldn't breathe. But nothing else. He moved on.

The man in the booth was alone. The chairs still in a pile around the booth, the other men all gone. I hadn't seen them go. The waitress set my burger and fries in front of me. I looked up. He was watching. Staring. Those dark eyes swallowed me whole. I looked down at the burger. Another Montana burger: prepressed patty, pickle chips and that special sauce of miracle whip, mustard and spiceless ketchup already sogging up the bun. He stood, picked up his back denim jacket and dropped a handful of wadded-up bills on the table. Then, like a Marlon Brando retake, he walked past me, slowly. Black t-shirt, muscular, tanned arms running into strong powerful hands. I watched his hands as he passed me: hard, caloused hands. A fresh cut on the thumb of his left hand as it passed within inches of my table. If I'd known him, I could have reached out and touched that cut. He walked outside to his friends.

I paid for the meal, packed up my stuff and left. The new photo, I'd hang next to Grandpa's once I got home. The man? He was a dream. I was twenty-eight years old and still living in a dream.

M O N D A Y I W O K E U P for work and realized I didn't even know what to wear. One of the small details the doctor had failed to mention. When I arrived at the office, I discovered there was one other small detail the doctor had failed to mention: me. His receptionist, a woman with brassy red hair and a mouth to match, didn't know who the hell I was. In fact, those were the first words out of her mouth.

I explained.

"I have no notice of your being hired," she said and made me sit in the reception area with the patients and fill out an application for employment.

While I filled out the form, she sat at her desk ignoring me. Not at all what I'd expected the receptionist to be like.

Instead of a uniform, or white blouse as I'd finally decided was proper, she wore a bright orange polyester peasant blouse with the shoulder elastic more than a little stretched out and needing constant readjusting, which she seemed to enjoy doing too much. And big, gold-colored wire hoop pierced earrings that made her look like a gypsy and got caught in her glasses when she turned too suddenly. She made a life's work that morning of not making sudden moves and sipping discreetly from a coffee cup hidden from patient's view under the lip of the counter.

She didn't fit in with the decor of the office either. The office was very rustic: old barn wood instead of trailer paneling and old leather horse harnesses nailed to the walls with the nails the doctor had told me about. *Still* shiny. And between the harnesses were animal heads—deer, elk and the entire body of a large white animal that looked vaguely like a sheep, but had large horns on its head. I supposed the doctor had his diploma somewhere in his office, but out in the reception room the only framed things were pictures of coyotes and foxes and other wild animals—all with their mouths wide open.

The receptionist looked up from her desk at me. "What did he tell you he'd pay?"

By then there were three patients sitting in the reception area with me, two of them filling out new patient information sheets. She'd turned on a radio, which was now blasting country western music. All three patients looked up.

"Well, he said he'd pay me twenty-four dollars a day, and said we'd be working a lot of days," I said, walking toward her. She offered nothing more than a "hmm" and bent back down to whatever it was she was writing. I sat down again.

"He can't give you that much," she said just as I got comfortable again. "That's what Vickie makes and she's worked here for four years. It wouldn't be fair to her. And you'll only work when the doctor decides to show up, which is four days a week, and not at all when he's off somewhere chasing ski bunnies and wild critters, which he does a lot of."

I didn't know what to say, so I just waited for the doctor like everybody else.

She was as straightforward with the doctor when he showed up at eight forty-five. He came in with an armful of sports equipment and dirty clothes, and started to lay it all down on the floor behind the receptionist's desk. She stopped him with that same look she'd given me when I said twenty-four dollars a day.

"Morning Susie-Q," Jack said.

"Dr. Paisley," she said. "We need to talk. In your office. Bring your dirty laundry with you."

Three minutes later, she stepped out and motioned for me to join them. Bright red nail polish on her short stubby nails pointed at me. The doctor had his sports bag on the floor between his feet with a pile of sweats to one side and soap, deodorant and shampoo bottles strewn on the other side of his size-twelve cowboy boots, swabbing it out with what looked like a sterile dish towel. He stopped long enough to look up at me when I came in the private office.

"Have a seat, Evelyn," he said. "I'm afraid I have to change what I said the other day. Suze's always on top of it. Vick only makes twenty-four dollars a day. So we'll have to start you out at twenty, move her up to twenty-five till she goes. And you'll only work the days I'm here. But I promise we'll be working a lot of days."

Sue Raffin took a pencil from behind her ear and jotted down what he'd said.

"He'll be gone a week in September, a week in October, two weeks in November and then skiing season starts. You're laid off when he's not here. You get a week vacation for every year you work, at the end of the year in question; and 75 percent off all dental bills, excluding any lab fees, which you pay 100 percent."

I nodded.

"Did the doctor promise you anything else?"

"No."

"Good. Then I'll type this up right now and you can go to work as soon as you've signed an employee's agreement." She closed the door behind her. Jack rummaged through his bag till she returned, not looking up or saying a word the whole five minutes. I wondered if I was supposed to leave and finally started to gather myself up in the the silence to go, but Sue came back with the papers.

There were four copies to the agreement, and she made Jack and me sign each one separately as if it was the original: one copy to the accountant, one to me, one to the corporation—Jack was incorporated for tax purposes and paid himself a salary like the rest of us—and the original Sue kept for her own files. She scooped up all but my copy once the doctor and I had signed.

"Put that in a safe place," she said.

Then she offered me her hand. "Welcome to the country club. I'm Sue Raffin. Don't call me Susie-Q like this dipshit. It's Sue. Not Susie or Sooooz. Sue Raffin. I'm Jack's finance and office manager. Speaking of which," she said turning to the doctor, "Vickie has been babysitting two emergencies back there in the operating rooms since 8:00 a.m. when you were supposed to be here, ready for work, including one guy who's proposed to her twice already, and your hygienist can't get going on her nine o'clock scrape and shine till you do an exam on her eight o'clock who's still parked in her dental seat, since you don't have a vacancy in one of yours. And Mrs. Peterson is going to love having jockstrap fingers groping her teeth. Now you get washed up and get to work."

"Mother Superior," Jack said as Sue Raffin walked back out. "I just work here."

ALL THE FIRST WEEK, I sat on a high stool Vickie brought into the operatory from the home care room and watched the two of them work together. I sat patients, put on bibs and then watched Vickie. Like watching a movie. But the second week we switched places. She set up the charts and instruments, prepped the patients and ran for coffee, and every time Jack showed up in the operatory to work, she pushed me into the assistant's chair, and Jack slowly, carefully, taught me the art of passing instruments. It was the muscle coordination that was the hardest to learn but that was only the half of it. To pass instruments we had to sit almost on top of each other. Jack sat with his knees straddling my right leg, and the patient's head lay in our collective lap. He did not let go of an instrument till he felt me pull it away, which meant, sometimes, if I didn't pull hard enough for him to feel it without looking or thinking about it, I'd end up with the sharp scrape of an explorer across the palm of my hand.

Jack said that would teach me the fastest.

What I found was that the easier I felt at the chair, the better I worked, the less my back ached at the end of the day. Vickie watched me constantly.

"You're leaning in too far," she'd say. "You need to keep your chair up close to Jack and lean against the backrest. Let it support you, take the pressure off your spine. He won't bite. He likes the instruments passed hard. You won't hurt him as long as you put it across the meat of his palm. You'll see. You'll get it right and he'll pick it up faster. You'll know without looking. And keep your elbows in against your sides."

Then one day Vickie started into the operatory and Jack suggested she go work up front with Sue for the morning.

From then on I was solo assistant. We worked five days a week, ten hours a day, putting a lot of silver fillings in baby teeth and first molars—the "bread and butter trade" Jack called it. I learned the preps for each tooth, the five surfaces for decay, retentive points for holding silver filling material. It was like engineering rather than the mystical, magical process I'd imagined dentistry to be when I was on the other end of the drill. There was logic to it. I could predict the instruments he'd need, place the correct burr in the high-speed drill just from looking at the chart. I could make the office more profitable. Increase our production.

That was the money and efficiency side of it. I could do that. But Vickie was like a bright red balloon in the office. She could be up at the front desk all morning, calling people in for their yearly checkups or running errands for Jack out of the office, but as long as she was around, as long as you could look forward to seeing her, she was this enormous smile. I could increase Jack's efficiency, but I didn't have that bubble inside of me. Vickie's bubble never burst. And the day came when her husband had passed his last final exam and it was time for Vickie to go back to Great Falls.

It was so obvious even Jack noticed it. The first day Vickie was gone. We were done for the morning, and he asked me into his office for a minute.

"I'm wondering, Evvy, how you're doing. Are you feeling okay?"

"I'm fine," I said.

"You don't seem to smile very much."

"No, I'm fine really. I kind of get into what I'm doing and just don't smile I guess while I'm concentrating."

"Not that I mind. Vickie, God bless her, she was a smiler. I just need to know it's not directed at me," he said. He was brushing his teeth with great bubbly clouds of toothpaste and between each sentence, he filled the spaces with 'umms' as if keeping his place in an open book. "You don't know this. You're new around here. Umm. I just got divorced and there wasn't a lot of smiling going on for a long time. I sure got tired of being the villain."

He went back in his private bathroom and rinsed his mouth. When he came out again, he seemed to have forgotten I was there.

"Evvy, I've got something to try out on you," he said after a long pause. "I've got this theory," he went on. "If a person could stand to floss their teeth while they still had a mouthful of foam, wouldn't it be a more thorough way of cleaning."

"I'm not sure I'd take that much trouble to floss," I said. "You'd have to do it over the sink, clean the sink and your face and chin when you're done. For most people, it's hard enough just flossing without having to mop up afterwards."

"You're probably right. Still. For some patients. If they were really motivated." He finished the thought in his own head as he got his Seattle Seahawks athletic bag out of the closet. He'd had his knee operated on by one of their surgeons in the off-season, and bought the bag as a get-well present to himself. That was just before the divorce, Sue said, when he was really feeling sorry for himself.

Anyway, Vickie and the big red balloon were gone and Sue and I started spending more time together. She began to tell me about Jack. In the first place, that horse tack Jack said he'd been saving for years, his ex-wife had collected for him, cleaning out all the junk shops and second-hand stores all over the state in two hard-driving weekends. She also picked out the bone-colored paint for the walls and the red, black and gray Navaho seat cushions for the chairs and couches in the reception room. He'd talked her into buying the fridge and coffee machine for the employee's lounge, the file cabinets for his private office—everything not specifically dental and not un-der Sue Raffin's nose—talked her into doing it after the divorce was final, after all the fighting and dividing up twenty-five years' worth of assets. Jack guilt-tripped her. He said she should earn at least part of the settlement—after all those years of feeding off the practice. And she did it. In a furious rage of creativity and final revenge, she decorated his entire office the way she'd always wanted to decorate their home.

"So Mrs. Paisley hung the animal heads and photos?"

"Oh no, the office was rather tasteful and relaxing when she got done. Jack drug those things in while the ex-old lady was backing out of the driveway," Sue explained. "Oh, and those galvanized nails he's always bitching about? She left Mr. Perfect in charge of the carpenters *one day*—had to go to Billings when her Dad was sick. The Doctor couldn't be bothered to come into the office."

I spent the first month elbow-deep in tongues and spit, it seemed, Jack holding to his promise of five-day weeks and still considering me a fast learner. If I made a mistake, he smiled, said, "It's only the people who never try, Evvy, who don't make mis-takes. You're always thinking." To be a beginner is a blessed post.

We had a good practice even though Sue often referred to the area beyond her pale as the Chinese Circus. That meant we were busy. Lots of dentists weren't busy, I pointed out to her more than once. More people wanted to be our patients than we had time to treat. And for all Sue's smart talk and brassy peroxide hair, I knew she couldn't turn down a potential client. That's what she called them, instead of patients: clients begging to give her money.

But, in order to keep from saying no to her clients, she had to appoint patients farther ahead than Jack liked. Every few months they'd get into it, building for a few days, then Jack pushing the button: some morning, some Tuesday, and it always seemed to be a Tuesday, he'd come in later than usual and tell Sue to cancel that Friday. And Monday. The first appointment book battle I saw was that first week Vickie was gone. It was already a terrible Tuesday morning. Our emergency patients and 8:30 appointments were no-shows and the 9:30 called just before Jack showed up and told Sue she wasn't going to make it either. That left nothing but time on hands already itching for trouble.

"Bring your appointment book, Susie-Q, and let's talk turkey," he said from his private office. But he didn't talk when she came in. He took the appointment book out of her hands and started rifling through it, marking off with one of his red tooth decay pencils the new days he was going hunting, marking a giant red X across the whole page—three potential days of clients gone with a stroke.

"I'll mark them if you can just speak. They do teach that in dental school?" She stood over him, behind his chair. "That red, greasy shit don't come off and it smears up all the other pages."

"I'm done already," he said. "Third and fourth week in October, last week in September."

She turned the book back to the last week in September. "Betty Condon comes down from Plentywood. Helen Scanlon comes from Anaconda. Helen's appointment's been made since last May to fit around her school schedule. These people plan their month around a trip to Missoula to see you."

"That's why you write their phone numbers in. Not like you've got to walk to Anaconda to talk to Helen. You got nothin' better to do, do ya?"

"Nothing better than to do everything twice," she said. When she was angry she stood very straight and took her glasses off so there'd be nothing between thee and those cold green eyes of hers. "Is this the lot?" she asked.

"Told you when you started not to appoint me more than

three weeks in advance. If I wanted to work myself to death, I'd'a been a real doctor. That's what some of those guys did, took another year of school. I could've done that. But hell's bells, there's a lot of other things I'd rather do than be tied to a beeper the rest of my life."

"Not while you're building that friggin' log home out of your checkbook, you don't leave your operating rooms anytime the fishin' or skiin' or goin' to Maui for the weekend or playin' drugstore cowboy bug bites you."

"Operatories," he said, correcting her.

"How would you know? You're not in 'em 150 days a year. A third grader spends more days in school than you do at the chair, and you forget your little three-hour, one-on-one basketball game 'lunches.' Someday you're going to jam your drilling finger and be out of business. Or get a dirty little index finger in your eye. Why the hell do you have to build that house out of your pocket money, big shot? The rest of the world gets a goddamn mortgage."

"Say, Suze. You know why a dog licks his balls?"

"I can take a gun and go shoot you, too. Doesn't mean I'm gonna do any goddamn stupid thing comes into my mind."

"That's what I like about you Suze. Don't even have to be married anymore and still get all the bennies."

That log house had been on the books ten months before I started working. Every payday, Jack took his paycheck and bought logs or bathroom fixtures or lights or windows and made Sue Raffin pay the workmen, all four of them, out of corporate funds. Someday, he wanted to semi-retire out there and run a part-time practice. That made it a "corp" expense, he said. That made it fraud, she said.

Jack was right; it was like they were married and the log house was one of those secret spots: the issue that ended all other fights, no matter how they started.

Sue Raffin followed Jack out of the office back into our main operatory, number two, where he made great gestures of reading his schedule for the morning.

"Those dildos you got working out there," she was saying as he was ignoring her, "they make more than any of your office help, and can't get hepatitis from some dickhead's bleeding gooms." (That's the way she always said it, 'gooms.' And she was absolutely phobic about catching anything: thank God it was just hepatitis in those days. Nobody had ever heard of AIDS yet.) "And couldn't get a job anywhere else if their lives depended on it. And you buy all your damned supplies at cut-rate, rip-off franchise parlors instead of supporting your local businessmen *and* patients, I might add. And what have you got in a year? A cabin six logs high. Hell of a deal."

"Six logs high and basement dug, plumbing and electrical, and hand peeling the bark off the logs before they can pile them six logs high," Jack said. He pointed at his 10:30 patient, Elizabeth Barsness, not due for another hour. "Get hold of Betty B and see if she can come in now. I'm going downstairs for a cup of real coffee and some breakfast."

Soon as his private door slammed, Sue threw the appointment book down on the floor and grabbed up three of Jack's newly sharpened red pencils. She broke them in half, threw them down on the floor and ceremoniously ground them into the carpet.

"Don't pick them up Evelyn. Don't you dare pick them up if you got any balls at all. If the asshole bitches about it, point him out my way." She collapsed in the dental chair, pressed the lay-back button and put her feet up. "I hope he chokes on his damned R-E-E-EAL coffee." She let up on the button and settled into the fold of the chair, letting her skirt ride way up over her knees.

"God protect me from a man with time on his hands. You'd think they could learn to scrub bathroom tiles or ovens or something to work off the tension." She pressed the up button a split second to bring her head up, but still didn't fix her skirt.

"You know I know you work hard, Evelyn. But I'm working in the ditches out there. By the time you got 'em, they're pleased as punch or at least as pleased as a dental patient can get. You hold their hands and fix their pain. I'm the one who takes the new snowmobile out of their garage."

"You want me to call Mrs. Barsness?"

"No, I'll call her. Then I'll call forty-seven-hundred other people in out-crop Montana and tell them I'll put them on a waiting list because the boss says he's feeling peak-ed."

So Vickie was gone, and I was totally responsible for everything behind that imaginary line strung between the coat closet and the employees' lounge. When we'd finished Mrs. Barsness' crown preps and started cleaning up for lunch, Jack asked me into his private office to talk. Sue and our hygienist, Terri, had already left for salad bar at Big Chief Pizza. I was supposed to join them.

Jack had a deal for me, he said. I'd get a raise if I worked out; if I could pick up the slack, if I could do the work of both assistants and not make Jack hire another full-timer.

"What about home care instruction?" I asked. I think it was Sue told me the move would allow Jack to fulfill his life-long dream of having a permanent full-time employee to teach nothing but the details of flossing and sulcular brushing.

"You can do it at the chair," he said. "While you're waiting for me. You'll be my top hand." He pulled his athletic bag out from under his desk and waved me good-bye. "Two o'clock?" he asked.

"One-thirty. Jaymie Porter and Kathy Hanson."

I locked up the office for the hundredth time and headed out to join Sue and Teri for lunch. It was all still very new and exciting despite the fights between Jack and Sue, and I looked forward to living up to Jack's expectations.

THREE

A L L T H A T C A M E to a screeching halt with Jaymie. There was no keeping me away from her after that first appointment in Jack's office. Maybe when I was thirteen. My mother would have taken one look and seen the trouble ahead. She would have forbidden me to see her, for my own good.

I think what drew me to her—she was the other side of me. I dropped out of college; she finished. I was the pink wheel in Daddy's office; she ran the family shop—J&B Lumber. Nails and hammers, posts and posthole diggers, doors, windows, drills, routers, and radial saws; she demonstrated them, sold them and kept a five-man crew on its toes, balancing the books to the penny and keeping the free maple bars on the counter plentiful and fresh. She introduced a computer inventory system and taught her dad how to use it; dreamed of taking over, letting Wally retire to fly rods and Winnebagos. And what did I dream of? She was what I feared my parents really wanted in a daughter, instead of the "sweet" child they had.

The way Jack worked, I spent a lot of time sitting with patients. He insisted that we seat patients as soon as they came in, whether he was there or not, and then insisted we never leave them unattended. Jaymie made her appointments for after lunch and Jack was always late. An hour the first time, two hours the third.

In the first place, I was grateful that it didn't upset her. Then, too, she didn't make me tell lies or make excuses.

"He's playing ball," she said the first time.

I nodded.

"It's okay. I know the Doctor. He still paying lousy wages and not offering health insurance?"

I nodded again. Trying to be noncommittal.

"You don't have to say. Pops tried to get me a job here after high school. He thought it was a nice ladylike job for his daughter. Then he found out the P wasn't paying any bennies. How many knee operations has he had now?"

"Just the two," I said. That seemed to be a safe enough subject.

Over the next two appointments she told me lots of stories about Jack. It was Wally gave Jack his first job—a high school kid hired to sweep out the office after work. Then Walls pulled some strings to get him hired on as a seasonal with the Forest Service. I told her about Grandpa's picture—why I'd come out here—and my picture last spring at the Bucking Horse Sale; I asked her if she'd ever heard of a town called Philbrook.

"Any idea what part of the state it's in?"

"No. I've never found it on a map."

She shrugged. "Might be on an old Forest Service map. Or a BLM map. Takes them forever to erase anything."

It was after the third appointment, the final one for that year, when there'd be no question of conflict of interest—because Jack seemed to bristle whenever Jaymie came in the office—only then did I get into her Bronco and ride away.

It was a simple errand. Her brother, Buck, had left his horse at their parents' house. Jaymie was simply going to retrieve the horse, to see that it got exercise and attention instead of sugar cubes and raisins. It had gotten fat, in short, with Rose and Wally.

I think I tried on ten different outfits for that errand. And when Jaymie showed up she had a pile of clothes with her to change into. My room looked like a rummage sale for a while. From her brand new jeans, green patent leather cowboy boots and dress shirt with pearl snap buttons, she changed into faded Levis, marigold yellow tank top and a pair of Nike running shoes. As she tucked the tank top into her jeans, she looked at the two Miles City photos on the living room wall. She stood there, quietly, for several minutes, then said, "Your grandfather was a handsome devil. That's your father's father, right?"

"Yes. He died long before I was born."

"Your family has long gaps between generations. I mean, I've got a photo just like that, but it's of Wall's *grand*father." She looked closer at the picture. "Same year, I think, he came out to homestead."

"What happened to the ranch?"

"There wasn't ever a ranch. He drove stagecoach for the Wells Fargo. Lewistown to Maiden and Gilt Edge. Grandma Bea taught school. They always intended to prove up the land and then sell it as an investment. They sold during World War I, when wheat and land prices were so high. A lot of people meant to do that. But not many were lucky enough to sell out in time. Market collapsed soon as the war was over. Then came a drought and finished most of them off."

"I suppose a lot of them went back east."

"Or ended up in the mines in Butte or cowboying for wage."

"Never got rich?"

"Just didn't starve to death. Towns dried up and blew away without anyone to notice. May be what happened to your Philbrook."

I went back into my closet looking for a hat, digging through a box of stuff I'd bought at rummage sales thinking they were treasures when I bought them and then never using any of them. There was one hat—a broken down straw cowboy hat. I put it on.

"So where is your brother and why doesn't he take care of his own horse?" I asked her.

"Peru this week, I think. Alaska? Mongolia? He's a geological engineer. Goes where there are mountains and people who want to buy the mountains and turn them into gold mines. Literally. Or silver mines. Or uranium, titanium, whatever. And I owe him. He talked Dad into taking me on as partner in the shop. I was the one who wanted to take over the business. Only piece of wood ever turned Bucky on was petrified— stone-cold prehistoric rock tree. Last thing he wanted was to be a lumber man, so he guilt-tripped them into letting me inherit the shop. I think he even threatened a sex discrimination suit—lots of talking long into the night that I never was invited into. So I'll take care of his neglected, spoiled old Kawasaki."

"Kawasaki?"

"He always wanted a motorcycle. They got him a horse."

She'd combed out her long French braid and pulled her hair tightly back into a silky black ponytail, and as she stood there in the kitchen doorway, she took a baseball cap and threaded the ponytail through the hole in the back, settling the cap down tight on her head. "He spent most of his time on horseback galloping down hills at top speed, making noises like a motorcycle. Poor horse. You like my outfit?" she asked.

The cap was red with black script lettering: "Legal Tender Saloon, Missoula, Montana." The shoes were sneakers.

"I thought we were going to play cowboy," I said.

"Wrong verb. Moving horses is work. Trying to outwit a thousand-pound animal with the brain of a zucchini while standing in slippery shit isn't fun. And it's hard on clothes. You wear your good jeans and boots to do that shit, you don't have a good pair of jeans and boots anymore."

"Am I dressed okay?" I asked.

I'd decided on my only pair of jeans, and a pair of brown leather loafers, which were my only pair of hard-heeled shoes, which I'd learned as a nine-year-old in summer camp was the only way to make a horse move at all. At camp, all I'd had was my black, patent leather church shoes. I wore them riding every day, then Sunday took them through the woods and across a swamp—the short cut—to church. I'd left them in the camp garbage bin at the end of summer.

"You don't own a pair of sneakers?" she asked.

"No."

"Well, I had a feeling that might be the case. What size shoe are you?"

"Nine. Narrow."

"Narrow is the only way girl cowboy boots come," she said and grabbed a grocery sack from the floor and set it on the dining room table. "Now I don't want you getting real excited about these," she said and pulled out a pair of dark leather cowboy boots. "They're just buffalo leather. I bought them a few years ago and never could get comfortable in them. They'll survive today. I'll show you how to clean them up again later."

She handed the boots over, and I started to put them on over my low socks.

She reached into the bag again and pulled out a pair of long white cotton socks. With the label still on them.

"These were in my drawer. I was afraid you wouldn't have real socks either." She waited patiently while I changed socks, then pulled the boots on and walked around the apartment in them. "You like them?"

I beamed.

She grinned. "All right now, there's three ways you can wear your boots."

I was still walking around, jeans fashionably bunched up over the tops of the boots. I turned and faced her.

"You can pull the jeans down straight and fold 'em up two folds like John Wayne did in all his B movies. You can tuck the jeans into the tops of your boots—like a Buckle Bunny. Or you can pull 'em down over the tops of the boots."

"What's a Buckle Bunny?"

"Girls who wear their silver belt buckles to the bar to get them polished."

"Rubbing them up against some loser's blue jeans?"

"You got it."

I struggled to pull the too-tight calves straight down over the boot tops.

"Next thing I'll have to buy you is a pair of boot-cut jeans."

THE HOUSE JAYMIE and her brother grew up in was ten miles south of Missoula. Thirty years before, as newlyweds, Wally and Rose built a little two-bedroom house on twenty acres in the middle of nowhere, planning to raise their children at the mouth of Lolo Creek where they could fish or swim, ride horses or play cowboys and Indians till the cows came home.

For ten years, they owned a little piece of Montana heaven. That's what Wally called it. They proceeded carefully, starting J&B Lumber (the initials of their two children, Jaymie and

Buck) with just the two of them—Wally hauling the goods in and out while Rose ran the office—and when they could afford to hire a real bookkeeper, Rose stayed home and had their family. A boy for him and a girl for her. Little by little, as they watched their children and the lumberyard grow, Wally and Rose added to their little cabin in the woods.

The problem was that in those ten years the little town of Lolo grew as well: from a small farming community with post office and steak house/lounge to a suburb of the sprawling metropolis north of them. Those who couldn't live with the citified rules of Missoula moved south to Lolo Creek and were quickly followed by three new bars to sustain them.

Jaymie's folks thought about moving when the first trailer park appeared, and again with the addition of the third bar, but by then they didn't have any kids in school and as long as no one on the south side of Lolo Creek sold out to the developers, they could close their eyes to what went on north of the cottonwood trees.

We said hi briefly, Wally, Rose and I, then Jaymie backed the horse trailer to the corral gate while Wally got a pail of oats to lure Kawasaki into the trailer. The buckskin walked into the trailer like he'd been living in it all summer. An hour later, we'd dropped him into Jaymie's Arabian Acres ten-acre ranchette to whinny and bite and kick the two permanent residents already in the pasture.

"Now what?" I asked, hoping to get an invitation to ride.

"What do you mean, 'Now what?' No Montana adventure is complete without at least one six-pack. I'm thirsty. I want beer. Cold beer, in a glass, with boys around to amuse us. Who knows, maybe this is your lucky day."

"I'm not dressed," I said.

"You're too dressed for the Legal Tender. And that little bit of horseshit you got on your boots will lend truth to advertising. It's supposed to be a cowboy bar."

It was heady stuff. All those years at high school and church dances, I never so much as danced with a boy, much less had a date. In seventh grade, at the Valentine's Day dance, my mother had made me a pretty new dress with hearts all over it and I sat with my friend Karen Glum holding up the walls. Finally, out of boredom and a weird sense of frustration, Karen asked me to dance or I asked her to dance and we slow danced, cheek to cheek, mocking the couples all around us but the teachers became offended and threw us out. It was the only time I ever danced in public. Before the Tender.

You had to follow some rules. If you let someone buy you a drink or danced with them after 1:00 a.m., they could get pushy. They'd think they owned you or at least that part of you that was dearest to their hearts. If you could figure out which guys wouldn't pull that on you at 1:00 a.m., you could sell it in a bottle.

The women always sat at the tables around the dance floor. The men sat on the stools at the bar or stood, beer in hand— on Saturday night—two and three deep. What Jaymie did was divide the hundred-foot length of bar into zones, and the men into three categories. Her theory was that the good men hung out in the middle section of the bar. Don't ask me why, but it was usually true. The guys who hung out on the bathroom-end of the bar were arm grabbers with missing fingers and a length of chain that ran from their belt loops to their wallets— men who knew you were their kind of woman just from the color of your drink. The guys on the other end of the bar, near the door, were on the shy side. But, somewhere between the Galliano and the Yukon Jack were the ones who could dance and chew snoose at the same time. Once or twice a month, if the man passed muster, Jaymie would take one home.

Apart from the bar was a large flat square of painted particle board floor where about two-hundred laminate bar tables were set up. FemaleLand. Then there was the bandstand and a dinky little dance floor. It was my job to take a table at the edge of the dance floor and watch the bar while Jaymie walked over to get our drinks or talked with the bartenders. Then I reported back to her—the reaction of the peanut gallery.

Actually, it wasn't a bad system, except what she said she wanted was not what she eventually plucked off the barstool. She said she wanted a real cowboy. But what drew her in like flies to honey were the urban orphans who fantasized about being cowboys—growing up on the ranch their great-grand-father had walked fifty miles into the wilderness to lay claim to or stolen outright from the savages. In truth, another me, except male.

She liked to dig the boy out of the man—take him home to her double-wide on Arabian Acres, feed him eggs still crusted with chicken droppings and custom-butchered hog meat, then take him horseback riding in the morning, naming the birds as she flushed them from the willow bottoms. The final criteria for this man-she-could-not-leave-alone was that he would have to look happy, but slightly uncomfortable in the saddle.

She found two the first summer I honky-tonked with her at the Tender. One was a high school biology teacher who took first place in a cowboy-jitterbug dance contest back home in Williamsport, Pennsylvania. He'd won a two-day vacation to the Elkhorn Ranch, a dude ranch outside of Missoula. The other was a wildlife photographer from Littleton, Colorado, on his way from Yellowstone to Glacier Park in search of an *Audubon* magazine cover photo. I, on the other hand, found one.

But first I learned something about myself—that I was always attracted to that man at the 600 Cafe. Jaymie explained it to me one night early in our Tender career.

"The guys you want are ones who disappear into the night just after you decide you like them," she told me. Then she started singing that Mac Davis song, "Baby, baby, don't get hooked on me," and she'd repeat the chorus every time I even glanced at a dark-haired man. Dark hair. Work muscles.

There's that old saw, "Men never make passes at women in glasses." I always made passes at *men* in glasses. Dark men in glasses.

"With leather jackets," Jaymie would point out. "You figure your mother will never notice the Harley Davidson logo on the back of the jacket if he's got glasses on. Hippy, wire-frame glasses."

"I never went out with a guy with a motorcycle jacket."

"Since I've known you, they're the only ones you look at. And you've looked at 'em enough, you're gonna have to start paying rent. Your mother's probably afraid of guys in leather jackets. Anything not in white shirt and tie. Afraid they'll steal her tires."

"My mother is 2,300 miles away. Besides, she married one."

"Your dad had a motorcycle? I thought he was a poor kid from the Catholic orphanage. What'd he do—rob a bank?"

"You can be dangerous without having a motorcycle. She's got pictures of him when he was in the CCC. Digging ditches in some state park out west. This one shot, he's got his face to the camera. Eyes that would kill you if you said one thing to him. And drop-dead, James Dean gorgeous at the same time. I've often wondered what he looked like the first time she saw him. It was at least six years after that photo."

"Maybe he didn't change all that much. You ought to go try one."

"I don't feel like it."

"I know. That's what I said."

So she'd send over all the blonde-haired, body-building pretty boys to our table, telling them I was a stewardess for Pan Am, and in love with them. She knew I was in no danger.

I'd let them sit about a minute and a half, then turn the conversation around to the fact that I worked in a dental office. One guy told me he didn't mind because his major medical included dental. So I told him about Milo McLeod and his motorcycle accident. Broke both upper front teeth off at the bone. Then Corey Huebner and his chain saw. One lower cuspid, an upper lateral and incisor, two lips and a chin. My third story would have been about the denture patient who woke up from the anesthetic halfway through his extractions, arms flailing, throat gurgling. His entire nervous system suddenly realizing it was awake. I never had to go that far.

This one night, there was a tall dark one with muscles he'd earned digging postholes and bucking bales on his ranch between fighting fires and training smoke jumpers, and the only reason I knew all that was because it was the second time I'd met him that day.

I don't think Jaymie ever figured I'd let anyone dance with me, much less take me home. But this was different. While she gave bonus points to out-of-towners, my one Saturday night date of the summer had been my eight-thirty emergency patient. "Possible root canal," Sue had penciled in on the schedule. Tall, dark and glasses. He asked me to dance. Jaymie sat back in her chair and watched me come unraveled, shaking her head and making moon eyes at me behind his back. By the time I got up to dance, my cheeks were fire-hot and the touch of his ear on my cheek did nothing to settle me down.

He'd cleaned up and changed out of his Forest Service–orange work shirt and jeans since his appointment. No root canal. Just a broken filling it took ten minutes to fix and two hours for Jack to finish talking about the good old days of smoke jumping. Gordy's first year had been Jack's last year, his last summer in dental school.

I don't know how many dances it takes to fall in love. I

know I had a head start before he walked into the Tender that night what with all the fuss Sue Raffin made over him at the office. Called him a 'gourmey hunk' (as if I hadn't figured it out for myself). Then she offered to assist for him, when she thought assisting ranked somewhere around having her chin instant-glued to the top of Jack's head. I fell in love bad that night.

"We could go for breakfast somewhere," Gordy said as the band finished its fourth set and took a break. "It'd be a heck of a lot quieter. Till the bars close down anyway."

"Or we could go to my house. I could fix us something, if you're hungry. It would be quiet."

"We won't wake up your neighbors?"

"My neighbors have a kid who bangs the door every time he goes in or out of the house. A dog that barks at night. But only when it's hot and I have my windows open. And a radio. Actually, it's a tape player. This little boy plays bible stories at full volume all day. That's the landlady's house. My downstairs neighbor wakes up at six with Mozart at maximum volume and moves on to Janis Ian, Taj Mahal and Rolling Stones by evening."

He was quiet while I babbled, looking into the bottom of his beer bottle. It was his shyness, what I took for shyness, that drew me in.

"I'm just pretty tired," I said. "You know, it's been a hard week. And this heat. It's different, the dryness of it. It kind of takes everything out of you." Mid-nineties all week. And dust and smoke from fires burning in Idaho and drifting with the trade winds.

All I could do was look at his hands. They were deeply tanned and covered with nicks and old scars. The nails cut short and freshly cleaned.

"We should leave before they start playing again," he said.

"I should tell Jaymie I'm leaving." I stood up. "I'll be right back," I said and walked off the dance floor in a daze.

I WASN'T USED TO taking people home. So far, Jack had been the only man; Jaymie was the only other person at all. I walked up the stairs and unlocked the apartment door, automatically flipping on the overhead, then noticing for the first time, all the bare bulbs screwed into overhead fixtures. I flicked the overhead off again, before Gordy caught up with me on the stairs. There was light from outside, a streetlight filtering through the two massive weeping willows in the front yard. I held my breath and waited for Gordy to come in, ready to turn back for the light switch if he said it was too dark, but he seemed comfortable and settled into my one good chair. He'd brought his shaving kit upstairs with him, setting it on the floor beside him after taking a small bottle of Jack Daniels from it.

I hadn't been able to afford much furniture besides what the apartment had to start with. Another table in the kitchen to have some counter space. A dresser with an art deco facade and round mirror. And one imitation cherry Victorian end table with an imitation porcelain reading lamp with a flower stencil stamped on it, and a paper shade with a red silk scarf wrapped around it to soften the light and a big old nubby-cloth armchair. That's where I spent most of my evenings, reading, and that's where Gordy sat. He set the Jack Daniels bottle next to my copy of *Pride and Prejudice.*

"My mother would have an ottoman to put your feet up on," he said.

"They're hard to come by secondhand," I said.

"Harder new. Now you have to buy a $500 Lazy Boy with the footrest already built in."

He unsnapped the cuffs of his pearl-snap, white cotton shirt and carefully folded the cuffs back twice, leaving just the wrist and a couple of inches of white forearm exposed above his tanned and scarred hands.

"Well, maybe I should put some music on," I said, "or find a glass for you." I couldn't sit. In the circle of light, he was almost a still life, a piece of art that shouldn't be disturbed. I brought the glass in and set it next to the Jack Daniels bottle.

"You look very tired," I said.

"Usually in bed hours ago. It's starting to tell."

I'd stayed by the table, leaning my leg against it lightly, waiting for something to happen. And he did. He reached out and touched my leg. Drew me toward him and wrapped both arms around my legs to draw me down. I knelt in front of his chair, my hands quivering with excitement, and realized his hands were shaking too, running up and down my arm.

"I should get some ice for your drink," I said.

"I'll drink it straight."

"Or fix you some breakfast."

He thought about that as his green eyes drifted over me. "Not yet," he said.

There we stayed, me a part of his still life, him slowly, carefully making love to me with our clothes on till the first pink light of dawn crawled up the living room wall, and then, only then, he walked me into the bedroom to finish what he'd started hours ago.

It was 6:00 a.m. before we fell asleep, the neighborhood already starting to wake up. We slept till noon, when Gordy got up to shower.

"I won't see you for a while," he said when he'd gotten dressed.

I nodded.

"Maybe a month or two months. And won't be near a phone to call most of the time." He snapped the cuffs of his shirt.

"I understand," I said.

He picked up his shaving kit from the bathroom counter and stuck it under his arm.

"It's Sunday," I said. "I'll make coffee and we can sit around and read the paper."

"I've got a new fire crew coming in from Alberta tomorrow bright and early, and lots of stuff to get lined out." He leaned down and kissed my forehead. "I would love to stay," he said and he left.

A boyfriend. Aren't they the ones who carve your name in a tree? Or sit on the front porch talking till 4:00 a.m., telling you their life story and wanting to know every moment of your life before they met you? He took me out twice that summer. Or once, if you didn't count the night he picked me up at the Tender which is how Sue Raffin described it even though I kept pointing out to her that I'd met him right there in the office. I knew him before he picked me up.

"One tooth," she'd point out, "does not a 'know' make. 'Know' is how many lumps of sugar he takes or how does he like his steak. You peered into his mouth, not his brain."

"We talked a long time," I said.

"Did he stay for juice and eggs? Has he called? Sent a postcard? Dropped by for coffee? Gordy's less than twenty miles away and you haven't heard from him since that night at the Tender. He's a cruiser. A one-night-stand."

"He's been married before."

"Ah." Sue reached back behind her to the B section of active patients and pulled out a chart. "According to this, he's been divorced six years. He may have been the marrying kind once, but he's a cruiser now."

"He just hasn't found the right person," I said.

She pulled out the dictionary. A tiny, paperback with it's cover torn off from being thrown at Jack so many times. "Cruiser," she said, "Let's see. C-R-U. Cruiser. 'An opportunistic feeder. See shark.' You won't see him till he needs another root canal."

"It wasn't a root canal," I said. "It was a single surface amalgam."

"You call home and tell Mom all about him?"

"No. Not yet."

"Case closed." She clapped the dictionary shut and tossed it into the filing basket.

And that case did feel closed till late August when he called and made a real date, dinner and the cartoon film festival at the Crystal Theater. He wore his new jeans and a white cotton shirt, but instead of cowboy boots and army surplus green wool socks, he wore Nikes, and white cotton socks, which he said was his only concession to the heat.

We'd had a summer of hot, smoky weather. Mornings you woke up and didn't want to put clothes on. Nights you walked past 2:00 a.m., hoping for a breath of air. I spent many evenings walking down the railroad tracks that rose past J&B Lumber and the sawmill, walking out over the trestle to sit on the edge of the railroad ties, waiting for the river's cool updraft to chill me down. If I walked home fast, I'd still have goose bumps when I got to the front porch steps.

When the show was over I suggested a walk down to the river, but Gordy said he was tired of the outdoors and bugs and the smell of wood chips and sawyers. That was his life seven days a week, twenty-four hours a day. What he wanted to do was sit. In a room with curtains, in a house with walls, with screens to keep the bugs out and a glass to pour the whiskey into.

"A bed, in a bedroom, with electric light and a woman in a dress, who is too beautiful for me to look at," he said.

I held my breath and prayed, "Please don't let him go away."

FOUR

IT WAS ONLY a week after that second date, the beginning of Labor Day weekend, when the trees started to turn yellow and nights were cool and Wally and Rose had their yearly end-of-summer bash. Something like my mother's New Year's Eve luau. Mom took two weeks to prepare the food: carving coconuts for drink containers, and making twelve varieties of Polynesian dishes to represent the twelve months of the year, seven flavors of mixed drinks for the days of the week and a carved watermelon boat—her specialty—with twenty-four varieties of fruit balls, one for each hour of the day.

Labor Day began early. Saturday night, I stayed at Jaymie's to simplify the planning for the Labor Day Party Provisions Expedition. Then five in the morning, while the sky was still dark, she woke me up, rolled me out of bed without break-fast, and took me for a predawn ride.

She had both horses saddled before I got out to the shed. Kawasaki for her—she said he still needed some schooling—and her gentle old mare, Rotten Bottom, for me.

"She's got the gentlest gait I ever rode. Like sitting in a rocking chair," Jaymie said. She said the same thing every time I rode Rotten Bottom, once a week for the last year. I'd been helping her school Bucky's bay gelding ever since she'd moved him into her pasture. Then she handed me the reins and pulled me closer. "We'll lead them down to the bottom of the hill then hop on and ride to the river."

We'd always gone the long way around before, avoiding the steep drop from the bench behind her house.

"It's shorter," she said, when I hesitated. "I want to get down there in the dark and be back at eight for Rose."

But it wasn't the dark I was worried about. It was getting on Rotten Bottom without a stool. We'd always saddled up at the corrals.

"I'll give you a boost up," she said, "when we get down there." And she did, almost vaulting me over the other side. She tapped my knee as I got settled. "We'll just take it slow down to the river. Not make any noise. Follow me."

Off in the east, a faint yellow wash hinted of morning. We crossed the half-mile of short brush, then slowly, carefully entered the low willows. I heard the owls hooting and the swoop of what sounded like bats over my head.

"Nighthawks," she whispered. "Birds." And I relaxed.

We never saw the owls, they had just gone to roost as we approached the tall cottonwoods lining the riverbanks. But as they gave their final hoots, the hawks, ospreys and eagles appeared. Jaymie pointed them all out, quietly, and led me under the osprey nests, then a mile further down river, under the heron rookery, their nests like Easter bonnets perched precariously on top of century-old trees.

Jaymie checked her watch, then pointed to the sun, just tipping over the curve of the earth. The pale yellow wash now concentrated into a hard orange knot. She'd bundled me up in a wool-lined denim jacket, warning that sitting on top of a horse wasn't like walking. "You get cold," she said, "I want you to enjoy this." She'd also warned that the coldest time of night was the half hour after sunrise. "Just when you think you have it licked," she'd said.

I was glad to have the jacket now. I turned the collar up against my ears and nestled deep into the sheepskin lining. That big orange knot would make it hot enough later as it climbed across the sky. Jaymie nudged me. We'd stopped on a gravel bar—the last spit of land that separated the Bitterroot River from the Clark Fork of the Columbia. From here, it was a straight shot to the Pacific. I was thinking about that. If I wanted, I could put a canoe in right here and get a free ride all the way to the Pacific Ocean. Jaymie had other things on her mind. She nudged me again.

Across the Bitterroot, on the sand and gravel bank straight ahead, two deer stood, heads down, drinking water. The larger one lifted her head, looked left and right, then lowered it again to drink. Rotten Bottom shifted her weight under me and bumped Kawasaki's rump.

"Whitetail deer. Doe and fawn," Jaymie said as she put a hand on my saddle. "Look how gray they are. They've lost their summer coats already. They'll have to stay pretty tight in the cover to keep cool till the weather changes."

I was watching them now as they drank and didn't notice Jaymie. She had taken her fly rod out—she'd been teaching me that, too—and stuck the four pieces together, unfastened the fly from the cork handle and started pulling line off the reel.

"I thought just for fun," she whispered, "I'd try to catch a little breakfast for you and Rose. Start the day off right." She nudged Kawasaki forward into the Clark's Fork, and made a wide arc downstream a hundred yards, angling back upstream to cast back into the seam of the two rivers. Three casts and she caught an eighteen-inch rainbow, stripped it in under Kawasaki's feet, then backed him up to me again, dragging the fish up onto the gravel.

"This will do for all three of us," she said, as she climbed down from the horse and unhooked the fish. "You do like fish, don't you?"

"I like tuna," I said. Despite Jaymie's patient lessons, I still hadn't actually brought a trout to hand. The question simply hadn't come up before.

"In a salad, from a can," she suggested, laughing quietly.

"And in casserole, with tomato sauce," I said, a little defensive.

"I might have leftovers, but that's okay, too." She took the creel out of the left saddlebag—a canvas creel, from Wall's father, with the initials W.H.P. imprinted on a bit of leather trim on the top—and wet it down in the river, then slid the fish into it. "Now, we have to get back for Rose. I'll race you."

"You'll win."

"I'll ride the long way around."

Of course she beat me and met me halfway back down the trail, afraid I'd gotten lost, and feeling guilty for leaving me alone—with Rose due in a few minutes. She'd have had a hard time explaining to her mother why she'd left me in the woods alone—Rose had already adopted me as her second daughter by then, which was why I was invited on the Labor Day Party Provisions Expedition at all. Traditionally it had been done only by the women of the family: Rose and Jaymie, Rose's sister Orene when she could make it from Seattle, and Rose's mother before she died.

Half an hour later, we were showered, dressed, powdered and primped, and Jaymie had the trout in a pile of breadcrumbs, gutted, beheaded and ready to fry. We heard Rose's radio before we actually caught sight of the Caddy—her white Eldorado convertible with red leather upholstery. Loud, old-timey country western music. Loud enough to split an atom, twangy enough to cure bacon, Jaymie said. Hank Williams senior and Eddy Arnold—the country equivalent of my mother's favorite, Frank Sinatra. Thirty minutes later, we were piling down the road with the top down at sixty miles an hour, singing

Why don't you love me like you used to do?
How come you treat me like a worn out shoe?
My hair's still curly and my eyes are still blue,
Why don't you love me like you used to do?
Ain't had no lovin' like a huggin' and a kissin' in a long long while.
We don't get further or closer than a country mile . . .

at the top of our lungs, with Rose's warning directed right at me that no one was allowed to live in Montana for more than five years unless they "proved up" their country music style.

"Ship you right back to New York City," Rose said and missed the turn for the liquor store. She slammed on the brakes and checked the rearview mirror. Pine Street, downtown Missoula, population 25,000, was clear for two blocks behind her, so she flipped the automatic transmission into reverse and backed up the half block to the liquor store, doing a moderately repressed—for her—forty-five miles per hour.

"Never has this Caddy known a more backward gear," Jaymie laughed.

"That sounds like poetry," I said.

Rose nosed into a parking spot against the steel back door of the State Liquor Store. "Oh, my dear, it is," she said and honked twice. "First stop. Everybody out, no dawdlers."

Another part of the tradition: getting the liquor store manager to open the store Sunday morning—not only on his day off, but hours before you could buy liquor, legally, anywhere in the state.

We loaded three cases of assorted half gallons of liquor into the trunk of the Caddy, which was why this was the first of four stops on Rose's well-planned Provision Expedition list. They would provide support for the round and rolling beer kegs we would pick up next at the Tender. Then we'd pick up the firecrackers, triple-wrapped and sealed in plastic, and tuck them around the kegs to keep the powder cool. Then to the pig—who was supposed to be 'spit ready' when we arrived at two o'clock. Except he wasn't. At 10:00 a.m., he was still walking around. That's when we arrived at the Legal Tender Saloon for the kegs and Rose strode behind the bar as if she owned the whole place. She called the Pig Farm.

"No, Ma'am, ain't dead yet. We figured we'd keep him fresh for you and dispatch him when you arrived."

"I want him shrink-wrapped when I arrive. Ready to put on the spit. We're four hours from your place and I'm not standing around once I get there. It's too goddamned hot to stand around a pig sty today."

She hung up the phone, turned to the bartender, "Thank you Teddy," she said—he was another of Jaymie's schoolmates—and walked back around to the customer side of the bar. "I don't suppose you have any ice tea back there?"

"Just pop, ma'am," he said. "Diet Coke, Coke, Coke Classic, Bubble Up, Seven Up, Mountain Dew, Sprite, Diet Sprite, Orange Sprite, Diet Orange Sprite."

"No Nehi?" Rose asked.

"No ma'am."

"Diet Classic Coke all around, then, Teddy."

"I'm sorry, Ma'am, we only have regular Coke Classic. I've got Diet New Coke, if that's okay."

"Diet New Coke, Teddy," Jaymie put in quickly before Rose could speak. "But only for these two. I'll have a Miller High Life, from a bottle please. And put it in a go-cup."

"Here," Rose said, correcting her. She dropped her purse onto the bar. "We're taking a ten minute break. Here. Out of the sun. Give the girl a glass."

Rose was taller than Jaymie, the product of her tall Blackfeet mother and a six-foot, four-inch white man who thought he wanted to be an Indian, but soon realized the heart of the Great Depression was no time to spend on an Indian Reservation. He stuck around long enough to sign Rose and her mother out of the hospital. I'd seen pictures of her parents. Rose had inherited that long, unbending spine from both of them and was carrying it elegantly and stubbornly into her forty-eighth year.

"I guess we're going to keep you company, Teddy," Jaymie said.

"You can keep an eye on the till, maybe serve the customers while I load up the kegs," Teddy suggested.

"No problemo," Jaymie said and grabbed her mother's keys off the bar and handed them to him.

By the time we got back to Lolo Creek, it was six o'clock. Rose had called the pig farm from every stop and was assured at every stop that the pig would be spit-ready when she arrived. When she pulled up after driving sixty-five miles per hour twenty-three miles down an all-weather gravel road, she coasted into the turn-around in front of a bunch of corrals, spun the car 180 degrees to the left and came to a stop. The twenty-foot plume of road dirt that had followed us all the way from the highway continued west, leaving us east-facing passengers clean, our vision unimpaired. The Caddy was a bit dusty, however. Elvis, Rose called it. The Spruce Goose, Jaymie said, because no matter how fast Rose drove it, it never got off the ground. But she never said it within Rose's hearing. The pig wasn't ready.

"Another forty-five minutes," the man said.

"That's what you said when I picked up my fireworks, Donny."

"Had a little trouble getting him dead. He was a bit opposed to the idea." Donny motioned to the house. He was older than Rose, heavy set and unshaven. Tired from a day of uncooperative swine and demanding women. But polite if it killed him. "If you'd like to go in the house, the missus will be happy to get you something cool to drink. Forty-five minutes."

"The missus"—a short thin woman named Betty fixed us each a tall glass of iced tea, and Rose and Betty talked an hour and a half. Kids and grass, and shrubs and husbands. Grandkids. Betty had three and one more on the way.

"The kids got this one tested, just to see. It's a girl, that makes it two and two."

"I'm hoping for one—any sex—before I die," Rose said.

"You know Bucky could settle down and make a family," Jaymie suggested. "I'm not the only baby factory."

With that left unsettled, and no more kids to rub her nose in, Rose led us back out into the brilliant, dry sunshine to a white Caddy with a big blue tarp full of pig laying across the back seat. We all piled into the front, Rose turned Hank Williams back on, and we headed home.

Wally was ready. A handful of guests had arrived early, and some were already setting up the volleyball net, some carting the pig-roasting machine out of the basement, some stringing lights on the roof for late night softball. Five guys met us as we pulled into the garage.

"Party Time," Rose hollered as she rolled to a stop. She hugged all the newcomers and introduced me—Fergie and Billy Byrnes, Iron Mike, Willie, Joe Yankowsky, Norman and Fireman Fred. Fireman Fred was in charge of the fireworks, but first, he and Norm each took a keg and gently rolled them out the back door of the garage, over the lawn and down the slope into the creek, turning them upright and settling them gently into the six inches of sand lining the shallow end of Wally's swimming hole.

The path was well worn—from kids on horses, to Wally's occasional fly-fishing excursions and his hot summer evening swims. It was the perfect swimming hole. (Almost perfect when they'd moved into the house twenty-five years before; perfect after Walls took a back hoe to it five years later. My father had made his own improvements on his personal swimming hole: putting in a forty-eight-inch, twelve-foot-diameter above-ground pool at our house in Franklin Square.) Natural improved, or totally artificial, both fathers took the same approach to water: Wally started at the top of the willows and took a running swan dive into the middle of the deep pool. My father did that too, but in the years before he bought his own pool, he mostly dove into bodies of water he knew nothing about. Once on our way to Florida on a family vacation, he saw a pond behind the motel and dove in, no questions asked. The pond was only six inches of water, camouflaging two feet of muddy sludge. It was cold and wet, he said, but he came up looking like the Creature from the Black Lagoon. And it never slowed him down, just flattened out his dive a bit. (It wouldn't have stopped Walls either.) It was nine years after the Black Lagoon incident before my father thought he could afford his own, more predictable, swimming hole.

Rose hung around long enough to see that the pig was properly deposited into an eight-foot aluminum horse trough filled with ice way back in the deep shadows of the three-car garage. Jaymie and I wouldn't start him till midnight. And until then, we'd be carrying charcoal—twenty-pound bags at a time—down to the pit, testing the electrically powered spit, bending the edges of the five-by-three by two-foot-high sheet metal box that enclosed the works and laying in provisions for a night of cooking. Sleeping bags, lawn chairs, a cooler full of soda and beer, sandwiches and candy bars.

It was after midnight when I crawled into a sleeping bag and started to drift off to sleep. The last I remember, the pig was on, the spit was turning, the coals were hot. Everyone else had gone to bed, and Rose came down to sprinkle garlic salt over the pig's hide and make one last check on her "chickens." She pulled up a lawn chair to the spit housing, holding her hands over the radiating warmth.

"Bucky hasn't called yet," Rose said.

I knew that was part of the excitement, because Jaymie's big brother hadn't made it to the party for four years. He'd been in Saudi Arabia and Afghanistan. He should have flown in on the 6:55 flight from Denver that night—the last leg of a twenty-seven-hour journey.

"He's wiped out," Jaymie said. "Probably drove to the first motel and got a room. He'll be here at noon tomorrow."

"You left his truck in the short-term parking at the airport?"

"Evelyn and I dropped it off last night."

The truck lived in a shed at J&B, up on blocks to save the tires. It was eight years old and had 25,000 miles on it—the only one who drove it was Bucky and only when he came to visit. We'd jump-started it Friday after work and drove it a hundred miles to the Hamilton Dairy Queen for nut whips just to be sure it would start when he got off the plane.

It was his job to take the pig off the spit, assigned time, noon Labor Day. My job to take the second watch. I listened to Rose and Jaymie as I snuggled deep into Wally's elk camp sleeping bag.

Jaymie made it up as she went along. "He'll walk in here with rings on his fingers and bells on his toes, acting like he never went away."

"I'm tired," Rose said. "You got everything you need down here for the night?"

"I could feed an army."

"You will." Rose stood and stretched, rubbing her forehead with both hands, then the sides of her long neck. Hair as black as her daughter's, still. Jaymie said it was because Rose cut samples of her hair while she was asleep and took them to the salon to match up with the Clairol bottle.

"You should go to bed. I've got this under control," Jaymie said.

"Yes," Rose agreed, but stood there, mesmerized by the sound of the river only twenty yards away and the whir of the electric spit. Rose nodded in my direction. "She's so thin. Is Jack paying that girl enough money to eat?"

"Evelyn?"

"Of course, Evelyn."

"No."

"He's always been so cheap. Your father should hire her."

"And what would she do?"

"He could teach her, like he taught you."

"She doesn't want to work in a lumberyard."

"The work's all the same. It's the wages. I'll bet he doesn't provide health care. Or dental."

"Seventy-five per cent. Just dental. No medical. No time and a half for holidays. No sick days. It's awful mother. But she's an adult. She hasn't applied for work. You can't just say, 'Here, little girl, this is the job we want you to do.'"

"I'm not treating her like a little girl."

"What do you call it?"

Rose sighed. A long, tired, intolerant sigh. "Your father should approach her about it. At least let her know the benefits—what she isn't getting with the P." Rose stood. "Tip the housing up on your end," she said.

"It's all right."

"I want to put out that grease fire." Rose had picked up one of a half dozen squirt guns loaded with water for just that purpose. "Lift it," she said again, and Jaymie did.

Grease fire out, Rose walked back to the cooler and set the water pistol down. She walked back to Jaymie and placing her hands on each shoulder, kissed her daughter gently on the top of her head.

Jaymie reached up with her right hand and touched her mother's arm.

"You don't know this," Rose said. "But every day I thank heaven that you didn't grow up and move away." She patted her daughter twice and turned, walking toward me as she headed back to the house. I thought I'd be asleep as soon as my head hit the pillow, but I was wide awake—eyes closed, not wanting to intrude. I felt a hand on my forehead, gently, resting there just a split second, then gone, and I wondered if I was hallucinating. But she spoke, her voice a whisper right above me.

"You tell her, Jaymie. Scrooge was a better boss."

"Yes, mother. Good night, mother," from the fire.

"I mean it," Rose said and then walked back up to the house.

She was back at six to help Jaymie and me lift the housing off the frame and add another couple of bags of coals to the pit. Then, while we stood and stretched — she'd woken both of us up—Rose sprinkled the pig again with garlic salt and we closed up the spit for another couple of hours. A couple, that is, if Rose kept busy up at the house. If not, she'd be down in a half hour—or even fifteen minutes, losing track of time and reality as the pitchers of gin and tonics, margaritas and black Russians started appearing around the breakfast table.

"I'll bring your breakfast down. Twenty minutes," she said and disappeared back up into the willows.

"I could go up to the house, save Rose the trip," I said.

"Uh-uh. Best place is right here," Jaymie said. "We get to see everyone two or three at a time, plus, in a couple hours, there'll be some pissant kid hanging around dying to put out the fat fires. We gotta be vigilant—supervise—make sure he doesn't fry his hand or something. Then when this baby's cooked, we're outta here. No washing plastic forks, no garbage detail. It's been organized so long, everyone's got a job. You don't want to be in the kitchen eating breakfast right now while Carol and Carole and Gail Van Ausdol and Barb Mosier are making potato salad, and macaroni salad with all those little shrimp, and three varieties of jello molds. And Fred the Fireman will have all his stuff stretched out on the deck, nailing Roman candles and whirligigs to pieces of plywood, running cordite between 'em, trying to outdo last year's fireworks."

Jaymie punched a dent out of a corner of the sheet metal, sealing the box tighter. "Four years ago. No one will ever top that. I went into the kitchen to get me a drink, thinking I'd miss the first, slow part—they always start out tentative—and before I got the black in the Russian the whole sky lit up like a lightning bolt blew right through the house. Five hundred dollars worth of pyrotechnics in 1.7 seconds. I missed the whole thing."

"You ever figure out what happened?"

"Bucky accidentally dropped a match into a box under the set-up table. Somehow triggered everything at once. That was the story he told. Actually, I've often wondered if he didn't rewire it while everyone else was playing volleyball."

"I would have liked to seen that."

"Yeah, me too. Mom saw it. I thought she was going to kill him."

"So, how old was he when he pulled this?"

"Evelyn. It was four years ago. He's been afraid to come back ever since. I say he's a brave boy to come back this soon."

I picked up a water pistol and put out another fat fire. "Adds a touch of excitement," I suggested.

"You don't have a brother, do you?"

"No."

"At five, he broke his leg trying to fly off the roof like Superman. Luckily the driveway was still dirt then. At six, he almost burned the house down trying to turn houseflies into fireflies. He was lighting their butts with matches while they flew around on his bedroom window beating their heads against the glass trying to escape. That was after he got tired of pulling off their wings—you know, making 'flies' into 'walks?' At my sweet sixteen birthday party, he swallowed a hot dog whole and almost choked to death. He's stuck raisins up his nose, peas in his ears. He snorted a spaghetti up his nose at dinner one night. Snorted it right up into his sinuses. Then he'd be eating and breathing out, and this little tail would start to show and Walls would grab for it trying to get the damn thing, but it scared Bucky having Walls lunge at him like that so he'd suck it right back up. Mom made him eat out on the porch till he could prove it was gone. Then, he used Mom's razor to shave his legs when he was eight, and almost bled to death in the bathtub, leaning a little too hard on that delicate, thin skin on his shins. He's still got scars from that. Tells everyone he got them riding his Kawasaki."

"His horse?"

"*You* know that. Everybody else assumes it's a macho dirt bike. Then he was mowing the lawn when he was fourteen and got to watching some girls riding their horses out on the highway. Halter tops and short, short cutoffs. Pulled the lawn mower back over his foot and whacked off his big toe."

Rose came with breakfast—orange juice and coffee, sweet rolls and a slice of watermelon apiece—then disappeared back up to the house.

The rolls were fresh-baked cinnamon sticky buns and I ate mine like it was the last sticky bun in the world.

"There used to be a restaurant in New York," I said. "Patricia Murphy's. You went there on Mother's Day or Christmas. Graduation. And put your name on the waiting list. Then you waited four hours. But you never knew. Sometimes it would be one hour. Sometimes two. So you couldn't eat before you went and by the time they finally seated you, you were about starving. Then you get to the table, and there's this big basket of sticky buns instead of the usual basket of pickles and olives. To hold you over till dinner arrived."

"What did you do for four hours? I don't think I've ever waited more than two black Russians."

"They had a big garden. Trees and shrubs, and little ponds with fish in them and brick walks all around. My sister and I would run around; play hide and seek and stuff."

"Older or younger?"

"My sister? Katherine's three years older. Always wanted to be a teacher. Always wanted to go to college and graduate school. She teaches college math. She's got two calculus classes now and a physics class."

"Are you close?"

"She thinks I'm a nitwit. I can't remember phone numbers. I'm always losing important things. Or breaking things.

Like Bucky and you, I guess. One sibling always has to be the responsible one."

"Like me? I'm responsible? I haven't even made Mumsy a grandmother yet."

"You will. Before your brother ever thinks about it. In the meantime, you're down here cooking the meats for the minions, instead of partying around the breakfast table. Waiting for the prodigal brother to show up so you can give him a hard time, and then you'll smooth things over with your Mom and Dad for him being late. If he ever shows."

"He's here. Came in at 3:00 a.m. Says he stopped in at the Tender for just one beer and ran into an old friend." She checked her watch.

"I haven't seen him yet."

"You will. He ran into town to get his old bud." He's going to surprise us. Says it's someone we both went to high school with."

Actually, Sherry didn't go to high school with either one of them. Jaymie and Buck were two years apart and Sherry fit in between. She was a junior when Bucky was a senior, but she never graduated. Sherry was tiny and cute and came on shy but friendly, and Bucky walked her around with one arm draped over her shoulder. A pint bottle of peppermint Schnapps in the back pocket of her painted-on jeans. He reintroduced her to everyone at the party, working his way down to the pit just about noon to remove the pig to the carving table. But doing it slowly, theatrically.

"Sherry," Rose said. "Sherry. Again."

Jaymie and I had the housing off, the spit unplugged, and while her two girls stood back out of the way, Rose stuffed six meat thermometers in various thick parts of the pig to test for doneness. But the pig was so tender and done it was falling off the spit.

"The stuffings falling into the coals, Mom. I think it's done." The more Jaymie said, however, the more terse Rose's answers got.

"Trichinosis. All I need is one person coming down with a lousy case of worms." But after checking the deepest, meatiest part of all four hams and both sides of the pig's thick neck, she declared it done. "Get your brother," Rose said. "And tell him to bring friends and a clean garbage bag to catch the stuffing while they're moving it."

Sherry came with the garbage bag—two garbage bags—long before Buck ever showed up.

"I've been here before," she said showing off both bags. "I don't want to miss a bite of your stuffing, Mizz Porter. And you let me know if there's anything else I can do." In a tube top and nothing to hide—unless you counted that pack of cigarettes she was trying to keep Rose from seeing. Her blonde hair was freshly bleached, long in the back and straight, but the top and sides had just been through the curling iron. It smelled of hair spray and peroxide and a touch of perfume— like Sue Raffin's, one of the Avon perfumes she was always trying to sell me—rolled in over the smell of pig and open fire and almost overpowered it.

"Evelyn," Rose said, "This is Sherry Fowler. Sherry this is Evelyn Holloran. Sherry's folks live just down the creek. I think you and Jaymie have fished down there a few times. Nice log house." Then as an afterthought she added, "And horses."

"Oh. The house with the two strawberry roans," I said. I'd never seen a horse like that at any riding academy in New York. I'd always thought sorrels with stars, and blacks with white stockings were my favorite colors till I saw those two roans. "They're really beautiful," I said.

"Oh, I don't even know what the folks got down there, now. I been away so long. Down in New Mexico."

"Oh, you going to school down there?" Rose asked.

"Oh, no ma'am, but now I'm getting divorced, I'm going to get my G.E.D., make something out of myself."

"So you're looking for work here now?"

"Well, no ma'am. I was working down there in a gold mine, hurt my back. I'm trying to get workman's comp to pay, but they say I'm faking it, and I'm going to a lot of doctors and stuff and got a lawyer down there, and if I can get that straightened out, maybe I could even go to college. Do some work that takes brains for a change. Like Jaymie and Bucky did."

Rose smiled. "Evelyn, why don't you go find Buck before this pig dies of old age."

I started to turn and Sherry touched my arm. "I'll go get him, I know where he is. Or where he was ten minutes ago." She walked away, not looking disabled at all.

"Only child," Rose said, softly. "I can't help but think she's always been a disappointment. But her father dotes on her."

Something about that hurt me. "That's what parents do," I said, but it wasn't what I wanted to say.

Rose touched my arm. "I'm sorry Evelyn. That sweet little girl has kept me awake watching for my son's truck to pull in the driveway more nights than I care to think. Maybe she's grown up. She must be twenty-eight by now."

She fussed at the coals, spreading them around with a stick. "You know I read in *Cosmo* or somewhere, some magazine, some big shot psychologist says a parent's job isn't done till they get the child through their first divorce. You ever have anyone get divorced in your family?"

"My grandmother. She married her childhood sweetheart just before he got shipped off to World War I. Then he comes back to a Mommy and baby—my mother—and told her he wanted a divorce. He didn't want any responsibilities. Went through enough in the war."

"And she was Catholic, too, wasn't she." Rose shook her head.

"Church wouldn't help her. But she came from a tough family. Twelve girls and all of them worked. Grandma went out and got a job as a nurse. When I was fourteen, I talked about becoming a nurse. She started telling me horror stories."

"Grandmas are good for that. My mother was always cutting out clippings from the newspapers. "Little Girl Killed When Horse Throws Her In Path Of Car." She'd show them to Jaymie, but Jaymie had no fear. One thing we did right, I think. Now, that Bucky. I think we should have made him afraid of jello. Where the hell is he?"

"He's coming. I see him through the trees there."

Rose walked up to the edge of the cottonwoods and yelled, "WALTER HENRY PORTER THE THIRD, YOU GET YOUR BUTT DOWN HERE AND GET TO WORK!"

He pretended not to hear, but she only yelled it again, louder. He stuck his finger in his near ear and continued talking, but only for a few minutes. Sherry appeared, laughing, and started gently pushing him. Then, when he refused to be herded, she grabbed his belt and pulled him backwards down through the cottonwoods.

"That's a sight I'd hoped never to see again. That girl leading him along by his pants." Rose shook her head.

But he came, and he brought friends, and the pig was carved and eaten, the kegs drunk dry, the fireworks fired off in magnificent and timely succession, and eventually, sometime around 3:00 a.m., I fell asleep, once more around the pig's roasting pit, but this time, the fire pit was empty—clean and tidy and cool. Sherry had come down once the pig was gone and cleaned the little cottonwood glade all up. Collected the garbage, got help to carry all but one of the coolers back up to the house and organized the cleaning, scrubbing and packing away of the pig roast equipment for next year. Even raked the ground for fifty yards around the clearing and refilled the last cooler with soda and beer in case anyone needed anything. I had barely fallen aleep when Jaymie came down too and crawled into her sleeping bag. I rolled over, nestled into the bag, to fall asleep again.

"Sherry's back. Good thing Bucky's only here three days," she said.

All was quiet at last.

FIVE

I GOT UP at six with Rose, had coffee, and the two of us began collecting paper trash all over the yard to burn later when the rest of the party leftovers were awake. There weren't many. Just four or five tents tucked under the trees, and within an easy walk of the back door. They had all stayed up late, Rose said, folding away the picnic tables and cleaning up the kitchen.

As Rose and I worked, a deputy sheriff's car turned into the driveway and coasted to a stop behind the Eldorado. There were two officers, and they walked very slowly toward us. At least it seems like that now when I remember. It was years before the older one spoke.

"Morning, Rose," he said.

She looked up at him into the rising sun and shaded her eyes with one hand. "Good morning Bobby."

"Rose. I've got some bad news for you. Would you like to call Wally?"

"No. Tell me now. Then we'll tell him. What's up?"

"It's Bucky. He's been found in the Piney Woods Motel parking lot. I'm sorry to tell you, Ma'am, your son has been killed."

He just got more and more formal the more he talked.

"He's in his bedroom," Rose said.

The deputy took a driver's license out of his chest pocket and handed it to her.

It was Bucky's. I felt my stomach rise in my throat, but Rose's breath—short shallow inhales, and you couldn't hear the exhales at all, as if right now she couldn't let anything out or it would all fall out—held me. She put a hand over her mouth.

"He's in his bedroom," she said again, but she didn't move.

"May we go and look?" the deputy asked.

"Of course. I'll show you," she said and walked the three of us inside, stopping at the kitchen sink to wash her hands, and then carrying the dish towel to Bucky's door. She opened it, and he wasn't there.

"I saw Sherry Fowler here last night," she said, turning to me. "He went off with Sherry last night didn't he, Evelyn?" she asked. "He's probably just off with Sherry," she said to the deputy.

But before I could agree or nod or anything, he explained that the Piney Woods Motel clerk had gone to school with Bucky, and knew Bucky, and he'd already identified the body. That was the first time he'd said it. A body.

"Who was that?" she asked.

The deputy told her the clerk's name.

"I guess I didn't know that boy," Rose said. "I thought I knew most of the boys in Bucky's class."

"I'm real sorry Rose," the deputy said, taking Rose by the arm and steering her into the kitchen again. He set her down in a chair in the dining room and asked me to go wake up the rest of the family, whoever was there, and he would stay with Rose till I got back.

What we decided to do—what Jaymie decided she was going to do, and Wally decided she wasn't going to do *alone*— was for me to go with Jaymie to the Piney Woods Motel while Wally stayed with Rose. The deputy tried hard to talk us out of it, but in the end, Jaymie loaded me into her Bronco and he followed behind.

The Piney Woods Motel was only three miles from the mouth of Lolo Creek, but the canyon closed up quickly upstream and hovered above the road there, like skyscrapers over a narrow street, except you didn't even have the luxury of patches of sky in the cross streets. This part of the canyon twisted through miles of old-growth evergreen trees, the sky a thin arm stretching ahead of you for a while, then disappearing into a slender thread. Later, as you approached the pass into Idaho, you topped the trees, then the pass, and drove for miles looking straight down the spines to the very roots of all those trees.

The Piney Woods Motel backed on the canyon wall. A depression-era building, it was white with green trim, one story high and twelve rooms long with the office less than a dozen steps from the creek. Bucky's truck, the black Ford four-by-four with the J&B Building & Lumber logo on the door, was parked head-in at room #8. There was a faded red Dodge Power Wagon parked beside it. Up close, the motel needed paint; the parking lot, more gravel. And the clerk who'd identified Buck, was no centurion in a hotel's star-spangled livery. He was one of those perennial students in torn jeans, t-shirt and sneakers. And in the cold and misty air rising off Lolo Creek, he was cold and shivering, still talking to a deputy at the tailgate of Bucky's truck.

Jaymie parked in the first parking space, for #12, and we walked over to the men. You had to talk above the roar of the creek.

"You shouldn't've come," the other deputy said. "We haven't moved him yet. Still waiting for the detectives."

Jaymie greeted both men by name, then smiled at the one deputy. "You gonna take fingerprints, Chester, or just trust the guy who did it will turn himself in out of the goodness of his heart?"

"They're on their way, Jaymie. Soon's the lab kit gets out here, we'll check the truck for prints and get Buck on his way."

"I want to see him."

"No, you don't."

"Don't tell me what I don't want." She started to push past him, but the deputy, Chester, took her arm and held her there with some effort.

"Why don'tcha just wait till the funeral parlor people get him all cleaned up?" Chester said.

"If it was your brother, you'd want to know what happened to him."

"I can tell you what happened to him. And if he was in my shoes, he wouldn't want you to see him like that."

He just held her. His meaty hand wrapped around her tanned arm. But as long as he held her, she watched him, stared him square in the eyes without blinking, and finally he looked away and let go of her arm. "I go with you, though," he said. "And when we're done, I have some questions I need to ask."

"Evelyn, you come with us, too," she said, and like an ocean tide, I got swept up behind them.

I hadn't planned on looking. I hadn't planned on getting out of the Bronco. But once my feet were on the gravel it took five more steps. I took them without thinking.

You take my father. I didn't see him. They didn't let me see him till he was laid out for the wake twenty-four hours after he'd died. They'd dressed him in his favorite suit, with his tiny enamel Big Apple pin on his lapel. That was his great love, New York—after my mother. He wouldn't wear the American flag pins everyone else was wearing. New York City was all he knew, and it had made his fortune.

They'd put his everyday set of rosary beads in his hands. Obsidian beads, pewter links. He looked the same, except his hands, they were different. Like parchment stretched over ice. And so quiet. I'd never walked up to my father when he didn't have something to say to me. The quick cough to clear his throat first. Then a story. Something that happened at work or he'd read somewhere. Or asking what was up with me. After the wake, Mom and I stayed behind to say goodbye alone, but when we walked up to the coffin, Mom took my arm and pulled me away.

"Come on Evelyn. He doesn't even look like Daddy anymore."

I'd stood there a second longer and realized she was right, then reached out to him, touched his arm. I just wanted that last comfort from him, but he was hard like a tree.

Now that truck—and Bucky—that was a whole other story.

You couldn't see him from the back of the truck; he'd fallen across the seat, perfectly sideways like he had a metal rod up his spine. It wasn't natural. He must've spent his last bit of energy trying to stay upright, trying to stick the key into the ignition. The keys were still in his right hand with the Ford key separated, pointed like a teacher's ruler at a misbehaving child.

There was only one wound, right in the middle of his shirt. But there was enough blood for a hundred wounds. Lying like he was, slightly tilted back and his body in the middle of the seat, the blood had all pooled at his waist, having nowhere to run. Or maybe he had tried to keep it there—his hands were covered with it—trying to keep it close enough to keep him alive. And then there were the flies everywhere inside the cab. But it was still cool. They sat, quietly. Not that they had far to go.

"How long was he conscious?" Jaymie asked.

Chester kept back from the truck window, having seen the whole thing already.

"Don't know," he said. "Hard to tell just now. He coulda been in pretty good shape when he started out here, but he was pretty disoriented. Too disoriented to start the engine or walk over to the office for help."

Jaymie took a step backward and backed straight into Chester. He touched her shoulders gently to help her balance.

"He was at Mom's party last night. Till about midnight." She turned and faced him. Took a step backward and leaned against the driver's side door of Bucky's truck, then thought better of that and stood straight again. "You ever run into Sherry Fowler?"

"Dick Fowler's girl?"

"When'd you graduate?"

"Year before you," he answered.

"She was in your class. Didn't graduate, though. Been down in New Mexico, she said. She was talking about going to school again—staying with her Mom and Dad till she got done getting divorced. She was there at the party, helping clean up and stuff, then next thing we knew Bucky and her took off."

It'd been sunlight for a couple of hours by then, but as Jaymie and the deputy talked, the sun finally made it into the canyon. Little by little, the white clapboard walls of the Pincy Woods Motel grew brighter and brighter, the cab of Bucky's truck hotter, and the flies—large black horse and blue bottle flies—woke from their lethargy and began buzzing around Bucky's open eyes.

Jaymie took a step away from the noise, keeping her back to it.

Chester took his pad and pen out and wrote down some notes. Names and times. When he'd caught up with what Jaymie had told him already he looked up at her again.

"The night clerk says there was two of 'em checked in. Bucky and a woman with blonde hair, five foot two, maybe hundred pounds."

"That's Sherry."

"Soon's we get done here, I'll go talk to her folks, see if they know where she is."

"What do you suppose she did it with?" Jaymie asked.

That took Chester by surprise. He kind of laughed, just a little cough, then put his professional face on again. He wasn't very tall, this deputy, barely taller than me, maybe five nine or ten, but he was very strong looking, with broad shoulders, large calves and thighs and no fat on him anywhere.

"I figure she did it with her old man," he said. "He'd been trailing her. Had a couple of calls Saturday night from the Hayloft and the Tender. Man and woman fighting. We'd send a car, and they'd move on to the next place before we could get there. There's a lot of that stuff floating around, but you say she's just divorced. And the description matches the woman."

"So you think he just followed her?"

"Or lost her, and was just driving around wondering where the hell she went, and bingo. Found 'em."

"Come on Chester, for Christ's sake, how the hell would some dickhead from New Mexico know what my brother's truck looked like?"

"Didn't have to. Clerk says Buck checked in with two vehicles. J&B's black Ford truck and this old red Dodge Power Wagon." He pointed to the truck next to Bucky's. "I'm pretty sure that's one of Dick Fowler's rigs. All the ex had to do was spot a familiar red truck in an empty motel parking lot twenty yards off the Lolo Pass highway. Howdy Doody coulda handled that. Especially since we're only four miles from her folk's place."

Jaymie thought about that, let it sift through her brain. "So what did he do it with?" she said finally.

"I ain't got no crystal ball, Jaymie. But I'll tell you this much. It was a small weapon. Skinny knife, or small caliber gun. He didn't die right away from the wound. From the looks of that cab, Buck was sitting there a long time before he passed out."

"They left him to die."

Chester nodded. "That's what I'd say, first impression. But don't you go quoting me around town, dammit. Wait for the coroner to tell you nice and official."

While they'd been talking, the lab kit arrived and two new men began working on the truck. Chester led Jaymie and me over to a small picnic table at the side of the motel office. If a person just looked away, you could imagine a nice, quiet, streamside picnic with no troubles in the world. You didn't have to witness any of this.

Chester left us for a while to call in an APB on Sherry. Then when the crew was done, the black Ford towed away, and Bucky loaded into the hearse, he walked Jaymie and me back to the Bronco, saying he was going to talk with Sherry's folks and get back to us when he knew something for sure.

So there was nothing left for us but to go back to tell Wally and Rose what little we knew.

It wasn't till seven that evening we heard from the sheriff's office. Wally had sent all the party people home, assured them it was all a mistake. Then Rose's doctor had come to give her a shot. Not that she was hysterical or screaming or anything. She couldn't sit. Not even for five seconds. And she wouldn't go outside. We could've taken her for a walk down to the river or something, worn her down somehow, leaving Wally to take care of the phone—you know, wait for information, but mostly just answer the questions—but you'd start her to the door and she'd pull back. She said she could hear Bucky's voice out there. So we gave up on the walk and around noon, Wally called the doctor.

While Rose slept, Wally, Jaymie and I took turns on the phone. Call after call: friends, neighbors. Just the curious.

Was he really dead? Yes.

Was he really murdered? We think so.

Where'd he get hit?

Who murdered him?

Let me know soon's you hear? Yes of course, we'd say, and kind of look at each other and shrug.

Wally called Rose's sister Orene in Seattle, telling her what happened, what we knew and asking her if she could get free. She promised to call back with her flight information.

We'd run out of things to say to each other, to keep ourselves going, and Jaymie had fallen asleep curled up on the couch when the sheriff finally called.

Wally picked up the phone and answered, falling into a rhythm of rote replies—"Right," "Okay," "Yes"—one every fifteen seconds or so, till five minutes later, he hung up the phone and turned toward Jaymie.

"That was John Clark," he said. That was the sheriff of Missoula County. "Sherry Fowler called him from St. Mary's Lodge up in Glacier Park. She claims her ex-husband kidnapped her from the Piney Woods Motel last night. She also claims he shot Buck in cold blood. Told everybody in twenty-two western states he would kill the first buckaroo he found her chippying around with." Wally was just saying what she'd said, but he still had one hand on the phone even after he'd returned it to the cradle.

"She says," he continued, "she tried to get help for Bucky and her ex wouldn't let her. She says he drug her off by her hair and broke her arm twisting it around her back, and drove her up to Glacier Park thinking that was Canada and he couldn't be brought back."

Jaymie started to talk, but Wally put his hand up to stop her.

"You just be quiet young lady, till I tell you the rest of it."

Jaymie sat back again and swallowed hard. Tears started rolling down her cheeks and she put her hand up to her lips to keep control.

Wally went on. "They got the husband down from the park and questioned him. He says there's been no divorce. He says they're still man and wife and he shot Bucky to protect his conjugal rights. He has those rights. If I found your mother with some half-ass, jackass Rambo, I'd shoot the both of 'em. Deader than ticks."

"It wasn't his fault," Jaymie said. "Sherry said she was celebrating her divorce. Bucky had no way of knowing."

"He's been pussying around since he was old enough to peek over a windowsill. A real clever little bastard." He was angry, his face almost as red as his thick, wiry beard, but his eyes were full of tears.

"He's an innocent bystander."

"Don't add no more bullshit to this thing, Jaymie."

"How was he supposed to know?"

"How long's he been hanging around that half-wit Sherry? She's been leading him around by his pecker long's I can remember."

"Look. Bucky didn't carry any gun. This guy must have brought his own gun, which makes it premeditated. That makes it murder."

"Nope. He didn't bring no gun. Sherry provided the gun. Except she claims she didn't even think about it being there.

She was driving her dad's old Power Wagon. He's always kept a loaded .22 in the gun rack to pick off varmints. Everybody knows that. Even Sherry's ex. Keeps it right out in sight. It's so beat up he figures no one would ever steal it. Like stealing a shovel. What kind of idiot would steal a shovel? Seems like there was here a trio of idiots. She didn't lock her Daddy's truck. Didn't even roll up the windows. Didn't lock the motel door behind 'em. Her old man stumbles across her tracks and here's a gun—loaded—right in front of him. Bang. Heat of passion. He gets off, the way I see it. We bury your brother and that's it. This family ain't gonna set up no memorial to this . . . this accident waiting to happen. I guess I just wish he'd shot Sherry, too—keep some other poor pecker-head from getting his nuts in a wringer someday down the line—then stuck the gun in his own mouth and blowed his brains out. As it is we're still a couple bricks shy of cleaning up the neighborhood, I'd say."

Jaymie looked at him as if he as a perfect stranger just sat down in her living room. Then looked down at her hands, which she'd held tightly clasped in her lap since Wally had started talking. She unclasped her hands and rubbed quietly at the knuckles.

In the silence, the phone ringing again sounded like a volcano exploding. Wally answered it on the first ring to shut it up. He listened for a minute then said, "No. We have no statement to make for the *Missoulian*." He hung up, pushing the phone back against the wall.

"Once your Aunt Orene calls back, you pull the plug on this damned phone, Jaymie."

"Where are you going?" she asked.

"I got work out in the garage," he said, and left the room. For a while we could hear quiet, safe little noises out in the garage, but after he'd been out there ten minutes or so, there was an enormous crash, followed by several more smaller banging sounds like an earthquake and aftershocks, and then the sound of yelling. It filled the entire house and made the windows rattle. Jaymie waited till he stopped, then hesitantly walked out to the garage. She'd been gone thirty seconds when she came running back in, grabbing a roll of paper towels from the top of the refrigerator.

"You stay here," she said breathlessly. "Stay with Rose. Pops sliced his hand open, I'm taking him to Community Hospital. I'll call you from there, in case Orene calls." And before I had time to answer, she was gone.

Oh Lord, it frightened me to be in that house alone. I went around first thing and turned on all the lights, looked in on Rose, who was sound asleep, and closed all the curtains and locked the doors. Then I sat on the living room floor, with my back against the wall waiting for something horrible to happen to me, too. And then the phone rang.

"Hello?" I said.

"This is Rene. Who is this?"

"Evelyn Holloran," I said with my hand shaking the receiver against my ear.

"Evelyn. You're Jaymie's friend from New York, right?"

"Yes, ma'am."

"I'm Rose's sister from Seattle. Are you okay, Evelyn?"

"Yes, ma'am."

"Is Rose still asleep?"

"Yes."

"Where's Walls and Jaymie? Why aren't they answering the phone?"

"Wally cut his hand. Jaymie took him to the hospital."

"Oh Christ. Listen. I'm coming in tonight, ten-thirty. Can someone come fetch me?"

"Jaymie's going to call here after she's done at the hospital. They'll probably come get you on the way home."

"Okay, well if they're not there by eleven-thirty, I'll just take a cab out. And listen, Evelyn. You turn the TV on real loud. Something funny. No news or horror movies, you hear?"

"I'll be okay."

"I know that. But right now you sound scared shitless. Turn on the TV. Loud. And don't forget to tell Jaymie ten-thirty."

"Ten-thirty."

"Okay then. You okay?"

I nodded. "Ten-thirty."

"Evelyn honey, turn on the TV."

When Orene hung up, I turned on the TV real loud like she said and waited. And finally, around midnight, when Wally and Jaymie showed up with Orene, I realized I'd fallen asleep, that kind of light sleep you don't know you're falling into till you wake up.

I got the details of Wally's injury as Jaymie drove me home. Thirty-five stitches in three places across the knuckles of his right hand. He'd put it through a safety glass panel in the garage door, then driven the glass into his fist, banging it against the wall.

And more details of Sherry's ex-husband. They had his name. Eugene Bofay. And they had checked some of his story. No, there had been no divorce filed yet. Sherry and Gene were still husband and wife. With none of the JPs in at ten o'clock on a Tuesday night, they left the legal proceedings for Wednesday morning.

Six

W E U S U A L L Y worked Labor day, usually worked all the holidays except high holy days like Christmas and Thanksgiving, and Jack didn't pay time and a half or anything. But that Monday we happened to have off. So I only had to take one unpaid day for Tuesday, and since Jack never worked Wednesdays anymore, it would be Thursday before he could grill me. All I had to do was live through this one Wednesday. The arraignment.

It was sunny and warm still, like Monday morning had been, with heavy dew on the lawns and windshields, and the maple trees around the courthouse crowned with red and yellow leaves.

"You should've gone to work," Wally said to me when we met on the south courthouse steps. "You can't afford it," he continued when I tried to explain that I wasn't being as brave as he thought. Then he hugged me and thanked me, and I quit trying.

Orene and Jaymie each had one of Rose's arms, holding her up between them. Rose looked tired. Her feet moved, she said "Good morning," but she was like a Jerry Mahoney doll controlled through a hollow in her back. Jaymie had called me at six saying she'd woken up to find her mother in the basement at the rec room wet bar, about three-quarters through a pitcher of Manhattans, sitting there in her nightgown and robe, barefoot, trying to tape three straws together so she could drink straight out of the crystal decanter. And then, when Orene came down to help Jaymie get her mother upstairs and dressed, Rose had insisted that she would wear red. Whore red, she told them, in honor of Sherry, and she'd insisted on keeping the pitcher full and at her elbow through breakfast, which Orene made, but no one ate.

Rose had finally listened to reason apparently and compromised: she wouldn't wear black like Jaymie and Walls, but she agreed on a very tasteful, simple, yellow cotton dress, with straw sandals and a straw hat that bumped into Orene and Jaymie as they walked her up the courthouse steps to the second floor rotunda to wait for the arraignment.

The district attorney was late, his office locked, and the five of us stood outside on the second floor balcony watching people below run errands. Above us blazed the rotunda with its Edgar Paxson murals of Lewis and Clark, discoverers of Montana, doing their business in two-story perspective. *Explorers Trade with the Flatheads*, looking as comfortable as we were in our Sunday shoes.

It was only the second time I'd seen Jaymie dressed like that, the other being four days in a row last winter when IRS auditors descended on J&B. One-inch heels instead of cowboy boots, tasteful black linen suit instead of Levis, and the ever-present pearl-snaps and button shirt replaced by a bone-white raw silk blouse with cap sleeves, and the initials JLP embroidered on the front in Gothic lettering. The 'L' was for Lamberta, Wall's mother.

The D.A., when he finally showed up, honed right in on her. Lawyers always pick one member of the family to chew on. He seemed to know it couldn't be either Wally or Rose, that neither of them would let him make a public spectacle of their loss in the courtroom every day. Because that's what he wanted—a sad but composed, grief-stricken face to sit and listen to the gruesome testimony. Sensing that he would strike out with the bereaved mother and father, he settled on the sister.

Or maybe it was just that when we all sat down, Jaymie left room on the bench for the guy to sit down. But there he was—the man with a reputation as a goody-two-shoes, who wanted to initiate helicopter surveillance of backyards to search for illicit marijuana plants and close down the Legal Tender for being a haven for prostitutes—sitting next to Jaymie Porter, the Queen Bee of Tender Pursuit, in close conversation. He held the jacket of his three-piece suit modestly closed with one hand, while he drew visions of revenge and "hard" truth in the air with the other.

His truth was murder. No accident, self-defense, or heat of passion, as he predicted the defense would try to claim. Deliberate, premeditated murder in the first degree. Murder with malice aforethought. If we're lucky, the death sentence, he proposed. Certainly no less than ninety-nine years, and with him being already forty-five—neither Mr. Aamold nor Jaymie ever said his name—with a designation of dangerous offender, which they could include in the presentence brief, then no chance of parole.

He floated the words in front of her and she tasted them. She believed him, that he was right, that he could put Eugene Bofay away forever and the family would never hear from him again. And he wanted her to believe he could do that. He wanted her to come to the trial every day: no tears and no hysterics or the judge would kick her out. He wanted the jury to watch her, and they would watch her, as if she were her brother's own dead and mangled body. Murder. A simple case of deliberate, cold-blooded murder. Lars Aamold would make Gene Bofay fall off the face of the earth.

Rose leaned across Jaymie, pointing a finger at him. "And what about Sherry Fowler?" she asked.

"No one sees Sherry till her hair grows out."

"That's not what I meant," Rose insisted. "What will she be charged with?"

"Sherry Fowler is our only witness, Mrs. Porter. We intend to build our case on her testimony. She makes our case stronger. In fact, without her, it's only circumstantial evidence."

"If the jury believes all her little lies," Rose said. The county attorney had been talking to Rose like she didn't have a brain, and she didn't like it. "And if the jury happily forgets who was married to whom."

Mr. Aamold stood up, stepped in front of Rose and leaned back on the balcony railing. "I can delay trial three or four months. Sherry has her instructions in the meantime. She's to live with her parents. Go to school. No booze. No bars. No boys. New clothes: quiet, feminine new clothes. Maybe lose a little weight. She has a small frame. If she could lose ten pounds, she'd look like a war orphan. Helpless against an enraged man. We'll make even Eugene Bofay wonder if he's not guilty."

Rose leaned into him across the narrow rotunda aisle, making the district attorney lean back over the railing to keep a comfortable distance. "He is guilty," she said. "And so is that little slut. She lured my son to his death."

"The evidence," Mr. Aamold said, "is not strong enough against Bofay without Sherry's testimony. Gene Bofay does not go to jail without an eyewitness. The eyewitness doesn't talk without immunity from prosecution. But with that eyewitness, we have a 95 percent chance of conviction. It's a simple deal. We do it all the time."

We heard heavy, slow footsteps on the stairs below us. Gene Bofay, in handcuffs and leg irons, headed toward us, seven armed sheriff's deputies and a German sheperd bringing him in for arraignment. It was the first time any of us had seen him. And with his escort, we got only the briefest look at his face, mostly just the back of his head and a white cotton county jail jumpsuit that looked like he'd slept in it for the last two days.

I still remember his eyes. I knew he'd be Indian: the deputy had told us that after they had him in custody. He was tall like Rose, with large eyes. But unlike her deep sparkling black eyes, Bofay's were flat black, like cold asphalt. Was he tired? Bored? Scared? Two officers escorted him into the courtroom in handcuffs, followed by the lawyer for the defense, an Irish man, obviously, wearing a suit that would have fit my father, and in the same quiet, expensive style, except that the man was several inches taller and fifty pounds lighter than my father, and the pants had been pressed till the seat was shiny and thin. Cameron, his name. He followed Bofay into the courtroom, and Jaymie, Orene, Wally, Rose and I slipped in behind him.

The first motion Cameron made that day was a motion to dismiss, on grounds of racial prejudice: Eugene Bofay was a full-blood, reservation-deprived Crow Indian.

Mr. Aamold pointed out that Rose was Native American herself, raised on a reservation, and in any case, that it was no excuse for committing murder.

"Then there should be a change of venue," Cameron said. "At least. Half the damned police force in this town went to school with Porter or his sister, and my client is in danger up there in the county jail."

"Son of a bitch," Rose said, not meaning to say it so loud, but loud, and as the judge denied this last motion for the defense, he shot her a cautioning look.

"The audience is here at the court's sufferance," he said. "It will not tolerate any outburst or delay in proceedings. Go on Mr. Cameron."

As Cameron went on, droning on, padding his bill with motion after motion that had no chance of being accepted by the court, his client sat quietly, almost drugged, rubbing his wrists as if none of this had anything to do with him.

Rose watched Bofay. Her black eyes added him up and threw him out as so much trash. It was clear for anyone to read on her face. He was Crow. I'd been around Rose enough to know the Crows were persona non grata in her book; not true high Plains people, she said, but Midwest river rats, fish-eaters pushed west by waves of white immigrants onto the backbone of the Blackfeet people. Beggars. Didn't even look like real Indians, the Crows, according to Rose. And, in fact, Gene Bofay could be a street vender on Times Square, selling roasted chestnuts or potato knish off a handcart. He entered a plea of not guilty.

"Not guilty, my ass," Rose whispered to Wally, once again catching the ear of the judge, and he threw us all out of the courtroom while they finished.

There was the business of his sister to take care of. The sister almost as tall as Bofay but heavy, carbohydrate-heavy, with fat torso and skinny legs. She'd driven all the way from Lodge Grass the day before, she said, and if the judge would grant her brother bail, she would promise to keep Bofay out of Missoula, out of Lolo, away from the Porter family and Sherry Fowler, at her place in Lodge Grass, till the trial started. The judge set bail at $50,000. The sister went off immediately to make bail.

We left the courtroom with our county attorney, because now he really was ours: the state versus Gene Bofay, and all of us, the family, swallowed up in the good of the state, the need to protect all of its citizens. Today, Rose even accepted this role and Lars Aamold himself, simply because he hadn't fallen for the bleeding-heart-liberal stance on Bofay's reservation upbringing. She told him so on the way down the marble steps.

Oh, of course they had softened, Mother and Father, once the initial shock had worn off. What else could they do? Bucky was their son, for better or worse, and they would bury him, love him, remember him and somehow make peace with themselves. And Jaymie would protect them from the details.

We walked out of the courthouse into the sun. It was noon already and summer was over. From the south steps of the courthouse, the tall cottonwoods on the river formed a third and fourth story over the downtown office buildings. One good frost would bleed the last of the summer green from those trees, and then a wind would knock all the leaves to the ground. Winter could slam in from Canada in the middle of the night and steal fall in one brutal blow, or it could linger at the border, turn east at Calgary, and let fall grow luxuriantly golden in the mountains and river bottoms of Montana.

For the moment, Orene was in charge; Mr. Aamold gone back to his office, Wally off to Great Falls to escort Bucky back from the forensic lab there to the funeral home here. Despite his sins, or his stupidity as Wally now called it, he could not let his son make that last trip alone. Rose gave Walls a small hug and sent him off to the bus station. Her chores finished for the moment, Rose wanted a drink, one drink only, she promised.

"Then we'll go home and take care of the little business we have to take care of, and get to bed early," she said. She ordered a pitcher of margaritas. And a second. Orene the calorie counter, who wouldn't drink the fattening margaritas, but sipped white wine instead, sat patiently beside her sister waiting for her to be done. Rose was the older of the two. The taller. The slimmer. Not just in body mass, but in bone structure. They both had the deep olive skin color of their Blackfeet mother, but Orene had inherited the small mouth and large front teeth of her own father, instead of the high cheekbones and regal walk Rose accentuated every chance she got. And while Rose continued to dye her gray hair, Orene had let hers go natural, and in that late summer sunlight streaming into the west facing bar windows, her hair shone clean and silver white.

Since Orene and her husband had no children, to be here burying her nephew was as close as she could come to burying a son. But for now, it was her job to help Rose get through it. She could do her grieving later.

Rose polished off her second pitcher. Jaymie and I still had half of the first glass she'd poured us, and Jaymie was intent on her last piece of business. She'd arranged for a gravesite, a funeral home, the notice in the newspaper, even the headstone, but she insisted on making her mother choose the inscription. It was the only big decision left to make.

Jaymie had handprinted six possible epitaphs from "Rest in Peace" to various quotes from the Bible, to the simple joint statement, "Beloved Son/Beloved Brother," and put them in front of Rose. "If you could just point, I'll call the stonecutter and get it started, maybe have it done for Bucky's birthday."

"You're too much like your father, Jaymie. Bucky, he's like me, he wouldn't care if we waited." Rose folded up the paper and put it in her purse, zipping the purse closed and setting it back on the booth beside her. "I've already made a decision. I want him cremated. I don't want anyone going out there on a toot and desecrating his grave. And that's all I'm going to think about it today. I've had enough of this whole thing. Orene and I are going out to dinner, to the steak house. You girls can come along if you like, but I want to have a happy evening now."

"I won't have him being cremated. I want a gravestone. I want him to *be* somewhere," Jaymie insisted.

"He'll be safe and sound. On my dresser," Rose said.

"Bullshit. This is already taken care of. Gravesite. Casket. It's paid for."

Rose smiled. "Fine. But no marker."

"Yes marker." Jaymie took a sip of her margarita. "I chose a very tasteful pearl gray granite. It's ordered. All they need is the inscription."

"The ones you picked are too common," Rose said.

Orene gave Jaymie an elbow, but it was the look that shut her up. Orene ordered another glass of white wine and tried to change the subject. "You would do well to count your calories, Rose, those margaritas are loaded."

A small detour. "Later," Rose said. "Much later, when I'm old and fat. I can sit in my garden with my floppy gardenia-picking hat and drink white wine with ice and orange slice garni," she said, and then she dropped her eyes as if she'd spilled something. "That's a pretty picture isn't it?" she said. "Sitting peacefully in my garden till I'm a hundred and one?" She ordered another pitcher of margaritas.

The place had filled up. A mixture of shorts, t-shirts and late summer sunburns—the last river floaters of the season; and wool, three piece suits—town folks who'd sat in over-heated offices all day, wishing summer would be over already. They all descended on the free buffet at four o'clock sharp.

A river float foursome slipped into the booth behind ours, plates heaped with cocktail franks and nachos, as the waitress brought our third pitcher to the table. The four of them were hot and heavy into boisterous conversation, two men and two women whom we ignored until one of them brought up the latest hot news. She was talking about Bucky of course. Rose picked it up a second before I did.

They said nasty things about Bucky. The blonde one with the sun screen plastered all over her nose said it served him right. She heard he'd been out at the Piney Woods Motel in Lolo and that was just a sleaze motel in a sleazier little burg and what did he expect. The girl was probably a prostitute anyway. That guy must have been a real loser.

"Natural selection at work," the PBS t-shirt man agreed. "Clearing out the gene pool."

"I wonder if he thought his last piece of ass was worth it," the blonde girl said.

And that was when Orene, who had the inside seat on Rose's side of our booth, pushed Rose to her feet and out the door. I followed close behind with Jaymie in tow, hoping she wouldn't open her mouth, not that she didn't have the right, but there just wasn't any point. You couldn't convince people like that. Jaymie seethed.

"Don't make it any worse for your mother," I told her halfway to the door.

She glared at me, but kept walking and I kept her as close behind Rose and Orene as I could, knowing I would have a hard time on my own keeping her under control if she really wanted to say something.

"Don't ever take me into that filthy rat hole again, Rene," Rose demanded as her sister pushed her into the back seat of the Eldorado. "Nothing but dirty little cuntbuckets in there."

"No, I promise," Orene answered and got in beside Rose. "Evelyn, you drive home. No stops."

Which I did, with the fear of God in me. I shook like a leaf trying to keep the Spruce Goose inside the little white lines, and worrying that I'd kill the rest of the family all by myself. I'd never driven a car as big as Rose's convertible.

Then Thursday I went to work and had to listen to it all over again: *Jack's* opinion this time on the whole thing, which he either described as a heroic act—he died with his boots on—or as utter selfishness—his father worked half his life to be able to leave his kid a livelihood and what does he do? His take on it depended on how angry he was at me that particular moment for turning the loss of only one day's pay into a three-day vacation. If he could've said what was really on his mind, he would have added that it was selfish of Bucky too, not planning his death during hunting season when I had lots of time to fool around without inconveniencing the Doctor.

"Just don't let that family get under your skin, E. They'll bleed you dry and throw you away," he warned, and disappeared for his ten o'clock coffee break.

I rolled my eyes at Sue who'd stayed out of it, behind her desk.

"He's right," she said, after the back door slammed shut and she was sure Jack was out of hearing. "Not about the family, though. Christ they're good people. But the situation. It's gonna knock 'em down and shit on 'em. And when it's all over they'll still have each other. What'll you have? You suppose Jack'll give you a paid mental health vacation for being a good Samaritan? Bull shit. He'll give you a swift kick in the ass out the door if you can't do your job. And another thing, I don't suppose Gordy's around for much hand holding. When you gonna find yourself a steady, homebody kind of guy?"

"Don't you start on me too, now. I'm dating Gordy. Until I break up with Gordy, I'm dating Gordy. One man at a time."

Sue was about to launch into another explanation of Cruisers. One nighters. How they couldn't make the Big C.

Commitment. Couldn't bear owning the same pickup more than four years; buy flour in one pound boxes. Write a postcard? Then, God forbid, there'd be something in writing.

"You sound like the doctor," I said, hoping to head her off.

"Sorry," she said and rearranged her coffee cup, napkin, donut and spoon. "You know this brother very well?"

"I spent three minutes with him—in a crowd of thousands—the night he died. I'll be fine."

"When's the funeral?" she asked.

"Saturday. Jack will be happy, I won't have to take any time off."

"I'm happy as a pig in shit I don't have to assist. I'll even take you to lunch today to show my gratitude."

"Can't. I'm having a working lunch with Jaymie. Help her with the details."

She gave me one of her patented looks. Mom calling me sweet was nothing compared to Sue's green-eyed stare.

"It's okay. It's a few days out of my life. The funeral will be Saturday and everything will get back to normal. I'll get back to normal. Jack won't miss his favorite assistant, and you won't get spit on your hands." She always reacted to that. Like scratching when someone starts talking about ticks, every time I said spit Sue Raffin wiped her hands on her pants. I laughed at her, watching her rub. "It will be over soon, I promise."

"Yes," she said. "That's what you said three minutes ago and you're still talking about it. I think this is one of those things that can grab you by the short and curly. Don't do it for Jack. Keep your head on your shoulders. For you."

These were the signs and I should've noticed them. Lunch with Jaymie at the salad bar of Big Chief Pizza, we didn't get anything done. She spent the whole time filling me in on the night before.

"I left you safe at home," I said. I was eating. She was pushing the food around the plate with her fork.

"Rose snuck out of the house. Rene and I just heard her pulling out of the driveway and followed her down to the Hayloft saloon."

"The Hayloft?"

"You know it. The old bar in beautiful downtown Lolo Village. She said she just wanted to see people she knew down there. It used to be a local bar, but now all the yahoos from Missoula come slumming out the ten miles and party hearty out there. Anyway, we weren't in there ten minutes when who the hell do you think rolls in?"

"I haven't any idea."

"Gene Bofay. In the flesh, despite the promises his sister made. He's in the bar, guys patting him on the back, getting glad-handed, they're making like he's a goddamn hero, and before Rene and me can get Mumsy out of there, she's calling him an asshole and worse. Thank goodness he didn't recognize her right off and just ignored her. But we got her out of there and stuck her in the middle between the two of us to get her home in the Eldorado, and left the Bronco there, 'cause she was ready to punch his headlights out."

"Well, what happened?"

"He didn't follow us. Rene called the sheriff as soon as we got Rose safely home. I tell you Evelyn, I had Pop's 12 gauge loaded and in my lap. If that asshole had walked in through the kitchen door there would have been brains on the refrigerator. I'm almost sorry I didn't get the chance."

"So he's in jail?"

"No." she said. "They gave him a second chance. The deputies found the sister and put them both on the road. They escorted him to the county line, sweet as you please. Like he was some damned VIP."

"So he's gone now."

"So they say."

"You better eat. It's getting late."

"Fuck eating." She got up and threw her salad plate into the garbage bin and headed out the door.

IT SHOULD'VE BEEN raining Saturday, it rained the whole week after my father died. But for Bucky, the birds sang and the sky glowed turquoise blue and the family laid Walter Henry Porter III in the ground amid a profusion of late summer flowers. They did it Jaymie's way. A casket, a plot; the stone on order.

Orene and I dressed Rose the best we knew how, choosing clothes we knew Rose would never in a million years wear together as an "ensemble," knowing she just wanted to be done with it, to live through the funeral and the days after without thinking. She did enough of that at night. She had dreams. Bucky was calling to her for help. He was right outside the patio door and she couldn't open it and he bled to death right in front of her. Then he was in his coffin, and the coffin was in Rose's bed and she saw tears running down his cheeks, but when she tried to comfort him in the dark, she couldn't tell where his arm started and the mahogany casket left off.

Bucky was in the new part of the cemetery. I'd been out twice with Jaymie picking the spot, learning from the groundskeeper more than I ever wanted to know about the logical, chronological disposition of graves throughout the hundred-plus-year history of the Missoula Municipal Cemetery. As the graveside services droned on, my eyes wandered up the row of newest graves searching out the date of death, testing out the exactness of the chronology. Bucky's was in the middle of the last narrow strip before the end of the cemetery property, one last sodded-in strip before the cyclone fence and then the vast, empty former home of Rocky Mountain Fiberboard Corporation. I calculated how long it would take to fill this last strip before the city would have to buy out the vacant fiberboard property.

Vaguely, I remembered the news stories when I'd first come to Missoula. Four hundred workers laid off. Then two hundred. Then the final hundred. But it was so far over on the north side of town I'd forgotten it was still closed. Two-foot-high weeds grew in the cracked asphalt and the giant storage hangars gaped like jack o'lanterns. It should have been scary. I guess if it had been empty and deserted the first time I'd seen it, it would have been scary. Now it just seemed sad. Like Buck. If you saw them alive, and they were your own, they had no power to scare you. Only other people's dead became horrible ghosts that made the hair on your neck stand up. Unless you had Rose's dreams.

When the service was over, Rose was the only one who wouldn't throw a handful of dirt on the coffin. Wally took Jaymie's place walking Rose back to the car. Jaymie walked back with me, but she never said a word or reached out to hold my hand. She was lost in thought, with her hands thrust deep in her pockets and her words deep in her head.

Jaymie moved into the house temporarily to take turns with Wally and Orene sitting up with Rose, then taking turns with her father going down to J&B, keeping the shop going. And I think, after the first week, after that night at the Hayloft, Rose started to trust that Bofay had really fallen off the face of the earth like Mr. Aamold had promised he would, and the nightmares became less and less frequent. She began to talk about Bucky in the past tense, "What happened, just happened," she said. "There was nothing I could have done to prevent it."

Orene had stayed a month to make sure Rose was on her feet before she went back home to Seattle, suggesting before she left that we get Bucky's truck out of police impoundment and clean it, wax it and try to sell it. Get rid of it.

It was a good idea, but I think it came too late. Instead of wanting to put the incident behind her, Jaymie had started collecting and storing things. Once she got the truck back to her place, she got a one-gallon mason jar from Rose's pantry and collected all the matchbooks from the dash and the glove compartment, the map pockets, all over his truck: The Crossroads, Miles City; Steve's Restaurant, Buffalo, Wyoming; Butte's Pekin Noodle Parlor; the Sun River Grotto and Steak House, Sun River, Montana. She took them home, sealed the jar and set them up on the windowsill over the sink.

"You should put them away somewhere," I said. "It's only going to make you feel miserable. Or use them. One at a time, carry them around till they're finally all gone."

But she kept the jar front and center, as if by just seeing the names on the matchbook covers she could keep him alive in those places at least. Still alive, and someday she would figure out how to snatch him back. The second night they were there, she added a book from The Tender. It was growing, becoming a living monument, and I worried about her. She thrived on her loss and that truck was the worst of it.

Saturday, after Orene left, I talked Jaymie into taking the truck down to Berg Ford to be sold on consignment. But Tuesday she had me take her down again on my lunch break and said, "Never mind. Thanks, we've had a change of heart," and she drove it back to her double-wide out on Arabian Acres and locked it up in the garage.

She bought me lunch at the Jumbo Elephant Drive-In and made excuses. "The inside's dusty," she said. "And it needs new tires before I try to sell it." But she didn't put new tires on it. And she wouldn't clean it up. It sat in her garage, and she had to park her pride and joy Bronco out in the driveway.

No matter what I said about getting rid of the truck, she answered with a "yes but" and told me a father dying of a heart attack in a nice clean hospital bed didn't equal a brother shot by a sleazy prairie nigger wino. She didn't mean that. A year from now she wouldn't say that. She just hurt and keeping the jar of matchbooks on her kitchen sink, and the truck, as is, in the garage, kept her a step away from letting him disappear forever.

"If I stop thinking about him," she told me finally, "he'll be gone."

"At least let me replace the seat cover."

But that was all she would let anyone do.

SEVEN

FOR ONCE Jack maybe was right: there is only so much you can do for another person. Besides, I had my own problems. My sister Katherine kept calling. One night after work, I was tired and hungry and while she talked, I stood with my back up against the refrigerator trying to rub the soreness out of my neck while spooning fruit-on-the-bottom yogurt into my mouth. It was a sorry excuse for a dinner, but at least it provided protein and vitamin C instead of fat, sugar and preservatives like the two bags of Oreo cookies I'd dined on the last two nights.

"You need to come back home and take care of mother. She's going soft. Says she talks with Daddy about taxes and investments and things. Says he's in the house, just like he's always been, and thinks I'm crazy for thinking he'd leave her."

"Well, at least she's not drinking," I said, thinking of Rose and her crystal pitcher.

"This isn't the Wild West," Katherine told me.

"*This* isn't the Wild West. There's houses, not tepees; nice wet bars in the rec room. I can't come home right now."

"It's not fair to leave me holding the bag."

"You can take care of it."

"Of course I can take care of it. But she needs someone in the house with her."

"Someone besides Dad, you mean. Why don't you move back home?" I suggested.

"That's impossible. I'd have to commute seventy-five miles each way. Don't think I haven't thought about it. The thing is this. She lost Daddy. Now she's lost you."

"I'm not lost. I call Mom. She knows where I am. She knows I'm okay. She never tells me any of these strange ghost stories."

"You haven't called in a month. You're out there on the Ponderosa chasing rainbows. When are you going to grow up Evelyn? Go to college? Get a real job?"

What I wanted to say was I wasn't ever coming back. But I knew that wasn't true. At least I thought I knew that.

"This isn't a good time," I said.

And I guess I said it loud enough that she could hear me, finally. If she'd been a smoker, she could have lit and smoked half a cigarette in the silence she gave me to change my mind.

"Are you all right?" she finally asked.

The thing was, I hadn't told Katherine, or my mother, about Bucky's accident. They wouldn't understand. I didn't understand. And I hadn't been gone from New York long enough not to hear for myself just how wild and woolly the whole Bucky thing was. Guns and love triangles. Sherry as the typical B-movie, bar half-wit who would innocently lead a willing boy astray.

"I'll call Mom tonight," I said.

"It's a pale substitute to sitting over coffee with her Sunday after church," she said.

"It's the thought that counts."

"Don't give me trite love-isms. I'm the one still in the picture, remember. I'll tell Mom you're planning on being home for Christmas."

"I can't do that. I've already made plans for Christmas." And I had. Jaymie's grand plan for the holidays was to keep me around, to keep Rose thinking about company in the house. That started with Columbus Day and included Thanksgiving, which was just around the corner.

"We'll put your picture on the dining room table," Katherine said.

"Just don't use the one of me at fifteen with the bouffant hairdo and little clip-on bow in my bangs," I said, which made Katherine laugh, and then she was quiet again. "I'll miss you both at Christmas."

"You know I love you," she said. "It's just scary to see Mom like this."

"They were married thirty-nine years. She's not going to let him go very easily."

"It just makes me scared," she said. "We've been going through his papers. You know how he told us he was a medic in the war? He was a harbor pilot. He was in Europe, June 7. The day after D-Day. He was ferrying troops and tanks and stuff to the coast of Normandy while the American army was hanging on to the coast by their toenails. I can't believe he never told us. And there's more of his father's papers. In the bottom of the boxes."

"Grandpa's papers?" It hit me like a hammer. What papers?

"He was a member of the Lather's Union in Butte, Montana. And married Grandma there. At Sacred Heart Church.

Dad's had their marriage license tucked away all these years. I can't find the cowboy photo though."

"I have that. Mom said I could take it with me."

"Oh. She must have forgotten."

"I can have a copy made. Send it to you," I suggested.

"That's okay. As long as we know where it is. Mom was tearing his dresser apart looking for it."

"She's still got his stuff in the dressers?"

"That's what I'm telling you. And the closet. And his bathrobe on the hook on the bathroom door. She's still got the book he was reading, sitting on his nightstand."

"Thirty-nine years doesn't stop overnight," I said, but it still sounded weird. "I'll call tonight."

"Promise?"

"Yes. But keep me posted. You know, if it gets worse or she starts expecting him home or something, for dinner." Then we said good-bye and hung up.

She was terrified. What would she feel watching Rose, as Jaymie was doing, drink herself into a stupor every night, taking pills, and still waking up screaming that Bucky was calling to her. It wasn't hard to start thinking Mother had it easy compared to Rose; that it was easier to accept death in a hospital bed, with your family around holding your hand.

So that was the real problem, you know, Katherine being scared for our mother. She was taking that on all by herself, because I couldn't tell her how lucky Mom was. I was scared for Rose. And what Jaymie was doing to herself kept me up at night, too. I'd thought once Gene Bofay had gone off to his sister's house in Lodge Grass, I could go back to work. But first it was the jar, then the truck, then about a month after the accident she'd gone down to the sheriff's office and weaseled a set of death scene photographs from the file clerk and every night after work she shuffled them on her dining room table, like playing solitaire, while she drank herself into oblivion, all the while reciting this litany about how Rose was not handling things as well as she could. Rose wouldn't let go. Rose is going to drive us all crazy, Jaymie said.

I sat with her for three nights running after she got them. The photos out on the dining room table, while I sat in the living room pretending to watch TV. Photos I'd seen once in real life and never wanted to see again. She was drinking, and the more she drank, the louder she complained about Rose. Rose wasn't being realistic. Rose wasn't facing reality.

"Rose hasn't got the slightest idea what really, really happened out at the motel that night. Not the slightest bit of curiosity what happened to her kid."

"What she imagines is probably a lot worse than the truth."

"Oh, I honestly doubt that. And I'll be damned if I spend another night out there baby-sitting the old hag."

"You don't mean that," I told her. I'd tried to talk her into drinking less or at least packing those damn pictures up in their manila envelope and stuffing them behind the couch.

"And if it comes to that, you'll do it," I told her. Rose, I meant, going out to baby-sit Rose.

"Thank you Dear Abby for your kind but meaningless words of comfort."

Not that I'd expected her to be grateful. That's not why you sit up with someone. But I had to set my limits. No matter what Mother or Rose or Jaymie did or said, or didn't do, I had to pay my rent. I had to get up at six-thirty and trot down to Dr. P's office and put in a productive day for him, and more, saving for the time Jack would be gone. Already it was tight and there wasn't much time before Jack's hunting would start. I needed a raise or some guaranteed days in the office while the Doctor was on vacation, and to get those, I had to show initiative and motivation and spunk, as Jack called it, in the workplace.

At the same time I had to be careful not to say I wanted him to work more. That was Sue Raffin's job. What I needed was for me to work more; for me to have more time for organizing and ordering replacement instruments for the office.

When I was a kid, my dentist just drilled. No numbing, no assistant, no laughing gas. He just stood at the chair and made holes, filled holes, answered his own phone, collected the money and drilled more holes with those old fashioned pulley drills. Now, you're on a compressor to keep the air/water syringe, the suction, the high-speed all operating; administering nitrous oxide to dry the mouth, and carbocaine for pain, and using all that stuff, somebody's got to sit with the patient every second to watch for anaphalactic shock. Not just a body—like Sue—and not someone who's worrying about the shortage of lower left molar anodized aluminum temporary crowns, or 25-mm root canal reamers starting to show signs of wear. Break one of those reamers off in a bifurcated root canal and Jack would want to know where the hell my head was at.

You don't watch people carefully enough when you're always digging in the operatory drawers, making lists and trying to keep track of which reamers you checked last time you had three minutes of "free" time. Oh sure, you can talk to the patient on nitrous, keep an ear out for silences and disoriented thoughts, but what if they get a rash, start to flush? By the time you turn around and actually notice, they could be dead. Sue Raffin said it would serve Jack right—getting himself sued—for not sticking to business. For being the only one in the office not treating the patient like a customer who has to be stroked. Has to feel good to keep coming back.

What it came down to was if I wanted that raise, it wouldn't pay to increase Jack's frustration level, and working with Sue Raffin as assistant would do that quick enough. So for the first three nights she had the photos, I'd slept in Jaymie's spare bedroom because she said she couldn't sleep in an empty house. But the fourth night, I explained to her that I wasn't staying over, that life went on, at least for me, and she would be healthier in the long run if she allowed Bucky to die once and for all. "I'm sleeping in my own bed tonight so I'll be up and at 'em tomorrow and ready to go to work," I said.

I went back to work the next morning, expecting to barely make it through the four-day week, and discovered Jack had added more days to his hunting vacation in October and Sue Raffin had consequently insisted on adding Wednesday to that week making room for the canceled patients. And we worked till seven and seven-thirty every night making up for Jack's ten o'clock breakfasts and three-hour, one-on-one lunch matches. I got more hours, and with that I was happy. If I wasn't at work, I was at my apartment with the phone un-plugged, sleeping twelve hours a night with no dreams, no tears, no handholding, and by Friday, I began to feel almost normal again. I got up early Friday, baked an apple pie for the office, for Jack, and walked to work with the two hot mitts barely keeping my fingers from melting. I smelled cinnamon and the crisp cool of morning instead of half-empty highball glasses and dirty ashtrays.

All day I anticipated correctly, setting up all the right in-struments before Jack came in to work the patient. I skipped lunch to catch up on filing x-rays and felt good, felt at home again in my office. As the last patient left, I was thinking maybe I wouldn't go down to see Jaymie and Rose, wouldn't check in on them. I'd call my mother, see how she was doing, and treat myself to a movie. I washed my hands for the last time that day, turned off all the electrical equipment, the compres-sor, the nitrous oxide gas system, armed the burglar alarm and walked home.

I had barely an hour of peace, when Jaymie knocked on my door. I had my slippers and bathrobe on and visions of a quiet evening still dancing in my head and like a fool, even seeing her on the doorstep, I thought I could salvage my peace and quiet.

"Is there something wrong with your phone or something?"

"It's unplugged."

"Unplugged? Why would you unplug your phone?" Jaymie, the social butterfly, would never understand that even before the accident. She looked tired. Tired and sad and worried. She sat down in my reading chair. "Never mind, don't answer. I need a favor. A big favor. Mother slammed her foot in the car door, and we've got auditors at the shop. Pop and I both have to be down at the place to answer questions, and somebody's got to stay with her."

She stood up in the middle of that speech and started turning off lights, picking up my coat, hat and gloves.

"Auditors?" I said. "What are the auditors doing back? They did you the last two years in a row, didn't they?"

"Not IRS. Pop's going to sell J&B right out from under me, now that Bucky isn't around to argue. He's got a couple of CPA's out there making up profit charts and all that, making the place more salable, he says, and gonna dump it at the first decent proposal. I gotta be out there to play it down, make sure he doesn't sell it right off, in the heat of passion. I'm sure I can talk him into just walking away from it and letting me have the store, but I need time, Evelyn. He wants to tie me up at home waiting on Mother, hand and broken foot, and keep me out of the way. Please come. I've worked my ass off at that place since I graduated from high school. I know that place as well as he does. Hell, I run it. It belongs to me." She got up and pushed me into the bedroom. "Come on, clothes and shoes. Dressed."

I dressed, locked up the apartment and walked down the

stairs behind her to the truck, and only after I was in it did I notice it was Bucky's.

"You shouldn't be driving this," I said.

"Alternator's out on the Bronco. And anyway, these four-wheel drives, you gotta drive them once in a while to keep the four-wheel greased." So she drove to the hospital at eighty-five miles an hour.

THAT WAS MY QUIET Friday night. Sitting with Rose in the emergency room watching the drunks waiting to get their ears sewn on again, while Rose lay on a gurney telling me over and over how the accident had happened. Occasionally a nurse would come out and check on her or wheel her into x-ray for another view of the ankle, but she never lost her spot in the story, no matter how many times she told it. You'd think it would all be alphabet soup by two in the morning, with the demerol, the pain—and there had to be pain, because what she'd done was slam the ankle in her Eldorado. Flying out of the house after another argument with Jaymie, alone, because Walls was down at J&B with the accountant, and slamming the Dorado's door hard as she could to make her escape *and* her anger more visible, not realizing her left foot wasn't inside.

Then there were the details of the argument. She told the whole story like she was peeling an orange. Each time in the same order. It started with the question: Where's Pops? Started with Rose deciding it was better for Jaymie to know the truth; telling Jaymie why Wally was working at ten o'clock at night.

"What do you mean you're selling the place?" Jaymie screamed at her.

"It's better that you know now," Rose said.

"What? Better than me finding out when they pack me up and throw me out the door? Great! Those are my choices, huh? Thanks a lot."

"You can't do the whole thing by yourself. We always hoped Bucky would come back and you'd have each other."

"So now I have diddly-squat."

"Don't talk to me like that, Jaymie."

"Don't *do* me like this, Mother."

"It's in your best interest. It'll take your entire life. You'll never have time for a family or anything."

"Let me worry about that."

"It's a parent's job to worry about their kids."

"But dammit, I'm not a kid."

"You'll think differently when you're older."

"I'm not getting any older at this rate. Not with you cutting me off at the knees. I've worked my ass off for the store. And you're just going to sell it out from under me with no asking—not even giving me a chance to beg for the goddamn place?"

"You're being impossible. I can't talk to you," Rose had said. And that's when she grabbed a coat, slammed the kitchen door and got in the Caddy.

We sat in the emergency room, waiting. She'd told me the story ten times before they finally took her in to surgery, set pins, reconstructed her ankle, set the bones and made a soft cast. They allowed me in when it was done—she'd lied and told them I was her second daughter when Jaymie left me off— and once I saw she was safely asleep, safely drugged and whispering about Elvis doing her wrong, I whispered good night to her and walked downstairs and out into the night, suddenly realizing it was morning. I started to call J&B to get a ride home, thinking it was the least they could do, but hung up at the first ring.

It would be less complicated to just walk.

EIGHT

WHEN I GOT home I decided not to play sitting duck, just waiting for them to come get me again. I spent the whole day wandering around the city, sitting in parks and watching other people walking two by two, walking to the movies, or downtown for dancing, or just standing on the Higgins Street Bridge holding hands as they looked down into the reflection of sunset in the slow-moving Clark Fork. Mostly they just leaned against each other in that intimate way: hip to hip, without embarrassment or self-consciousness. I didn't go back home till midnight, made sure the phone was unplugged and my door locked, and fell into bed.

As soon as the light was off though, in the darkness and warm hum of the refrigerator motor, with nothing left to watch go by or entertain me, I thought of Gordy. How I missed

Gordy. Even the long sitting in the chair unwinding from his month on the road. It was something to anticipate. Somebody else's problems.

It wasn't just Gene Bofay who'd fallen off the face of the earth. It was Gordy, too. I knew he was around. I read about the fire season in the newspapers, but I never heard word one from Gordy. If it hadn't been for the rest of what was going on taking up all my time to just think my way through, I would've gone out to the Tender one of those weekend nights, and maybe just try to meet someone nice, maybe just once have someone to talk to in the morning. Except I was too chicken to really do it. Sue kept inviting me to go out Friday night after work—to the Gay Nineties or the Office bar—but I didn't want a computer nerd or an accountant, or an insurance adjuster who calls himself a private eye. There had to be the magic of chance. And I was still in love with Gordy. What I didn't know about him could fill a book, but what I felt around him, I had no words for. He'd come to me in my dreams and be everything I wanted him to be. Then I'd wake up and no one was there.

Jack started to pressure me, again, to let him get me dates for my football tickets. The free football tickets I got for assisting with the University of Montana's football team's yearly dental exams.

"You need to get out and get some sunshine, quit staring at your four walls," he told me. And there was some truth to that.

"I gave the tickets away," I lied.

"This is me you're talking to, kid," he said. "You don't give anything away." He stared at me then. We had a denture adjustment in the chair, ninety-two-year-old Catherine Henry, who'd been in the week before for a long overdue reline. Tuesday, 8:00 a.m., she'd given us a tea-stained plastic denture with two missing plastic teeth that she couldn't hold in her mouth with epoxy cement, and 5:00 p.m., we'd given her back a sparkling, perfect, ultratight-fitting denture, and warned her she would have sore spots and to call us immediately when she hurt. This morning Catherine was in the office at the insistence of her granddaughter.

"She took a whole jar of Skippy peanut butter, the extra creamy kind, and started whittling away where they hurt her," the granddaughter explained. Using the peanut butter to pinpoint the tight spots.

In spite of the peanut butter, Catherine didn't have a spare ounce of flesh on her four-foot, six-inch frame; the granddaughter had it all. Jack said she'd dress out at 250 pounds, which was his idea of a joke. He liked to talk about fat women that way—as if they were elk or deer he'd shot, gutted and hung on a meat hook to age, like prime beef. It didn't matter that she was a nice, honest, hard-working woman either, which Catherine's granddaughter was. A very devoted and gentle caretaker of a very frail but headstrong old lady.

She'd walked Catherine in, set her safely in the dental chair, and then perched on the cabinets in operatory two to make sure the Doctor fixed what was hurting the old lady, and make sure the old lady didn't call the Doctor a quack or worse, as she'd done out in the reception area once already.

"I've never heard Grandma cuss before, Doc. You really got her riled up," the granddaughter said from her perch.

I think if Jack ever took any freebies, his choice would always be the old folks. He loved the little old ladies and gentlemen. So he took the denture, winced, and quietly went to work at re-creating the seal on his brand new reline. (If Catherine had been forty years younger, Jack would have given her the "Reason You Pay the Doctor" lecture.) He had to add quick-cure plastic, since Catherine's pocketknife and her skills at wielding it weren't quite what her myopic eyes thought they were, and she'd left big gouges where there was supposed to be a vacuum seal. Then he had to start over with a mouth exam to find and grind out the real trouble spots.

He gave Catherine back her denture, handed her a stack of crackers to chew on to see how they felt, and while we waited, he gave me the third degree about the season football tickets. He glared at me across Catherine's blue-haired head that only came about halfway up the back of the dental chair.

"You've got them stashed away for safekeeping," he said. "You're as bad a pack rat as I am."

So I gave in and admitted they were indeed stashed under the silverware tray, feeling shamed at lying in front of Catherine and her granddaughter, and Jack told me not to worry. He'd fix me up with six very nice, up-scale dates for the six regular season games of football season. One up-scale guy at a time, in case I fell in love.

"Stop me when you get to Mr. Right," Jack said. The dates, and football games, started in two days.

Well, bachelor number one wore a fake lizard-skin shirt and polyester pants, all beige and brown-tones with lots of gold jewelry on his neck, fingers, wrists and shoes. And a fine Italian-made, knee-length leather jacket. Luckily it was warm at the stadium. After the game, he took me to the Alumni Elks Club no-host post-game cocktail party and quickly fell into conversation with other men with jewelry on their shoes. I went home, wondering how long it would take him to miss me. The home team had lost, 27-6.

Number two had a harder time. Game day dawned cold, windy and damp. Neither one of us dressed warm enough and in the second quarter, noticing I was shivering badly, he brought out a pint bottle in a brown paper bag from his inside jacket pocket. Apricot brandy.

"It will warm you up," he said.

I drank. It warmed me. I drank some more. By the time the band had finished the halftime entertainment and the sky divers had picked up their purple-and-orange striped mini-parachutes and gone home, bachelor number two had me bundled off to his apartment and I spent the rest of the afternoon throwing up in his downstairs bathroom and fending off his groping hands. The second time he forced his way into the bathroom, I pushed him out and locked the door, passing out on his faux marble bathroom floor with the laundry hamper and my feet propped against the door.

Bachelor number six had some potential. He wasn't a friend of Jack's. He was a friend of a friend of Jack's stockbroker, a fellow stockbroker and native of Missoula, who lived in San Francisco. Tony. He drank rye. The first person I'd known since my father who drank rye—and only one in an evening. He dressed warmly for the game—in layers—pale yellow oxford cloth shirt, slate gray crew neck sweater, herringbone wool sports jacket and a heavy, sheepskin-lined suede coat with a deep collar he buttoned up to cover half his face when the Hellgate wind started blowing through the stadium in the fourth quarter.

"Poor planning and engineering," Tony explained. "Setting the open ends of the stadium in such a way as to create a chute for the Hellgate winds."

A thoughtful man. He'd even brought a stadium blanket which I wrapped myself in to keep warm and bought me hot spiced wine at the Edgewater Restaurant, lobster for dinner, and thanked me for a wonderful afternoon and evening. The home team lost that game, too. (They had lost the third, fourth and fifth as well. But the sixth and final game was what Tony called a "rout," 67–12.) Tony said nothing had changed since his college days, and he went back to San Francisco and I never heard from him again.

When I told Sue, she said, "He must've been one of those gay boys, didn't even try to give you a tumble. You've got to beware of the real polite boys, you know."

"Not everyone who lives in San Francisco is gay," I said.

"Everyone who moves from Montana to San Francisco is gay. Now a boy who likes to fondle sheep, that's pretty well normal. But these pink boys they learn real fast they're not gonna last long or stay pretty in Big Guy Country."

"I just don't think because somebody's polite he's necessarily a homosexual."

"Well," she said. "Personally, I like a man knows how to fix my carburetor and doesn't wear rubber gloves to do it."

There were just some times you couldn't reason with Sue Raffin. You had to accept that about her. Like when I showed her my can of mace—for self-defense—and she said, "Just don't use it on Indians. It don't work on Indians."

And that's how fall went, which wasn't exactly the happiest fall in my life.

December, just before Christmas, Jack had a bright idea. A pal of his from dental school was coming out to visit for a week, and the guy was a prince. Smart. Honest as the day is long.

"He's here four days," Jack said. "I'd give him up for one. For you."

"If you bring him to the office, I'll see what I think," I said.

"Of course. That's what I'd planned."

So he brought Johnny B. into the office, and smiled that knowing smile at me. Johnny B. was not tall, but tall enough. Handsome, dark, with gold-rimmed granny glasses and slow. Shook hands with me, talked dentistry with me, sat quietly in the reception room with me over the lunch hour and never once mentioned the word date, or later, or anything resembling any expectations. Finally at one o'clock, he mentioned that Jack and him and three other dentists and their wives were going out to dinner together that night and would I consider joining them?

"Yes, I'd like to," I said.

"I'm glad I had the chance to talk to you," he said. "Jack's kind of a fast mover, I didn't know what he'd said about me, you know, in the office."

"Or what he told you about me," I added.

"I'm going to enjoy having dinner with you," he said. "And in the meantime, I should get out of your way."

S U E R A F F I N H A D come back from lunch. On time for once. But only because she was curious about the new boy Jack picked out. And as soon as Johnny B. had left, she grilled me.

"Got to be something wrong. Maybe he's got the clap," she said, but I went back into the sterilization area, ignoring her. Every once in a while, she'd come back to the operatory when Jack was out of range and say, "He's got seven children he pays alimony for and hasn't got a penny left for himself." Or "Mass murderer," just to get my attention. But I never answered her, hoping to put in a good day—no foul ups— and five o'clock came, time for her last dig.

"He's fixed you up with a limp wrist; an over the-hill swinger; he get you one with herpes, yet? No matter, you wouldn't know anyway. I don't know, Evelyn. Maybe he still lives with his mother. Irons her sheets."

But she still wasn't happy. It tugged at her. When she got her coat on, she came back again, zipping it up, tying her scarf, pulling on her mittens. (Jack was down having his last cup of real coffee, so she had lots of time to luxuriate in my date's possible fatal flaw.) "It's like playing Russian roulette, Evelyn. Six dates—you haven't got hurt yet—but I know Jack's got a real asshole out there with your name tattooed on his butt. Could be Doc the Jock's really good buddy."

"Go home, Sue. Take care of your decrepit puppy. Watch TV. It's only dinner. He's a nice guy."

"Take a gun. Slip it in your purse."

"Five oh three," I said, nodding at the clock.

"Shit." And her little red head was out the door.

So I went home, took a shower and put on my best dress which was less than a tenth the best dress those doctor's wives had on, and they were so nice to me, smiling and politely nodding but never talked to me except halfway through dessert when one of them leaned over her New York cheesecake and let slip that good old Johnny B. had a little woman back home.

All I could think was, I'm a fool, I'm a fool again. Just what I need. So I politely finish my dessert—chocolate mousse—slowly and with great concentration ate it, goddammit, licked the spoon and excused myself.

Christ have mercy. Christ have mercy. Christ have mercy.

"Had a lovely evening," I said to the waiter and walked back home along the railroad tracks. Fool.

Jack, in his usual way, took offense, and didn't say anything right away. It was a week or so later, he said "We need an office meeting. To clear the air." He scheduled it for Christmas Eve. Even had Sue Raffin block out an hour in the appointment book.

We were in Terri's kitchen, our hygienist's house, Friday before Christmas Eve when he announced it—Jack's once-a-year treat party rather than the usual potluck office parties. His idea of a "treat" meaning to have Sue Raffin go out and buy all the raw ingredients with petty cash and have us cook them in our "spare time," including a twenty-five-pound turkey, which was Sue's specialty. She put the bird in a brown paper bag, turned the oven on at 250 degrees and let it cook at Terri's house all day, while we worked. It came out a bit dry, but it was hot and ready when the party started, and since no one else wanted to take responsibility for the bird, we all oohed and ahhed over the finished product.

Sue and I were setting out the deviled eggs on a platter, another of her specialties, when she told me, warned me, that the old goat was on the warpath again.

"I was going to ask him for a raise after Christmas," I said.

"Well, you were gonna and you were gonna and now he's at it again with his damned austerity program. He says finances are tight and payroll is too high and you believe him. And you know who payroll is—he's 99 percent of payroll. And he's renting a helicopter for a week in January so he can ski on virgin snow. Poor little bankrupt boy."

"He needs some time off once in a while," I said.

"A hundred bucks an hour, the helicopter," she said. "Besides the only one those cuts are gonna hurt is you. You know damn well I got a special deal with the asshole. And Terri's got six other doctors waiting for her to quit the old Scrooge. Ain't gonna make one bit of difference what he cuts out to anybody but you. You're the one working for slave wages, not to mention dating his married friends and other misfits." She picked up the tray of deviled eggs and headed out for the dining room.

There I was, all alone in the kitchen, listening to the clitter clatter of her high heels down the linoleum hallway back to her date—another long-distance trucker—and Terri and her husband in the living room, Jack with his newest "forever love," as Sue called them, a woman named Madeline, who worked as a legal secretary for one of Jack's lawyer pals, all of them laughing it up. (So where the hell was Gordy? Was he pining away for me like I was pining away for him?)

I started down the hallway thinking to catch up with Sue before she reached the living room, to hear more of what Jack was up to. What he was up to was having his arm around Sue as Madeline stared up at him from the floor—she'd been sitting at his feet all night.

"Hell of a party," he was saying. "What'd I tell you, Maddy girl, I've got a great bunch of girls in my office."

Some of what Sue had said sunk in, 'cause that made me mad. The whole office meeting would be directed at me and I'd be nothing but an office joke. Someone Jack could pick on who wouldn't even fight back.

WELL, THE DAY BEFORE Christmas he had his damned office meeting, making his pronouncements about the financial status of the office, offering his new austerity program. No raises. No new office staff. When the going gets tough, the tough get going. No one said anything to dispute his figures. Then he handed out the Christmas bonus envelopes, which were all flat except mine I noticed. Mine was thick with bills, and I thought after all that Sue had misinterpreted Jack's intentions. I waited till I was alone in the x-ray room to open it.

Inside was a collection of bills, all ones, all crumpled, used bills, fifteen of them, like he'd raided the till at Dorothy's Coffee Cup Cafe downstairs at the last minute. It kind of took my breath away and I stood there in the x-ray room, leaning against the wall, just barely breathing. I heard Sue and Terri leave, heard the door close behind them, and in the quiet of the office, heard Jack moving around in his private office.

I cleaned up the x-ray room, taking all the racks out of the rinse water, hanging them carefully so they didn't touch. Then I went into the sterilization area and cleaned instruments. Jack was still in his office puttering around. I was done. Nothing else to do. I went to his office door and knocked, not really knowing what I would say.

"I'd like to have a few words with you soon, over a beer, or a drink somewhere," I said when he opened the door. "I haven't had a chance to sit down and talk with you in a while. There's some things I want to talk about."

He looked about to turn me down, plead another date.

"It's important to me," I said.

"How about right now?"

"No. I think some real time. You know, take off your coat and listen, for a few minutes, half hour or so."

He looked like I'd asked him to do three free root canals.

"Okay," he said. "I'm having dinner with Maddy, then I'll be heading home, out to the range, about eightish, is that okay for you kid?"

"Thank you, yes." Of course what he didn't say was that Madeline would be outside freezing, 'cause he wouldn't leave the motor running for her while we talked inside, but that was his fault, nothing I could do about it.

I'd stopped at the grocery store for a six-pack of beer, in case he wanted one, and then went straight home, to figure for the third time on a sheet of stationery paper, the hours I worked, hours Sue worked, times off per year for each of us. She had started three months before me, but even figuring Sue's wages the same as mine, I ended up with 40 percent less, given her five days a week, fifty-two weeks a year guaranteed. I got the compliments for how well I kept the office running, while Sue Raffin got the wages, and bonuses besides. She had the Cobblestone Condo, big fancy four-wheel-drive truck with snowplow and hydraulic winch. She didn't even need Jack. She could go into business for herself, plowing parking lots. I had student district housing, no storm windows, no furniture, no Christmas tree, despite the fact I was too "valuable" in the operatories to move me up front last time Sue Raffin threatened to quit.

He was late and walked into my apartment like he owned the place, putting his coat in the hall closet and helping himself to the beer in the fridge. He got out two glasses and poured a glass for each of us.

"I gotta hand it to you, kid. Most women, they spend themselves into a hole, fixing up a place like this, you know, fancy dish towels, paintings on the wall. Maddy, that's the one fault she has. With Christmas and everything else, she always has her credit cards charged up to the max. But you and me, E, we're just alike. Since my divorce, just getting a couple things at a time, you know, replacing what Dolores Anne took as I can afford it." He took a swallow of beer and settled into the other end of the couch. My Salvation Army couch. Goodwill pillows. When he was settled, he looked back at me. "What's eating at you, Evvy?"

"I wouldn't say anything's eating at me. Just, you know, I heard what you've been saying about collections and expenses and all."

He got up, grabbed a chair from the dining room and brought it in front of the couch, slumped down again in the corner and put his big cowboy boots up on my dining room chair. "It's terrible, just been terrible. Going to be a lean Christmas," he said.

"Well," I continued. "It's just that if you look here," I offered him my piece of lined stationery, which he held with both hands in front of him, squinting like he needed glasses, which he didn't. "If you look there, on the right, it's what I earn, number of days I work, all that. On the left, there's Sue, you know, a comparison, and then at the bottom, the totals of possible incomes for each of us."

The visuals seemed to help, at least he wasn't arguing, and was looking at the page, tracking the numbers, or so I thought. I elaborated on days of enforced vacations. "Since we started at approximately the same time," I told him, "I'll assume we make the same per hour wage. If so, then Sue has the ability to earn 60 percent more than I do, when we both have jobs that require a lot of the same qualities. And in fact, you don't want me to apply for Sue's job, if she leaves, because you need me in back, you tell me. Now," I looked at him before I started the big push. I couldn't believe he was so quiet, not arguing already. He just sat there. "What I would like," I said, "is more quiet time in the office to be able to do inventory of root canal reamers, for instance, extra cleaning, cleaning I can't do in an hour, or half hour or between patients. You know, take things apart and really clean. Organize. I barely have enough time now to keep things clean and put away. If I had one day a week, Wednesdays, alone in the operatories, all the things that get forgotten, neglected or done at the last minute while you're standing around waiting, like last Friday I had to make up those sutures, it would save you time and frustration."

He looked at me. He nodded. "Always thinking, Evvy," he said. "Can I get back to you in a week?"

"That would be wonderful," I said. "I appreciate your coming over tonight and listening to me rant."

"Hey, no problem E," he said, picking himself off the couch. He left the dining room chair there, went out in the kitchen and got himself another beer, popped it open and with two strides was back in front of me. "I'll take one more for the road and leave the others in there for Gordy," he said.

Right. Heard from Gordy? He didn't even have to say it exactly anymore.

That week, then, between Christmas and New Years, he acted like nothing had been said. I waited. I developed my x-rays, cleaned instruments, changed sterile towels, as usual, between patients, before he got back from lunch. But Thursday, New Year's Eve was payday, and still he didn't say anything. Five o'clock, I still had one more patient in the waiting room, one on nitrous, and Jack downstairs getting a last cup of real coffee, when Sue came back in the operatory and laid my paycheck on the counter by the sterilization sink.

"Sorry kid, the asshole's a tightwad," she said and headed back up front.

"Wait," I said, getting up, turning the patient's nitrous off. "What did you say?"

She'd gone back to her copying machine, closing the lid, putting the plastic cover on, locking up the filing cabinets. "You know him, Evelyn. He just tells me what to do. He doesn't explain himself."

"He told you to give me a raise," I insisted.

"He said, and I quote, 'Give Evvy a fifty cent an hour raise. She's really stressed out. Poor kid deserves it,' end quote. And I'll bet that doesn't make you feel any better."

"Is that all?"

"That's all Doc the Jock said," she told me putting on her coat. "And it's five o'clock. I'm outta here."

"Oh Christ," I said and left it at that. When Jack came back upstairs to finish off our two patients, I kept quiet. I left it up to him to broach the subject and of course he did. About seven-thirty, we were on the last patient, finished drilling and digging out decay and had only to fill the two cavities. Just the three of us and the steady pitter patter of cowboy music, plus three phone calls: two from Maddy, twenty minutes apiece, and one from Monday's one-on-one partner who couldn't make the match and Jack spent ten minutes trying to make him reconsider.

Jack slid his chair back from the patient's head to let me put the matrix bands on and to get himself another cup of instant coffee, but then he just sat there, half in and half out of the way.

"Do you want me to put the bands on?" I said, hoping he'd take the hint and get out of the way.

He sat. He pondered his cup. "You know what women's greatest fault is?" he finally said.

"No what?" Not again. The "Women's Greatest Fault" lecture. Last time it was lack of stick-to-it-iveness and mental toughness. Except Sue Raffin of course, he always pointed out. I had my matrix bands ready, a double alloy ready to mix, plug, carve and get out of here on New Year's Eve, and he wanted to discuss the faults of women?

He stood, stretched, and looked down at me, still obstructing my way to the patient's teeth. "They're ungrateful," he said. "You give them a raise and they don't even say thank you."

It was Barney Barrett in the chair again, again our last patient. He looked at me, waited for Jack to leave the room. "Is something going on here?"

"Oh no," I said lying through my teeth. "It must be the nitrous," I told him.

"Oh," he said, and settled back into his self-protective, going-to-the-dentist cocoon.

In the meantime, Jack mixed up his cup of instant coffee in the employee's lounge, while I steamed in the operatory. He knew I had an eight o'clock appointment and when he finally did come back to finish the amalgam, he was as charming as a snake and never mentioned women or raises or gratitude and who had more than their share. Our patient never closed his eyes the whole time we were finishing up. Barney was a large man with large brown eyes, and he tried as hard as he could to keep both of us in range as we stuffed and carved his new silver filling.

I walked him out when we were done. Jack had run out of the operatory like a shot and hit his back, private door before I'd gotten Barney out of the chair. So we were alone, Barney and I.

"I'd make you another appointment," I said, "but Sue's got the books locked up for safekeeping."

Barney nodded. "Nothing going on?" he asked again.

"No," I said. "It's an office joke."

"Hummmm." He stood there for a second, then shrugged his shoulders. "Okay," he said and went out the door.

NINE

W H A T I H A D waiting for me after finishing with Jack for New Year's Eve, was Jaymie. I hadn't seen her since Christmas Day. Then the night before, she'd called me out of the blue.

"We'll have drinks tomorrow night, you're free aren't you?" she said.

It's what everyone assumed, that I was always free. Gordy, if he ever appeared again, would just show up or call an hour before he wanted to see me. Sue just dropped in now and then with a six-pack of Oly and a bag of pork rinds, wanting to sit at my kitchen table and watch the neighbors while she explained the latest problem with her latest trucker boyfriend. And Jack. He assumed I had nothing better to do every weekend and every day off than to sit and wait for him to trip the burglar alarm, so I could go down to the office, meet the policemen and explain to them that the system must be weird and I'll tell the doctor so it would never happen again. Of course they would nod their heads at me, and get back in their car. Jack? He was in and out before the call went into the cops.

Like Christmas morning. Jaymie had showed up at my doorstep at 7:00 a.m.

"You don't have any turkey," she said, walking through my little apartment. At times it felt like a fortress; times like that morning, more like Grand Central Station. "There's no little pieces of bread chopped up. No Christmas tree. No mistletoe." She had on a silky red blouse and black slacks and a navy blue wool coat with a funny little Santa Claus pinned to her lapel whose nose lit up when you pulled the string.

"I was planning to put my feet up," I said. I still had my flannel nightgown on. Jaymie got my bathrobe out of the closet for me and draped it over my shoulders. This was going to be the slow pitch.

"How would you feel about coming out to Mom and Pop's for the day? I promise a good turkey dinner with all the fixings, lots of hot dishwater and the absolute corniest collection of Christmas music you've ever heard in your life. Doris Day, Elvis Presley, Frankie Laine. Even the Chipmunks."

"Who's cooking?" I asked. I'd been to Thanksgiving. Rose had started the turkey at six a.m., after she'd finished her first pitcher of martinis. (Margaritas were only suitable from Memorial Day till Labor Day—like my mother used to say about our white pleated skirts—then Labor Day through Memorial Day, it was back to martinis.) At dinner, she'd insisted on setting Bucky a place at the table and propping his high school graduation photo on the empty plate.

The evening had ended in a fight. The usual fight. Rose and Jaymie deified the lost son. Wally thought he'd been a chump, had always been a chump and was now succeeding at tearing the rest of his family apart, months after he was dead and buried. Rose had grabbed her end of the tablecloth and ripped it off the table. Coffee cups, dessert dishes and silverware crashed to the floor.

"Now that, Walter, is what I think of your opinion," she'd said and gone off to her bedroom. She was sleeping in Bucky's old room by then, and she locked the door behind her, not letting Walter come in no matter how long he stood outside the room, gently knocking and repeating Rosey, Rosey, Rosey, slowly, as if the words and the sound of his voice passing through the door were a carpet he could ride to the bottom of her pain.

"Mother's better," Jaymie said. "She's really better. I promise."

I got up from my dining room table and dressed, believing it because Jaymie wanted to believe it so badly.

It had started out okay. Jaymie and Wally and I dug out the Christmas china and crystal from the basement while Rose sat at the kitchen table—her ankle was still in a cast—and stuffed the turkey. The tree was a monster—eight feet tall and almost as broad—with not an inch of branch, needle or crown left undecorated. Snowball lights, blinkies, bubbling candles. And lots of tinsel: tinsel applied, retrieved, and stored each Christmas for the last thirty years — saved like a family heirloom—like at our house. They even had plastic cranberry and popcorn garlands, because like our family, all the busy little hands had grown up and moved away before Mom had grown tired of the gaily strung berries. And like our house, there was an angel for the top of the tree. Ours was pure white, with silken hair and wide skirt like the Good Witch in *The Wizard of Oz*. The Porter's angel had a Norse look, with rosy cheeks and a white, angora-trimmed cape.

We had spent the morning stuffing the turkey, then making creamed onions, candied yams, mashed potatoes, rutabagas and succotash, while Rose supervised all of us from Wally's Lazy Boy. By noon, we were ready to slide the pies in the oven and put the final touches on gravy and mashed potatoes as the aroma of turkey and fixings filled the whole house.

But then the meal was done, and Rose, without purpose anymore, but with more martinis than she needed, couldn't relax and continued to find chores for all of us to do. Jaymie and I started with polishing the sterling silver while Rose emptied all her cupboards and washed them down, rewashing all the dishes, and scrubbing cans of cling peaches and fruit cocktail before she put them away again, this time in size places. (They had been in alphabetical order.)

She tried to get Wally to help, but he refused, and rather than fight with her, he retreated into the living room to watch football. Jaymie ran back and forth between the two of them, telling Rose how great the game was and that she should come in and watch. Telling Wally to go drag her out of the kitchen. But neither budged and at midnight, after we'd put the oven and stove top back together, and I sat at the kitchen table with q-tips, toothpicks and scouring powder cleaning the range top control knobs, I leaned over to Jaymie and whispered it was time to go home.

In Bucky's pickup, on the way back to Missoula, I said, "Never again." And meant it.

So here was Jaymie calling the night before New Year's Eve, and I started backpedaling before she even said anything.

"YOU AREN'T DOING anything tomorrow night," she repeated, except this time she wasn't asking a question. "Look. I just want to sit down with you and have a drink for old time's sake. I'm not dragging you out to Mom and Pop's or anything. You know. People go out and have a few drinks on New Year's Eve. They get happy. That's all."

"We'll take the Bronco?"

"The Bronco's fixed. No more truck."

"Okay then," I said.

"Eight then?" she said. "Meet you at Maxwell's."

I MANAGED TO ARRIVE at eight ten and had gulped down two glasses of Chablis before Jaymie arrived; I guess I dreaded the meeting. I felt guilty for deserting the family. But now Jack was tightening the screws. I wanted to make a clean cut. Find some other job. I spent the half hour or so that I waited fantasizing about a new job.

She sat down opposite me in the booth. "You look like the cat that swallowed the canary," she said.

I smiled and my cheeks started aching, and Jaymie started to laugh at me.

"So tell me what's up already. I could stand a good joke myself."

"Oh, nothing much. Just that I'm never going to take another insult from Jack P."

"He's moving his practice to Hawaii?"

She was perfectly serious. As if that was the only way I could ever be free of him.

"No," I said. "But Monday morning, I'm quitting. No more dental office."

"I'll believe it when I see it. And what brought even this minor movement on?"

I began telling her, over my third glass of Chablis, about our private conference and my organized lists of potential money earned, and potential days worked, and Jack's reaction. Before I was done, there were three more glasses lined up behind my one, bought by gentlemen sitting at other tables, busy watching the two women alone on New Year's Eve. Jaymie's mood turned blacker and blacker the more attention I got.

The men who came around the table started out talking to Jaymie—they knew Jaymie. But they bought me drinks. They sat next to *me* and put their arms around *me*. Whenever they'd lean in just a little too much, she'd start in on me about how I'd handled the negotiations with Jack all wrong: I'd pushed too hard, too suddenly, after being too meek; I should've done it sooner, better. And now I was smiling too much. "Drunk," Jaymie told me.

All I felt was flush. Monday morning my key ring would be lighter, no chance of being called in to meet the patrol car at the office at 2:00 a.m. No more P-brain tormenting me about Gordy Bennett. Fixing me up with dates. So I listened to Jaymie's criticisms for a while and then I said, "That's easy for you to say, when the only one you're negotiating with is your own Daddy. Your Daddy isn't going to kick you out on the street anytime soon."

"Oh no, but he'll sell the company out from under me. If I'm lucky, the new guy will let me stay on and run the place for him for half my current salary."

"Welcome to the real world," I said. Then I regretted saying it. I didn't need to be so petty. "Is he really going to sell?" I asked, trying to be more understanding.

"Is there a guy in Connecticut calling him twice a day?"

"It sounds serious?"

She shrugged her shoulders. "He whooshes me out of the office every time Connecticut's on the line."

"Listen Jaymie, I didn't mean to say that about Wally. I just feel twenty pounds lighter, like a monkey's off my back. I guess I just wish you could feel good about my good news," I said.

A tall blonde man came over, said hello to Jaymie, talked lumber, nails, putty, and radial saws for a minute, then he sat down, quietly, beside me to talk to Jaymie some more, but pushing me against the corner of the booth and leaving his leg up against mine.

"Who's your friend?" he asked Jaymie after they'd exhausted the shop talk.

"Evelyn Holloran. She's a dental assistant."

That was the first time she'd ever called me that.

"Oh no, I'm not. I've worked my last day as a dental assistant. In fact, I think my new career is going to be airline stewardess. I'll fly to Hawaii. I've always wanted to fly to Hawaii. Or Ireland."

Jaymie looked at me with a sour face and at the guy, who seemed pleased enough at the prospects of Hawaii.

"Jaymie was kidding you about my being a dental assistant," I said. "Tell him, Jaymie."

"I was kidding you, Tommy. She's not a dental assistant anymore. But she doesn't go out with men who don't floss."

Tom looked pensive which made his brow ridge more prominent.

"That's not true," I said. "But I will probably always draw the line at men who wear dentures."

Tom smiled at me broadly, showing off his coffee-stained, but natural teeth. I considered asking Tom to dance, he was such a handsome man and so close, but still a friend of Jaymie's so not really a stranger, but in the middle of weighing the merits of Tom, Jaymie picked up her coat and purse and walked out of the bar without saying a word. I grabbed up my stuff and followed her out to the parking lot. She was waiting in Bucky's truck, lighting up a cigarette, with her Maxwell's glass on the dashboard. I got in the passenger side and closed the door.

"I hate that bar," she said. "Slimy men who don't have any respect for two women who have things to talk about."

"It's New Year's Eve," I said. Walking out to the truck made me realize that I was more drunk that I'd realized when

I was just sitting down inside. So be it. New Year's Eve is a time to party, I told myself. But being around Jaymie had turned the mood from party to morose. Or maybe there couldn't be a party without Jaymie anyway. "I don't want to listen to anymore anything," I said.

"That's a pretty profound thought," Jaymie said and sipped from her glass of Jack Daniels. When she'd finished the bar whiskey, she reached across me into the glove box for a pint of Jack and poured that over the remaining ice.

"You're hitting that pretty hard," I said.

"Not hardly hard enough." She put the glass on the dashboard, watching it slide back down against the windshield. Then she relaxed, sinking back into the bucket seat. "I'm sorry. I'm being a real bitch tonight." She took a drink. A sip. "I'll stop drinking as soon as I get everything settled."

"The gravestone?"

"The gravestone," she said and nodded. "Bucky's birthday is April 10. I promised myself he'd have a marker by then. But mother won't even look. I've got sample books. Full color and black and white. Photos, psalms, Shakespeare, nursery rhymes, famous last words of famous Indian chiefs from Geronimo to Black Elk." She turned in the seat and looked at me.

"Oh no. Not me. I'm not getting in the middle of that one again."

"Evelyn, I've done all the homework. He's been four months in the ground and he's got this four-inch cement block with his plot number stamped into it. Looks like a well cap."

"I know," I said. "I've been down there."

"We could go funky: put his high school graduation picture under glass, or engrave a dirt bike on the stone. Or tasteful: beloved son/beloved brother. It's boring, but it's easy on the head, you know? Or veteran of foreign war, all that serious stuff. An angel. Anything."

"Why don't you just go out and buy it?"

"It's a family thing. The family should decide."

"The family can't deal with it. I don't think you realize how much they hurt. They'd be happy if you just let them off the hook on this."

"They can make one little decision. Take five minutes."

"You're getting off on it."

"That's a cheap shot. You used to be a nice girl, Evelyn."

"Sell this truck. Take the money and buy a tombstone. Something that will make you happy. Help you leave it all behind."

She looked at me like I was telling her to sell her firstborn. She poured another shot of Jack into her glass.

"What did you do for your Dad?" she asked.

"I didn't. He had it all planned out. Part of setting up his will. I guess that's the advantage of dying when you're sixty-eight." Advantages. I thought about that for a minute. There really had to be some, no matter how hard it felt at the time. I went on slowly with the thought out loud. "You know what I mean. Feeling like you've done everything. Kids. A house. He'd seen his kids grow up. I think sometimes if he could come back for five minutes, he'd say it was okay."

"You still miss him?" she asked.

"We were together a lot once I was out of school. Three hours a day commuting. Like you and your Dad—we worked together. He was my cheerleader. I could've been thrown in jail in Timbuktu, he would've come every week to see me, to tell me things would get better."

The truck had gotten cold and the windshield fogged up with our breath. Jaymie turned on the engine and flipped the defroster on. People walked out of Maxwell's back door, two by two, like Noah's Ark, pulling a little of the warm light from inside the bar out into the parking lot, lighting up the backs of the brick buildings in the alley.

"You notice how much leather these people wear into this bar? Just think of all the cattle who have given up their skins to make them look pretty," she said. She fiddled with the defroster controls. "So you been out there? To Bucky's grave?"

"Couple of times."

"You talk to him?"

I looked at her, trying to figure out what she'd say. If she'd think I was stealing him or something.

"I talk to him," she said finally. "I miss telling him stuff. Funny stuff that goes on at the shop. You know?"

"I've told him about Jack's new girlfriend. And about Rose breaking her foot."

"You shouldn't tell him that. I try to only tell him the good things. Make up for that last day."

"I don't think it would hurt him to know about Rose's foot. He might think it was funny—his mother, grace in action—clobbering her foot. From what you told me, he wouldn't take on any guilt about how it was all his fault or anything."

Jaymie laughed, a very quiet choking laugh, then lit another cigarette and slipped the match out the fly window. "I can't believe you talk to him," she said. "I didn't think you were into being morbid."

I'd accused her of being morbid many times. Over the truck. Over the mason jar full of matchbooks—which she was still adding to. I'm sure she felt I was thinking 'morbid' every time the tombstone issue came up.

"It's not morbid," I said. "At least I hope it's not morbid. It's just something I miss. Bucky's down in the ground. Stuck. A captive audience. Even if I was back in New York, I wouldn't have that. My dad was cremated. I know he was here. On earth. I know he was born. He had an office in the basement of the Coliseum for twenty years. He knew the city better than anyone I ever knew. Give him an address, he'd tell you what subway to take, the name of the station, which way to turn when you walked up to the street. He was here. But he isn't—here—anymore. Bucky is here." I shrugged. It was so personal—your dead ones. Who do they belong to? Half the time it wasn't Bucky I was talking to anyway. It was my father. I was just using Bucky as a substitute. Or maybe he was a messenger. There was no way to guess what Jaymie would think.

But she nodded. "I wish I felt as sure as you do. Sometimes I want to dig the son of a bitch up and see if he is down there. Not playing hide and seek on me or something."

"You're still trying to hold him. I guess I'm just wishing for ten minutes, just to say good-bye. I never got to say good-bye."

"I hear you, Evelyn. It's been three years for you. Maybe in three years, I'll want those ten minutes. But not yet."

"That's why you want the tombstone," I said.

"So his name's on the thing. Maybe even his damned picture."

"I could go with you and pick it out. Can you afford one?"

"I can make payments," she said.

"J&B Lumber can make the payments. Wally would never know. Just find a way to hide it from the IRS.

"I am having some effect on you, aren't I? You're getting sneaky in your old age."

"Just seems like a logical business expense. Get everybody back to work."

"You just solved the biggest problem in the world. Would you let me buy you a drink? One drink. On J&B Lumber's tab?"

"One. And then we can celebrate the solving of both our problems. Your tombstone and my albatross, Jack P."

"That's right. He's moving to Hawaii," she said, putting the Ford into reverse and pulling out of the parking space.

"No. I'm quitting, dear," I said.

"Call me Monday noon and give me the particulars, and I'll believe it," she said, and drove us out to the Legal Tender and laid claim to that piece of dirt, too. We stayed and danced with a different boy each dance till closing time, and Jaymie drove us home, just the two of us, a little better for wear. Almost happy. If ignorance is bliss, temporary amnesia can be almost happy.

But paradise gained was soon lost. Monday morning at nine o'clock, Sue Raffin called asking where the hell I was and what the hell happened Friday night and get your ass down here.

"You know I hate assisting," she said.

"I'm quitting," I answered and rolled over in bed to see what time it was. "I'm going down to Frontier Airline's employment office and apply for a real job. Besides, I think he fired me."

"Oh God. He didn't fire you honey. Trust me. He's running around here like a chicken with his head cut off. He didn't fire you. Now get up and get dressed. Your God didn't mean for nice Catholic girls to fly around heaven all day in short skirts. You were born to be a dental assistant. God gave you great hands. Now get down here, please."

"You didn't hear what he said to me Friday night."

"What did he say to you Friday night?"

"He said I was ungrateful. No. He said *all* women are ungrateful. He gave me a raise and I was ungrateful for not saying thank you—for fifty cents, Sue."

"Oh, sweetheart, why do you listen to him? He's just another change-of-life crybaby. Listen. I've got him talked into two dollars more a day, same as I'm getting. He won't go for the extra Wednesday hours, but he's come a long way. Don't blow it now."

"But I don't want to come back. I really want to quit."

"Evelyn. I won't survive around here without you. I mean that."

I knew she meant it, and I knew it was hard for her to say.

"He's paying you better than he's ever paid any assistant," she said.

"Okay. For the time being. I'll be in for the afternoon."

"I have to assist all morning? Oh goody," she said and hung up on me.

TEN

I MADE ONE special request before signing my new employee's agreement form: I needed the week of January fifth off for the trial—to hold Jaymie's hand because she was the only one in the family who wanted to see Gene Bofay in court. Jack agreed. As he said, "It's no skin off my nose, I'll be out of town then anyway, kid." So he didn't have to work without his assistant, and Sue Raffin didn't have to stick her fingers in anyone's spit. And me? I was relieved the trial would finally be over.

Jack left for helicopter skiing on the fourth, the day before the trial started, taking me out to lunch our last working day to the International House of Pancakes and warning me to rest up while he was gone, since he was going to be dog-tired from playing so hard and needed an assistant who could pick up the load. A word of advice to the wise, he offered: don't get drug into Jaymie Porter's problem life, when we've got enough problems *of our own*. That's what he said.

That night, Wally and Rose left for an Inland Empire cruise, fourteen days up and back from Alaska. No newspapers, no radio. Leaving from Vancouver the sixth, with the intervening time spent with Orene in Seattle, eating fresh seafood from fisherman's wharf and touring the fine local wineries for free sips. They left Jaymie in charge of J&B, thinking that would be the only thing that might keep her away from the trial, yet knowing that wouldn't work either, warning her as they went through airport security at Missoula to take care of business. "Be responsible," Wally said as we waved good-bye.

A lot of good any of that advice did us, because Monday morning we were both in the courtroom, front row center for act two of The Piney Woods Tryst.

Jaymie played her role of the bereaved interested party to the hilt. Every stitch on her body was brand new. New shoes— high heels even. New white wool, double-breasted suit, real cowgirl-go-to-town clothes. She told me a couple of times when we first met, when I kept giving her a bad time about her city clothes, how she'd fallen in love with a New York City boy buckarooing on the Ox-Tail Ranch the summer between high school and college. He left in September, headed back to Columbia University, and Jaymie followed a week later, landing in Penn Station at four in the morning in "nice" flats and A-line skirt, the epitome of a Pillsbury-clothes girl, or so Jaymie's summer boyfriend felt, because he hightailed it out of the train station leaving his Wild West cowgirl stranded. Of course *he* was wearing cowboy, she said, dime-store cowboy only big-city money can buy: lizard boots and twenty-seven hundred miles of genuine Indian beadwork, accented by many more miles of leather fringe. You can't wear that stuff at a branding; it gets torn off or dirty, she told me. In fact, after telling me the story the third time, she allowed as it might have been the perfect outfit for Grand Central Station. She couldn't think of any other place he could've safely worn it. And if you thought about it, there were few other places Jaymie could have worn this outfit. I'd worn one just like it Easter Sunday 1966.

It was another story she told me that morning, waiting in the rotunda for the participants to arrive. "I want the jury to think I respect the law. Like they've got to do their duty, because I'm not the type to go out and pop the bastard if they let him off. They've got to punish him for me."

Whatever. The jury bought it. They respected her, read what they were supposed to read from her clothes. They watched her from the first day, the first time they all walked into the courtroom together as a unit, anxious to begin making mental notes to lead them to the path of right decisions.

Mr. Aamold couldn't introduce Jaymie as the bereaved sister or me—the girl from New York City who just happened to show up to hold the sister's hand. Not directly. But he planned ahead. Moments before the jury entered the courtroom, he came over to us, squatted in the aisle and began whispering, very softly, so Jaymie and I both had to lean very close to hear him. He didn't want her to watch the jury ever, so they would feel free to stare at her, and he used that moment to tell her, to keep her occupied, to make sure that first time, the first day, as the jury walked past within inches of the three of us, they had a long, slow stare at this poor young woman. A hundred different ways you could see she wasn't anything but a nice young lady, the sister of what must have been a nice young man, who had sinned only once in his life: the night he was murdered. And she had a nice young friend to hold her hand—to get her through the ordeal. There was something they could do about making that ordeal worthwhile.

Now Sherry Fowler, she was what Rose would have called a pistol. Minutes before the jury walked in, she'd turned up out of breath and brunette, but in a pair of pink plastic high heels.

"After all the tutoring and time, they let her show up in fucking Barbie doll shoes," Jaymie said. "And she's on our side. This is going to be some circus."

But Sherry's outfit wasn't all that bad. She too had bought all new clothes, on Mr. Aamold's orders. She'd shown up that first morning in a pink calico granny dress. She hadn't lost those ten pounds Mr. Aamold said would make her look like an orphan. Instead, she'd gained ten. Or more. It made her look pudgy—even cherubic. Until you saw the shoes—or heard them. Sounded like a cheap girl snapping bubble gum.

Sherry click-clacked past us to a seat as Jaymie rolled her eyes. There'd been no time to fix the shoes before court convened, but luckily the first order of business was to rule witnesses out of the courtroom, which left Sherry cooling her plastic heels in the third-floor rotunda, where prospective jurors wouldn't see her. At the first recess, Mr. Aamold sent his assistant out to the secretarial pool to find a pair of presentable size fives.

"You can't dress up a sow's ear," Jaymie whispered. "Dress it up and it still looks like a sow's ear."

And sounded that way, too, because when Sherry came back wearing that other woman's sensible shoes, she still clacked across the marble lobby. It didn't matter what you put on her, or that she was as sweet looking as Annette Funicello. She was cheap as secondhand gum. You could see Mr. Aamold's mind working, trying to figure how he could magically levitate this woman from courtroom door to witness stand, without having the jury see or hear her walk. He didn't need them adding that spectacle to their little fountain of knowledge.

"THIS IS HER MOMENT in the sun," Mr. Aamold told me before court convened. "Aside from getting on 'Wheel of Fortune,' being in court's the one time she'll ever have a captive audience. Her kind," he said more quietly, "some are less equal than others. But she's all we've got."

That was the circus outside the courtroom, before the trial started.

Inside, that first morning was easy. It began with forensic experts, the pathologist who'd performed the autopsy, first on-the-scene police reports, the death-scene photos I'd seen a thousand times. Everyone used the word murder, but with such clinical detachment you didn't really have to pay attention. It was no one. I'd read the word five million times in my life: *Dial M for Murder*; *Murder on the Orient Express*, one of eleven murders committed in the last seventy-two hours in the South Bronx. Clinical, clean and dry. I listened to the patter of fact sayers, quietly, with immense reserve and dignity. Then, after the lunch break, Sherry Fowler was called to the stand.

Oh, it was easy to imagine her in the Piney Woods Motel with nothing but sex on her mind.

MR. AAMOLD PLACED himself squarely between Sherry and the jury's view of the witness stand. "Miss Fowler, how long have you known the Porter family?" he asked.

"Since I was ten, eleven years old. My mom and dad bought the place next to theirs. Myself and Bucky, we were in sixth grade together."

The jury, rather than stare into Aamold's back, did exactly as he had predicted: they watched Jaymie and me.

"And your parents knew each other?"

Overnight camping trips, Jaymie and Bucky and Sherry, school dances, water fights at the J&B Lumber Company swimming pool while their fathers negotiated the price of fence over a six-pack of beer.

"Swimming pool," Jaymie muttered. "She always called it a swimming pool. It was an aluminum cattle trough Pops stuck out in the stacks to keep us kids out of his hair."

"We were engaged once to be married, in the old days," she said. "Before Bucky went off to college."

"And you married Gene Bofay?"

"Yes."

"What was it like to be married to Gene Bofay?"

"Put me in the hospital twice," she said. "Jealous old goat. Expected me to stay home twenty-four hours a day. I'm just not that kind of person. I can't just sit. You know."

Mr. Aamold gave her some kind of signal, telling her to say just yes or no, just the lines they'd rehearsed, and the rest of her testimony fell out that way, a one- and two-syllable recitation of seven years of drinking, fighting and pitched glass. Bofay sat quietly through this whole recitation, barely moving, and slumped down in his seat like he was at a Saturday matinee.

Mr. Aamold turned back to the evidence table and picked up the manila envelope of photos.

"Why did you and Bucky go to the Piney Woods that night?" he asked.

"He had some photos he wanted to show me, from when he was in Peru for this oil company. One thing led to another."

He must have given her another signal because she stopped that sentence cold. "Would you describe the events leading up to the murder?"

"Sure." You could almost see her turn the page in her lesson book. "Well, we were both asleep then. And we both heard some noise right outside, like someone walking around on the gravel. I thought I'd locked the door, but he just walked in. It was Eu-gene. He was really angry and had a high-powered rifle in his hand. Eu-gene said something, I don't know what, about wanting 'his woman' and Bucky, he pulled me over and behind himself to protect me. And they argued."

"You were standing up?" he asked. She nodded, like what else would they be doing after someone barged into their room.

"What did Bucky say?"

"Well, they weren't really arguing. Bucky wasn't anyway. He just kept saying there wasn't anything wrong, we could just talk, sit down and talk, get some clothes on, which would have pleased me no end. But Eu-gene, he wouldn't let me. He said, 'No, don't get anything on, you look like the chippie you really are,' he said to me. And he pointed the rifle at me, so I didn't go nowhere."

"Bucky was trying to talk Bofay down, then. What did Bofay say then?"

"It's not polite to say in mixed company."

Gene Bofay relaxed at this statement, stretching his legs out in front of him, and sliding even further down in his chair. Not despondent mind you, but relaxing, because maybe she wasn't telling the whole truth about the event, but the tone of her voice, it was the tone he knew, that was truth. Truth, and what he would consider beauty coming through his ex-wife's lips. Perhaps he thought he had a chance then.

Of course the judge would have no part of Sherry's coy tricks. He leaned into her like an Irish priest and told her in no uncertain terms that truth is what we were here for and she would not be allowed to censor or substitute truth for fiction, for whatever reason.

Mr. Aamold repeated his question.

Sherry squirmed a little, then put a smug little smile on her face. "Well, what he said was that he was gonna cut off Bucky's balls, make a tobacco pouch out of the scrotum and eat the Rocky Mountain oysters for breakfast right in front of him. That was when I first thought maybe he was serious."

"You said he was carrying a high-powered rifle. Where would he get this knife to do the cutting?"

"Pocketknife," she said, as if she was saying pass the salt for the third time. "And he was always losing 'em. Had to stop at the K-Mart every two days cause he was losing this stupid, worthless little cheapshit pocketknife. With an imitation pearl handle. And soft brass pin. If he didn't lose the stupid thing, he busted it."

"You're saying, it was important to him to always have a knife on his person?"

That was obviously the answer they had rehearsed. Sherry nodded her head. The judge instructed her to answer verbally yes or no.

"Yes," she said, then waited to give the next answer.

"You'd heard him make threats before. Did he ever follow through?"

"Sometimes. He promised to put me in the hospital and by God he did. And he promised before I left him, that he'd kill the next guy I hooked up with. He, by God, kept those two promises."

"Would you describe what happened after Bofay threatened to mutilate Bucky Porter?"

"Well, he started to come after me, said he was gonna teach me a lesson, but Bucky kept in between and finally—what it looked like to me, 'cause I was in back and not seeing very much, thank God—it looked like to me Gene just hauled off and sucker-punched Bucky. But what it was, it was the rifle. I was so scared, I guess, I didn't even hear the shot. Or I was yelling too loud. I was yelling at Gene to get the hell out of the room. Which he wasn't listening to. Anyway, he shot Bucky in the stomach. Bucky dropped to his knees right there in front of me, and soon as he fell, then Eugene reached over him and got hold of me and walloped me good in the face a half dozen times and drug me out on the gravel."

"What was Bucky's condition when you were forced from the room?"

She gave Aamold a puzzled look.

"Was he still on his knees? Sitting on the bed? Did he talk to you?"

A light bulb went off and Sherry smiled quickly and then stifled it. "He was rolling around on the floor and I noticed there was blood on his stomach."

"Why didn't you try to call an ambulance for your friend?"

"Eu-gene wouldn't let me." She kept saying his name like that, Yooo-gene. "Eu-gene had me by the hair, leading me out buck-naked to his truck and telling me to shut up or he'd beat the living crap out of me," she said. As an afterthought, she added, "I reiterated to him several times we should call an ambulance."

"One more question, Miss Fowler. The high-powered rifle that Gene Bofay used, this was your father's rifle, was it not?"

"Yes," she said.

"How did Gene end up with it?"

"He went rabbit hunting with Daddy a couple of times with it. He knew Daddy kept it in the truck. In case he saw a coyote or something near the house. Or dogs chasing deer. Daddy hated when those high-breed dogs from the subdivision came down on the river and chased the does and fawns."

"No further questions," Aamold said.

Sherry considered the last part of her testimony the climax of her whole trip to town, really the climax of the last four months, and was puffed up like a penguin when Cameron began his cross-examination.

He called her Sherry, and Mrs. Bofay, which didn't sit well after Mr. Aamold had called her Miss Fowler for the two hours or more he'd been questioning her. Aamold had warned us he wasn't going to object.

"Just bring attention to it," he'd said during the break before cross-examination. "My job is to discredit Cameron and his witnesses. When I get that done, the jury won't believe that Mrs. stuff or anything else he says for that matter."

Cameron stood to the side of the witness stand, leaving the jury a clear view of the girl. "Isn't it true, Mrs. Bofay," he said, "That you were the only one to pick up the telephone that night and that you were the one who pulled the phone out of the wall?"

"No. That's a lie."

"Isn't it true that you went voluntarily with Gene?"

"No."

"That's why your fingerprints are the only ones on the doorknob, isn't it Sherry? You opened the door all by yourself. You were leading Gene out of that motel room."

"You bet I was. He just shot my childhood friend and beat the living hell out of me. Just look at the pictures they took at the hospital. As long as he quit hitting me, I did anything he said."

"Sherry, you didn't think Porter was fatally wounded."

"Don't tell me what I thought. I'm the only one knows what's in my head."

She sat there in the witness chair surrounded by fine mahogany, but the word you could almost taste in the room, it was Sue Raffin's favorite word: asshole. Sherry sat straighter in the chair than before, and her lips almost disappeared inside her mouth she had them so tightly closed. Assholes. You're all a bunch of assholes, the words seemed to come out of her eyes. And Cameron let her stew in her juices for a few minutes.

Then just as the judge stirred, Cameron moved in again. "No, Mrs. Bofay," he said. "You didn't think Porter was dying, did you?" He returned to the defense table and picked up a piece of paper, unfolded it and waved it in front of her. "You told the officer the day they arrested you, he was sitting on the bed getting dressed when you waltzed out of that motel room. 'He was fine,' you told them."

"That's what Eu-gene told me to say or he'd come back and get me when the whole thing was over. Bucky was bleeding like a stuffed pig. I told them that, too. Any dimwit would have called an ambulance."

"But you didn't. That must have been an awful mess for a man sitting on the bed, putting his pants back on."

"Well I don't suppose he was thinking about the dry cleaning bills then," she said. "Besides, I told you, that's just what Eu-gene told me to say."

All through this part of her testimony, Jaymie had hold of my hand like if she'd let go for an instant, she would have flown off into space. What she saw in her mind—I know because it's what I saw in my mind—wasn't those photos. It was the real Bucky, dead in the front seat of his truck, trying to stick the key in the ignition to drive three miles back to Walls and Rose for help. Or at least that's what everyone guessed, trying to figure what a man would do, knowing he was bleeding to death—somewhere in his brain—but too much blood flowing out too fast to put that information to any good use. Maybe he just sat there, pointing the key nowhere in particular, *talking* to the ignition—cursing or trying to talk the key into the hole—for half an hour or more, doing and undoing the same thing over and over, not knowing what he was doing when all he really had to do was slump against the horn. The motel clerk would have come out to shut up the racket.

Cameron walked back to the defense table, put his piece of paper down, squared it up next to his leather folder and paused there, his hand still and calm steadying the paper.

"So what kind of shape was he in when you left the motel, Sherry?"

"He was in piss-poor shape," Sherry answered. "If you'll excuse the French."

I don't know why he asked that. It didn't make any sense for the defense to let the prosecution witness rattle on about the severity of wounds his client had inflicted. And I think the jury felt that, too. Instead of just watching Sherry, their heads swiveled back and forth like at a tennis match. They looked at Cameron when he spoke; at Aamold when he objected; at Sherry when she started a sentence. And everytime she said anything about Bucky, they whipped back to Jaymie and me, expecting hysterics or tears. Something to reinforce their own horror at first hearing the facts. Imagining their son. Or their brother at the mercy of Mr. and Mrs. Eugene Bofay.

Cameron ended it, finally, sitting on the edge of the defense table while Sherry rolled her eyes, examined her fingernails and stared at him. Giving her time to make the point Cameron hoped to make: to Sherry, the whole process was an intrusion on her nail-polishing time. Bucky was no more than a broken fingernail. Not worth messing up her fresh polish to call an ambulance for her lifelong friend. But the other damage—that was impossible to measure until the jury finished their work.

"What is your reputation, Sherry," Cameron asked, "For truth and veracity?"

But Sherry looked at Mr. Aamold who rose halfway out of his chair. "Objection your honor, irrelevant."

The judge sustained the objection. "Have you any other questions of this witness, Mr. Cameron?"

"No further your honor."

And he adjourned court for the day.

JAYMIE AND I STOOD on the courthouse steps in the freezing late afternoon air and told each other we were fine, we were okay, we would sleep fine, really, and hugged each other, but the hug was more like two statues clanking against each other, not Jaymie and me. Then we each went home our separate ways.

I was fine. I drove home. I made supper. I washed dishes. I ate only seventeen—counted out and stacked by the side of the bed—seventeen oreo cream cookies. Counted them and timed them so they would last till one minute after nine, which I'd already decided was the earliest proper hour an adult could go to bed for the night. I split them with a slight, deft, separating twist and ate the cream first, then the wafers. I waited the next nine minutes quietly lying on top of the bed with the bed still made and my clothes still on until the proper bedtime arrived at which time I rose and undressed for bed and tucked myself in. Then I ate the rest of the oreos in the package. No time restrictions now, no deft twist. One after the other like a chain smoker with a pack of cigarettes.

I dreamt of a man standing by my car in Jack Paisley's parking lot, demanding that I tell him the truth about his bridgework, and when I did, he slid a long, paper-thin knife between my ribs. Just that. He didn't twist it. Or pull it out. And all I had to do was stand perfectly still, perfectly straight not to bleed to death. I slept that way all night.

In the morning, as if Sherry Fowler's lies and tap-tapping heels across the floor hadn't been enough, Gene Bofay got on the stand for his required turn at the alleged evidence and told the jury that everything Sherry had said was a lie. And while he talked, I tried to find a comfortable way to sit on the wooden bench, my body so sore and stiff, my ribs stitched together so tight that anything but the most shallow breathing felt like fire.

This was not a very dark man, and not a very Indian-looking man—much less than Rose—though the defense had made a big issue of his Indian heritage. Mostly he was a man who talked very slowly, very deliberately, as if he was spelling out each word in his head very carefully before he uttered it. Cameron had told the court early and often that Gene Bofay was a victim too—culturally deprived and intellectually undeveloped.

But apparently he was more adept at memorization than Sherry. That, or he told some version of the truth. The one word he used most often was "wife." Sherry was "his wife." And through an error in Mr. Aamold's office, the divorce papers, in fact, still had not been filed. In court now, as well as four months before at the time of the accident, Sherry and Gene Bofay were man and wife. Gene said that nearly everything "his wife" had said was a lie. That she was prone to do that sometimes. He had not shot the rifle on his own.

"My wife, she told me to kill him. And then, when he was just kneeling there, to finish him off. I thought Porter was already pretty much dead. Then my wife said, 'Let's get out of here.' She led me out of the motel room. I was in a daze. She told me 'Drive, you stupid-ass son of a bitch.'"

Those last words he said quickly, more softly, as if he didn't believe them. The rest of it, he just kept saying monotone lies, like a string of glow-in-the-dark rosary beads, no lie different from the last and all easier to listen to than what Sherry said happened, maybe because it was the second time I'd heard it, and I believed he was only telling those lies for his sister, who was there in the courtroom. I would have told lies for Katherine if I'd been caught like that. He wore a brand-new suit; she must have bought it for him for the trial to make him look good. It was a two-piece leisure suit, beige with brown contrasting stitching all around the edges and a dark brown polyester shirt.

When Sherry left him, he said, he'd been off work, broken his leg on the job. He was a cat skinner, drove heavy equipment, made lots of money. But he was on worker's comp, and Sherry liked to spend big money at Hart Albins, you know, like most wives, he said. They like to spend the money and we were low then. His wife couldn't adjust. He'd borrowed two hundred dollars to come up to Missoula to find her the day he got his cast off. Four days before the accident.

"I called her folk's place first, but they didn't even know she was around yet. Or they weren't letting on what they knew. Then I called all the bars up Lolo Creek. At the first one she got on the phone, to see if it was really me and I'd drive eleven hundred miles just to take her home. Which I would, I promise you. But when I got down there, she told the bartender to tell me she wasn't there anymore. Just left, he said, probably headed for home. But she was still there, I saw her daddy's truck, still out in front of the Hayloft Saloon. So I just hung out in the parking lot and followed her when she left, down to the Tavern Bar, where she always used to hang out before I married her."

"What was it like being married to Sherry?" Cameron asked.

"She was a pistol," he said. "A real pistol." Bofay smiled and one of the men on the jury, a man about Bofay's own age and with stained teeth, smiled too. "Kept me guessing, you know? One day she's throwing things at me, and the next she wants me to not go to work so we can stay in the sack all day."

"And when you found your wife in the sack with Porter, how did you feel?"

"Well, my first reaction was to haul off and hit him, which I did. But that wasn't enough. He came at me like a tiger, scratching and biting, going for my eyes. And then he grabbed for the rifle, trying to take it away from me, and I got scared, honest to God, but the next thing I know, he folds over."

"Why did you leave him there?"

"I was worried about Sherry's safety and my survival. He could have jumped up again and taken that gun away and shot me."

"Did you pull the phone wires out of the wall?"

"No. I never done that. Jeez, the phone company would never let you off if you pulled their wires out of the wall. I started to call for help for Porter, that's probably why they got pulled. Sherry said, 'Put the damned phone down you stupid idiot,' and pulled me out by my arm. I guess I didn't let go of the phone till I got back in the truck."

"Did you enter that motel room to kill Porter?"

"I never meant to hurt nobody at that particular time."

Cameron moved back to the defense table, slouched like he was going to sit down, then righted himself again. He stood, his feet crossed and his back twisted over the table, held there like a marionette for several seconds. "And the tires, Gene. Did you let the air out of two tires on Porter's truck?"

"Now. I did that. But I did it before I went in. I didn't want the guy, whoever it was, to get away without my knowing for sure he was in there. You know what I mean? I wanted to know it was somebody and not just me going off half-cocked. Then on the way out I was so upset I guess I forgot."

"Did you break into that room?"

"No sir. When I got to the door, the key was still in the lock."

"And the gun, Gene. Did you mean to take that in the room and shoot whoever was with your wife?"

"Man, I never thought of shooting no one. I was scared, you know, and I knew Sherry's old man kept that gun in his truck. When I saw his truck out there in the parking lot, I guess I just picked up the gun automatically."

"And loaded it?"

Bofay held both hands up in front of him as if surrendering. "As God is my witness, I just picked up the gun. I was only going to scare the guy off so I could get my wife back. You know? I never even checked to see if the thing was loaded."

"So as far as you knew, you were going in there with an empty gun?"

"You bet."

Cameron now sat on the defense table. "Gene, I want you to think about this before you answer. Knowing what you know now, would you take Sherry back?"

"I love that woman. She's a handful, that's the truth. But I never loved no other woman."

"Would you take her back, lock, stock and barrel?"

"You bet."

Before Cameron could untwist his body and declare himself finished with the witness, Jaymie leaned closer to me and whispered, "Up close and personal with Howdy Doody and Princess Summer Fall Winter Bed-Spring. I've got to get out of here, Evelyn. I can't stand much more of this lovey-dovey bullshit."

"We can't go anywhere till court is recessed. Mr. Aamold needs you for his case."

"The fool can remember only so many lies at one time," Jaymie said. "It's like a soap opera. We're not going to miss anything. I need some time at the shop."

"An hour isn't going to help the shop at this point."

"You're right. As usual."

Cameron sat down, adjusted his pant legs one at a time, pulling the fabric free over his knees and then crossing his legs. Mr. Aamold stood to begin cross-examination.

As he went through his paces with Bofay, it became obvious that Jaymie was also right. Each response came out a carbon copy of the one he'd given under direct examination. Like a tape recorder playing back the same statement, with the same monotone delivery. Cameron had succeeded in convincing Bofay not to think. Or Bofay did not think on his feet, so Cameron had no choice. Let him give the answers they had carefully worked out, even if the question didn't quite fit his answer.

For the rest of the afternoon, Bofay's sister, Lillian Yellow Bird, the sister who cared enough to go to K-Mart for his leisure suit, and put her house and twenty acres in Lodge Grass, Montana, up for bail, his only sister, she said, held the jury rapt, with her strong melodic voice. Cameron just let her talk. Aside from teaching Bofay his testimonial catechism, it was the smartest thing he'd done in three days.

Lillian Yellow Bird took possession of the jury.

"I been around that girl a long time," she said, "when Eugene lost his job two years ago, they come live with me."

She chose one of the women in the jury to tell her story to. A slightly fat woman about forty-five years old, who had worn the same well-washed baby blue sweater and medium brown wig to court every day.

"He gave up whiskey and cigarettes more'n once those nine months they lived with me. She took him down there to the bar. She led him astray —more he tried, more she teased. Say to him, 'You're not man enough to quit drinking.' Couldn't stay away from those city bars. 'I'm going to Billings,' she say. 'You two couch potatoes can come if'n you want.' All the time I'm the one's buying them groceries, then, and mascara for the girl, and the girl, she's getting money from her daddy or she's selling herself over there in Billings and putting it in her pocket."

"She fights with him all the time those times. He paddles her, she throws the iron at his head, turned up on high, on linen, she throws it and she burns a spot in my carpet, in my brand-new trailer house. Throws him out of the house altogether one time, he tries to tell her she can't go to Billings again. Then she tells me we're women's libbers and we don't need no men. He sits around the house worrying about her when she's gone. She brings him whiskey so he gets drunk and pass out and she can go party. He's better off without her, that's what I say. Now he can get his life back together. Get his self-respect."

Cameron approached the witness stand. "You've heard what Sherry said happened," he said. "Do you believe she's telling the truth?"

"I think maybe now she worries what her family thinks," Lillian said.

Cameron nodded. "When you put up Gene's bail, did you ever worry about him skipping out and leaving you without your home?"

"I raised him, since he was ten years old. He won't do anything to hurt me."

"Thank you, Mrs. Bird. That's all."

Mr. Aamold stood halfway. "No questions, your honor," he said, and we adjourned for the day.

I walked out with Jaymie to her Bronco.

"Pops called last night," she said. "They're halfway to Alaska and mother's driving him crazy. Won't come out of their room. Says it's too wet, too cold, too many people."

"And he's happy he can count on you to take care of business," I added.

"Oh, of course." Jaymie unlocked her Bronco. "Are you holding up okay?" she asked.

"What? You going to call it off if I'm not?" I said. "No, I'm fine." What I didn't need was for her to start worrying about me. I was supposed to be there for her. To hold her hand and help her through the ordeal. "I'm fine," I said again, patted Jaymie on the shoulder, and put her in the Bronco.

On Friday, Cameron introduced a string of defense witnesses, all swearing they knew Gene Bofay, swearing he was a good old boy who never hurt anyone who didn't need it. A string of men who lived up Lolo Creek, loggers and truckers whose faces showed more sunburn than alcohol use, and whose hands were more used to barb wire, wood and mud than the comforts of indoor pencil-pushing, and who made the jury wonder if this was another side of Gene Bofay worth looking at. But when Mr. Aamold began his cross-examination, we discovered that all six men also knew Buck Porter, something that took not only Mr. Aamold by surprise, but Cameron as well. Lars Aamold waded in, not knowing what they would say.

"What kind of guy was Bucky Porter?" the D.A. asked each man.

Buck was a "nice" guy, salt of the earth, never got in fights. Two of the men were even young enough to have gone to high school with Bucky, and all of them ended up presenting an interesting picture to the jury. Gene Bofay: hard drinker, hard hitter, hard-luck sort; not averse to taking a guy down a peg or two if he needed it, or getting his ear chewed off in a fight to back up his buddy. Buck Porter: hard worker, occasional party drinker, give you the shirt off his back, help you push your truck uphill, or change your wife's tire if he found her out there alone, no matter if he was dressed up for the evening or in his work clothes, and he'd follow her home to make sure she got there safe. So there was Gene Bofay sitting at their kitchen table with their sons and brothers. They all leaned back a bit in their chairs.

That woman on the jury with the wig, the one Lillian had talked to for all her testimony, she watched each of the six men go up and testify and then sit back down again, and at the end she just gave Cameron a look and shook her head. None of it made sense at that point, none of what Cameron had to say. And when the defense and prosecution were through with the parade of Lolo Creek natives, Cameron sat down briefly, to listen to Mr. Aamold's closing statement and then stood up and made a fool of himself again. He'd hired a private investigator for the afternoon, a man who looked twice as prosperous as Cameron, and still not fit to chauffeur Mr. Aamold around.

His job was to pretend to be Bucky in a re-creation of the struggle that ended in self-defense. Cameron played Bofay. His pen, the rifle. He pointed it with both hands at the investigator. But Cameron had made the mistake of using a pen with red ink, not thinking of the consequences, and halfway through the charade, the investigator pulled hard on the pen the same way Bofay said Bucky did in the motel that night. The pen broke into a dozen pieces in the investigator's hand, leaving a large red stain on his shirt just slightly lower than Bucky's wound but close enough. Cameron made a joke of it and sat down. And the listening part was over for once and for all.

As the jury picked up sweaters and papers and pens and waited to file out, Mr. Aamold walked through the little swinging gate straight to Jaymie and me. He checked his watch. "Timing's on our side," he said. "They've been on the hot seat all week and it's Friday night. Most of them would rather have a cold beer and a pizza than argue over whether Gene Bofay's 85 or 95 percent guilty. Fast decisions always work for the prosecution. But don't expect anything for an hour and a half. It'll take that long just to get them herded over to dinner and back up to the jury room.

Mr. Aamold rose from his last squatting conference, as the jury exited the courtroom. "You'll stay close?"

"I'll be at Evelyn's apartment."

"Before you leave here, make sure my assistant has that number."

So it came down to the waiting. The first hour and a half, Jaymie busied herself cleaning up my apartment. Washed the dishes, which were mostly just morning orange juice glasses—

Monday through Friday—and evening ice cream and Hershey's chocolate sauce binge bowls. Then she hung up my clothes, made the bed, folded my towels, and marked the day, Friday, January ninth, with a big black magic marker on the calendar.

She turned and saw me watching her and put down the pen. "I'd mark it a red letter day, but you don't have a red pen and I don't know what letter I'd use," she said. Then, rather than give me a chance to ask her a question, she turned on the offensive. "What are you thinking about all quiet there in the living room, while I've been puttering up your house?"

"Mostly how long I've been here in Montana, and I've been kind of wasting my time."

"Working for the P?"

"That too. But I came out here to find some trace of my grandfather, and I've just been sitting here in Missoula, trying to balance a checkbook with no money."

"You have any whiskey around?" she asked.

"No."

"I could sure use a belt. Just one." She opened the kitchen cupboards, looking for something. Anything. She found the oreos and hauled them out.

"I think I could probably use one too."

"You know what I've been thinking?" she asked, stacking a pile of oreos on the counter. "Last week one night, before the trial started and all that, I was thinking it's been a long four months. I haven't really given Pops much reason to let me take over the business. All he's been seeing is a lush. I think if the situation was reversed, Bucky would have been all right. He would have told the old man to fuck off and just packed his bags for Istanbul, or wherever the next rock pile was waiting. He would've gone on with his life. Me, I was thinking how good I'd been. You know. Took care the best I could, hung around. Did the dirty work. Like always. Now I want my reward. You know what I'm talking about. I've been good, and now Bucky can just stop fucking around and come out of hiding." She picked up an oreo cookie off the pile and twisted it open. "Well, buckaroos, that's not gonna happen. You'll be glad to know I know that, Evelyn. Last week, finally, I came face to face with that. You know what? He wasn't in that courtroom this week. No matter how many times they said his name or showed his pictures around. I packed him up and put him in his coffin, but I guess I always expected to be able to call him back. When I really needed him. It's the rest of my life now, and no Bucky Beaver to play with. And whatever the jury says it doesn't make any difference in the world." She popped an oreo cookie in her mouth and spit it back out. "Jesus, how do you stand these things? You gotta start buying a better class of chocolate."

WHAT THE JURY DID was to convict Eugene Bofay on the toughest charge possible: premeditated, deliberate homicide. It was barely dark when the phone rang, barely a half hour from when we figured they'd start deliberating. If they'd had supper. If they'd thought about their homes and families and a cold beer, like Mr. Aamold said, and come at once to a decision, each one feeling the consensus without even a straw vote. Or maybe they had all just believed in Mr. Aamold's system of justice.

Eugene Bofay was led back into the courtroom for the verdict the same way he'd been presented for arraignment: in ankle and wrist irons and with seven deputies and a German shepherd to guard him. Guilty. And held over for sentencing March 4.

It was over.

ELEVEN

WE HELD COURT together that night, Jaymie and I, at the Legal Tender Saloon. All sweetness and light and everlasting serendipity it was, at least for the first three hours and the first ten shots. Then all hell broke loose. It was my fault for getting as drunk on two shots as she was on eight. Sober, I would have kept my mouth shut. But all I said was the truth: that Gene Bofay's lawyer was a down-and-outer unable to provide a competent defense and surely, when the appeal came—which was inevitable—the conviction would be thrown out. Period. She was there. If she'd had eyes, she would have seen the same thing I did.

"Evelyn," she said to me across two very clean-cut Ohio tourists. "You don't get the point. He's going to the slammer, no matter. He's guilty. I drink to his guiltiness. Not just me that thinks so anymore, but twelve honest and pure men and women of the jury."

"I'm just looking down the road," I said. "His sister's no dummy and she loves him. Maybe as much as you love Bucky. She's sure to hire a new lawyer to file an appeal. And in all probability, she'll win a new trial. Maybe even, you know, like your father says, a guy has the right to kill his wife's lover, just once, as long as he doesn't make a habit of it."

That's all I said. Wally said he'd've done the same thing if, God forbid, he found Rose with someone. Maybe even shoot her too, and himself, save the taxpayer the cost of adjudicating the damned mess, he said. He'd said it the day Bucky was found, and said it again, this time out of Jaymie's hearing. We were alone in the shop the Saturday before the trial, closing up, locking the floor safe. He stood up again, and leaning on the desk to unlock his right knee, he told me "You're the one's gonna be around picking up the pieces when Jaymie sees it in the paper. When he walks."

Jaymie still didn't get it. But then she was fresh from victory, still celebrating the wisdom of juries and had four drinks lined up in front of her like tin soldiers, and these two clean-cut tourist guys, drawn to her fire and her glow. Clean, blonde boys with no dust or sweat or five o'clock grime on them.

"All he needs is some hotshot lawyer who says, 'Who brought the gun? Not *my* client. Who was married and fooling around? Not *my* client. Who taunted her spouse for days, leading him on a wild goose chase? Not *my* client.'" I took a drink of Jack. "Hell. Who loaded the gun? Not *my* client."

She looked at me sideways, not really wanting to take her attention from either of her blonde boys for a second. "It's not that he did it," she said. "Everyone, even him, admits that he did it. It was how he did it—for Christ's sake, leaving his victim to bleed to death, the corpse to rot. Nobody wants to think of their brother or son or father lying in his own blood and begging for mercy and no one giving a flying fuck. Do you forget he beat Sherry to within an inch of her life, so even she was too afraid to snitch? Poor old Sherry. She's always depended on her cute face, and then he beats her face to a screaming pulp. She still has a scar on her left cheek where it swelled so hard it split the skin. Wouldn't let her get medical treatment. Wouldn't even let her put free motel ice on it. Does that make you like him a little less?"

"I'm not saying I like him, Jaymie."

"Well you sure enough lean on his side of the argument."

One of the clean boys said he was going for drinks. The other one stood and offered to help carry them back.

"All I said was don't be surprised if the verdict is overturned. It happens."

"Oh, Miss Courtroom Procedure Expert, now, after one trial."

"I read the papers."

"This is different."

"Because it's your brother?"

"Because he's guilty as hell and gonna spend the rest of his life in prison for it."

"Only because the defense attorney was more incompetent than the prosecution. He should've objected to half the stuff Aamold presented. Aamold spent half his time leading his witnesses through their testimony. What is the new lawyer going to do with that? If Aamold isn't any better with the new guy—the guy they know they have to hire out of their own pocket now, since the free attorney didn't earn his money—he's going to lose the case."

"Bullshit. Where did those two cute little assholes go to anyway?"

"They said they were going for more drinks," I said.

"A lot you know. They've flown the coop. You chased them away."

"If the truth scared them, good riddance," I said. "Look at those alleged character witnesses Cameron paraded through the courtroom. They knew Bucky better than they knew Eugene. All Cameron had to do was spend three minutes questioning the lot of them. 'Did you know anyone else involved in the case?' But no. He was too busy inventing a skit to entertain the jury, which probably hung his client all by itself. I don't like it any more than you do. Maybe the truth scares the hell out of you."

Oh, but that really made her mad, and she swept the shot glasses off the table, skipping broken glass halfway across the dance floor. The band was on break—which was also the only time she could actually hear every word I said—and out of the line of fire.

The broken glass brought the bouncer to our table, and before he even grabbed her by the arm, he's talking to her—he knows her—talking to her by name and telling her he'd lose his job if he didn't kick her out of the bar. So I apologized. I explained to him that Jaymie had a very bad day, and I'd been upset and said things to her that upset her and I shouldn't have, and if he'd just let go of her once we got out the door, I'd take her home. Well, he was a big guy with nothing really to prove, and knowing Jaymie and really only wanting someone else to take care of the problem, he let her go and let me walk her out of the bar by myself.

We got in the Dorado and Jaymie was definitely not driving, no matter what she said, 'cause the car had just gotten out of the garage again—the third time the mechanics had tried to adjust the hinge after Rose's ankle-smashing whacked it out of alignment. That gives you some idea how hard she'd slammed it. And Rose expected that car at the airport two weeks from Saturday, 6:02 sharp, to pick her up from her miserable three-week cruise.

"If I'm not driving, you're taking me where I want to go," Jaymie told me.

"I'm taking you home."

"You take me home and I'll just go where I want after you're gone. And I want to go to pissant Maxwell's. Time they had some real people in there."

I knew it was true—soon as I left her she'd be in the Dorado again, so I drove her back downtown to Maxwell's, across from the courthouse, which I told her was probably an unwise decision, that now she should start forgetting for sure. But she said she wanted to sit on a bar stool with a fine glass of Tennessee sipping whiskey and look up at the county jail. Fine. But Maxwell's was where the accountants and lawyers gathered. They went slumming out at the Tender, but this was their living room—complete with homespun-covered overstuffed sofas and oversized arrangements of mauve silk flowers. You didn't jostle anything there. It was not a good place to have Jaymie plopped down in the middle of with a glass of sipping whiskey, after sipping eight at the Tender and more on the road into town. By the time we hit Maxwell's, she was little more than a common drunk.

It only took about fifteen minutes for the manager to come over and ask me to remove Jaymie from the premises. She wasn't saying anything or breaking anything, she just looked drunk, and while it was fine to buy Maxwell's liquor, it was bad taste to show its effects.

Now this manager, who Jaymie was calling "the pretty boy," exhausted his litany of manager-school tact in three minutes. He nodded to his bartender, and with one swift movement, they lifted Jaymie off her barstool and levitated her out the front door and onto the pavement. Then he stood with arms crossed, blocking the doorway.

"I'm going back inside pretty boy," Jaymie said. "I'm a paying customer."

"I already called the police. If you don't leave now, they will arrest you for drunk and disorderly conduct. I suggest you leave now."

"Fuck you," Jaymie said and the force of it just about tipped her over on her face. "This is a two-bit, horse-face, sissy bar."

Moving her was impossible. I had her elbow from behind, trying to move her back from the doors and the confrontation, to take her home and put her to bed for the night, but all her weight leaned into the manager and no amount of pulling budged her. And he was no help at all, reminding us every thirty seconds that the cops were on their way. Jaymie cursed him and tried to kick him, but didn't have the balance to carry it off. And me, I tried to talk the guy into helping me put Jaymie in the car. He would have none of it.

About the third time he told me that Jaymie was *my* responsibility and if I couldn't handle her, she deserved to be arrested, the cops showed up. They double-parked the patrol car right in front of the door and came around and took Jaymie by each arm.

By this time there were people all over the place on the street, none of them quiet and most of them offering the manager tips on how to handle a drunk. And I'm in the middle. Like the time my father took offense at something some guy named "Mack" said in front of his daughter, and I'd be left standing on the sidewalks of New York, holding his top coat and newspaper while he waded into the crowd after the guy. Who knew what his real name was? Till I was ten years old, I thought half the men in New York City were named Mack.

The difference was that Dad knew enough to leave before the cops showed up. Jaymie didn't. They'd started to drag

Jaymie off to the squad car when she turned on them, neither of them really holding on tight since she was a woman, I guess, and I don't think they expected any more than token resistance. First, she kicked the right one on the shin, and then, barely keeping her feet under her at the edge of the sidewalk, Jaymie hauled off and punched the left-side cop with a hard right to the jaw. Had this been the Tender, the crowd would have cheered. But Maxwell's being the fern bar that Jaymie often accused it of being, the crowd quieted and disappeared into the faux brickwork. I was the only one to watch them put the handcuffs on and read Jaymie her rights. I was allowed to follow along behind in the Dorado.

S H E G O T V E R Y L U C K Y. When they booked her, instead of assault on a police officer or anything like that, they only charged her with disorderly conduct. That would be a small fine and two weekends in jail, since she was an upstanding member of the community. In the meantime, I arranged her bail, getting her out about five a.m., which maybe I shouldn't have. I thought about letting her sit, at least just for the night, to cool down. But I couldn't leave her in the same jail as Gene Bofay. Instead, I bailed her out, then waited till I'd loaded her up in Rose's big, white Eldorado to tell her in no uncertain terms how she'd embarrassed me.

"I've never had to talk to one of those bail bondsmen or sit outside the drunk tank. Or even been in a police station."

"Join J&B Lumber and see the world."

"I'm serious. Why did you hit that cop? I mean that's big-time stupid. All-time stupid. I'm sorry about your brother. But goddammit, I'm not going to babysit you anymore. That's it. Don't call me unless you grow up."

I started the Dorado, turned on the windshield wipers and looked up to see if they were clearing off the window and realized, slowly, that it wasn't rain on the windshield, it was broken glass. And a brick, a common house brick sat on the left windshield wiper blade keeping it from working.

Jaymie waved a hand at it. "It's out of the shop for one night and it's broken again, goddamn thing."

"That's hardly what I'd call broken," I said. I really should've just kept my mouth shut, but I guess I was about as angry as she was by then. I just couldn't leave it alone. "It was stupid to take it out tonight."

"Can you just drive me home?"

I drove her home, walked her to the door and unlocked it, since she couldn't unlock it by herself, and helped her out of her lovely go-to-town clothes.

She put on her long white terry-cloth bathrobe, gathered up her dirty clothes and headed back out the door.

"Now where are you going?" I said, sounding even to myself like her mother.

"Trash," she said not rising to it.

"With your new clothes?"

"Uh-huh," she agreed.

"Let me take them to a dry cleaner tomorrow. I'll bring them back good as new."

"I don't want them back. You can't fix them, Evelyn. You can't make these goddamn clothes good as new."

She kicked open the storm door, took two steps out on her redwood deck and pitched the pile of new clothes at the lawn. Then she went into the garage, while I watched from the door, and came out with a two-gallon can of gasoline and poured it all over the clothes, emptying the can, and throwing it out on the lawn.

"Get my shoes, would ya?"

"This is ridiculous. I'm not getting your shoes. I'm not helping you destroy three hundred dollar's worth of brand-new clothes."

"They're not paid for, yet. They don't count." She walked around the frozen grass in her bare feet. "Get me a match, then," she said.

"Only if you burn up all the matches with them." Buck's collection, I meant. She knew what I meant.

"Don't nag, Evelyn. It's not becoming," she said, patting her bathrobe pockets. She found a book of matches in the right pocket and set fire to the whole book before throwing it on the gasoline-soaked clothes.

"It'll be a short, happy fire," she yelled, and staggered back as the flames leapt over her head.

I got the hose and turned on the outside spigot but nothing came out.

"City girl," Jaymie said laughing. "Pipes freeze if you leave the water in 'em all winter."

The fire died down immediately with so little fuel to keep it going, and I realized it was not much of a threat anymore to the house, or Jaymie. I'd been most worried about the hem of her robe catching fire, maybe with some gasoline on it. But she'd been careful enough and escaped unscathed. With the fire out, the yard turned dark again, inky dark like a midnight ocean, and Jaymie's white robe glowed neon-bright in the reflection of living room lights.

"I'll tuck you in," I said. "If you'll come inside now."

She did. But she immediately fixed herself another large whiskey on ice and sat down on the living room couch.

"You know those Buddhist monks weren't so brave," she said, tucking her feet under the pillows at the end of the couch. "And don't give me that more-innocent-than-thou look."

I didn't catch on, not right off.

"Walter Concrete. Viet Nam. Buddhist monks. If you use enough gasoline it doesn't take very long at all." She looked down in her drink for a moment, then looked at me innocently.

"You suppose they cheated and did a presoak in the monastery—you know before going out to torch themselves?"

"I think there probably isn't any completely painless way to die."

"Maybe burning up a pile of clothes isn't such a weird thing to do. Instead of cremating a body, you cremate some remains, so to speak. You think I'm getting morbid?"

I shrugged. "You do what you need to do and then you get on with it."

"With life? That must be Catholic," she said. She got up and fixed herself another drink in the kitchen.

"It's healthy," I said to the back of her robe. "People do it. There's nothing wrong with it."

"You give your mourning clothes to the Salvation Army and wash your hands of it?"

"Or you keep them in your closet and wear them somewhere else. Somewhere happy."

"You'd remember," she said, stirring the ice cubes around with her finger. She lay her head back on the couch.

"Yes. I hope so. I think in some rule book somewhere it's written: it's a sin to forget people just because it's not fun to remember them anymore." I'd tried not to say anything. Not wanting to say anything else that would stimulate her, upset her. I just wanted her to relax, talk herself out, maybe go to sleep. But I fell asleep first, sitting up in the Barcalounger and woke up at dawn, stiff-necked and feeling dirty and sweaty despite the January cold. The sky was clean and clear, the mountains all around the valley snowcapped, white as new baby teeth. Jaymie had passed out on the couch. I thought about covering her with a blanket, then thought it might waken her. Instead, I slipped out the back door and walked home.

And that was the last I spoke to her or saw her for two weeks. Monday through Friday, she ran the shop from 7:00 a.m. till midnight, trying to catch up for the trial week she missed and getting started on the tax preparation for April, and serving her time in jail, two weekends in a row.

At least that's what she told me two weeks later when she called. It was the only time she called, to remind me to pick up the folks at the airport Saturday, while she was in jail. So it was me picked up Rose and Wally in the Bronco with their luggage and presents, and me who had to explain why the Eldorado—and Jaymie—wasn't there.

But at least after that, after I took Rose and Wally home and Jaymie was finished with her jail sentence, my life returned to normal. Jaymie was busy trying to prove to Wally that she could run J&B as well as he could. No more melodrama, no more fisticuffs. And Monday, Tuesday, Thursday and Friday I worked with Jack, came home and cooked dinner—real dinner—with vegetables and meat and salad. I walked around the block once or twice for exercise, and for a change of scenery followed the railroad tracks at the end of my block down to the river and to the back end of J&B's lumberyard. I sat on the trestle and watched the trucks come and go and the neon-eyed front-end loader grab raw logs from the piles and carry them into the mill building. And I wrote home to my mother, things I could write home about.

March fourth, it was in the papers: Gene Bofay got ninety-nine years or some such unrealistic number. It probably meaning he'd serve twenty-five, which would make him seventy-two when he got out of jail, and maybe smart enough to not get married to another Sherry Fowler. He'd used up all his luck, such as it was, in that first marriage not getting the death sentence. That *was* luck. Bucky hadn't come out nearly as well.

So that night in March, the sheriff's deputies got the dogs out, and the leg irons and handcuffs, and bundled Gene Bofay out of the county jail and into a county van with bars on the windows to take him to Deer Lodge for a long time. I would be willing to bet a nickel that Jaymie watched the transfer from Bucky's black Ford truck in the parking lot at Maxwell's and followed the van all the way to the state prison's front gates. She probably sat there for a long time after the gate was locked shut, making sure it didn't open up again like a swinging door. Starting the truck up she would breath deeply—first time in six months. Then maybe she would drive home and fall into bed, to sleep without dreams. Without nightmares. Without waking up in the night to his voice. By then, it wasn't just Rose having those dreams.

TWELVE

ABOUT A MONTH later Gordy Bennett turned up on my doorstep. Sue Raffin had talked about him many times over lunch that winter. I was spending a lot of time with Sue then. What she said was that I had put Gordy in the driver's seat.

"No," I'd told her. "There just isn't any way to reach him. He has to get in contact with me. I'm the stationary one."

"Right. Fine. But you don't always have to act like you're waiting for him to call."

"I can't play hard to get."

"Not hard to get. A person with a life. The asshole doesn't exactly make himself available to you—give you a phone number or a post office box where you could write. And he doesn't write, does he? A post card every six months would be an improvement from what I've seen."

"You just don't understand."

"You're dead right there. I don't understand how you can let him walk all over you."

So a week after the sentencing, I come home from work and there's Gordy on my doorstep. In my mind, I'm counting off how many months it's been, to keep from hearing those things Sue Raffin said about him.

"Where've you been?" I finally said.

"West Virginia," he said. "Slinging concrete. Did I tell you my brother found me that job?"

"You're on call," I said. He was sitting on the porch step, chewing on a stalk of celery with cut and dirty hands. Maybe already clearing firebreaks in the woods.

He shook his head and laughed. "Just started. April one. And we won't be in the woods for a while. All that snow you had this winter, the roads'll be a swampy mess."

"I hadn't noticed."

"Not exactly a requisite in the dental assisting profession, I suppose," he said pointing the celery stalk at me like a seventh grade geography teacher's ruler. "Of course when it raises the price of your celery and other fresh vegetables, it'll be on your mind."

"That one probably grew in Peru," I said. "I don't think we get those weather reports here." Part of me thought Sue didn't know what she was talking about. That she spent too much time worrying about how much time a guy spent thinking about her, and too little time wondering how it felt to have his hand, calluses and all, touch her arm. That was part of it anyway. The other part was he was just never there. He offered me a stalk of celery and a seat on the front porch beside him. I took both, keeping about a yardstick between us.

"Just get back?" I asked him.

"Oh, 'bout a month."

"I would've liked to have heard from you."

"They've had me out at smoke jumper headquarters since I got back, filling the cracks from last year's fire season," he said. "And then in my spare time, I'm out at the place trying to catch a few calves before they hit the ground. But listen, for tonight, I brought a bunch of groceries over, maybe could make you some supper. I'll cook. Chicken fried steaks and milk gravy, mashed potatoes, peas and carrots, and twinkies. Good cowboy food."

"Twinkies?" I said. He'd pulled the grocery sack onto his lap and wrapped his arms around it. That was the first time I was ever jealous of a grocery sack.

"Cut in half with strawberries on top. Ummboy. You been working for that old coyote Jack P. too long, getting uppity about good American cuisine."

I'm not at all sure I would have let him in even then, if it hadn't been for my landlady's six-year-old, Michael, next door coming out in the middle of the conversation, swinging the broken aluminum door BANG shut, then plopping himself on the squeaky porch swing, kicking his sneakers into the wood, and BANGing the back of the swing against the side of the house each time it swung back again. BANG.

"Cute kid," Gordy said, watching my face.

"I forgot how noisy spring was around here," I said. "How 'bout we go upstairs and you fix me a drink. I assume you brought drink?"

"Red wine for the lady, and whiskey for the gent."

"Good. But I'll have one shot of whiskey while you open the red wine." I started up the stairs. "You can make the drinks while I wash tooth grime off my face."

No, still not at all sure what I wanted. I washed my hands, rinsed, lathered them again to wash my face, taking my time. It would have been nice if Gordy had called. If he could have shown up for a traditional date. I folded the towel in thirds, matched the corners, slipped it in behind the towel rack and draped it over, folded exactly in half. He had to make money. Like me, he had to pay the bills. No one standing around the edges to bail him out. And I wasn't the only person in his life. I could make an argument for being very understanding, all by myself in the bathroom, but I knew it wouldn't stand up for beans at lunch with Sue Raffin. I wasn't convinced she was right. But she might not be wrong.

Gordy came in and set the drink beside me on the counter. "Maybe I should go," he said.

"No." I realized I still had the corner of the towel in my hands. I let it go. "It just hasn't been the best of days, or the best of years for that matter."

I told him about Jaymie. I started anyway. I hadn't talked to her in a month, or seen her since the verdict. He told me about West Virginia and his brother's family. Three kids, two dogs, a wood stove and an unfinished house outside of Wheeling. And the best way to tape and sand Sheetrock for a smooth finish. I told him how I'd stop outside Arabian Acres, about to just drive up to Jaymie's place, and sit there waiting for something or someone to push me, or for Jaymie to accidentally come driving out at that moment and invite me in, sit me down to a cup of coffee and some news about the family or J&B. Good news—that all was well and Rose was healthy. Jaymie would be sober and tell me funny stories all night, like the old days, and I would tell her about Jack P. and his latest girlfriend. I hadn't told her any Maddy stories since Christmas. Maddy, the one who wore a see-through blouse to a Paisley family dinner and a pair of Fredericks of Hollywood padded-rump jeans seven days a week.

I would start, then Gordy would tell me what fun it was to paint indoors, in the winter, with rug rats under his feet and working around the living room furniture which included a radial saw and electric sander and, during hunting season, a whitetail buck hanging from the exposed rafters behind the television. Then he went back to his favorite topic, the Forest Service and going back to work for the Forest Service for another summer. He told me about the long drive back from West Virginia, after all winter with his brother's family, driving alone in his pickup truck and thinking about the next paycheck, the next job that would pay for more fencing and hay till the grass started coming in fresh and green. Maybe he could stay in Montana next winter, stay with his cows instead of depending on the neighbors.

Maybe even quit the seasonal Forest Service work. Too many dickheads, he said, working seasonal. People who never paid attention to details. Drunks, dopers. Losers.

You could have done that whole evening in slow motion and added it to the movie of all the other evenings we'd spent together. He set me down in the rocking chair and placed himself in my easy chair with his coat and boots still on, as if he could leave anytime he wanted to. It didn't matter if I was there or not. Being out there on the road screwed him down inside himself and the longer he'd been gone, the more lonely arguments he'd had with himself, the longer he'd take to talk them all back out of his head. The fire crews, the bureaucracy, the equipment; the man on the backhoe moving equipment at the jump center today, not watching the rearview mirror, backing up within inches of him, almost pinning him to a power pole.

"Would've squashed me like a fly," he said. "First I nailed the driver, hauled him out of the rig and pounded a couple of fingers into his chest. Then the supervisor, he's standing there watching the whole thing picking his nose. I almost quit. In fact, I think I did quit. Except they can't afford to let me quit.

I was two inches from dusting that super. That would've put the cherry on top."

It was the same thing every time he came to visit. Different stories, but the same people and places, the same frustration. He'd talk and talk and talk, and then there'd be this slow sudden quiet. He'd collect himself again and start in with the list, a long, slow list of everything, until he realized the bottle was getting low; sitting in the dark, by now with his coat off and his shirt sleeves folded once above his gnarled hands. Like sterile white surgical linen surrounding an open wound.

That night I watched him fold his cuffs back, about an hour before he was all talked down; somewhere on a piece of Montana interstate or flashing back to the blinking lights of the backhoe. He realized he was still alive, that he was warm, sitting in a house with windows and electric lights. And had another season with the Forest Service guaranteed. Another season with cash money to support the ranch for another generation. He was working on his fifteenth summer now. The ranch, its fourth generation. And always the men had to have cash jobs. His grandfather had broken horses. His father worked in the talc mine. And then silence. He got up and turned on the light and said, "I'm done, honest," like a little boy caught banging his pink rubber ball against the side of the house seventeen times more than his mother could stand it.

"Haven't you heard enough of this bullshit yet?" he said, and then he was embarrassed and sat down again.

Too embarrassed for me to tell him I was not done talking, I was not done stringing out my litany of lost chances. I still missed Jaymie. Not the one out at Arabian Acres now. The one I'd known before the accident. All the nights I'd sit out on the highway watching her place, wondering what she was doing. Or, if I had extra money for gas, running out to

Lolo Creek and watching her mother's house, watching the lights go on and off.

I'd given up the VW, or actually, it had died a couple years before. And Wally had given me the old yard truck, a '55 International Harvester pickup with a fresh coat of cherry apple red metallic paint, J&B's logo and only 10,000 real miles. He even spent one Saturday afternoon last summer showing me how to work the synchromesh transmission, running up and down twenty-foot-high stacks of kiln-dried lumber, listening to the revving of the motor to tell me when to shift, learning the natural progression of gear changing, without benefit of a clutch. I was proud of learning how to drive it, proud of owning the old beater. But it ate gas like chocolate and I couldn't afford to drive it down to Lolo much.

Gordy nudged me, looked up at me wondering if I thought he was crazy; if I would still let him hold me.

"I'm hungry," I said. "I'm going to start the broiler."

"Come here," he said, holding his hand out to me.

His one hand, the size of both of mine, drew me back to him mind and body, those familiar calluses sliding up the side of my leg. I missed him. Those four months gone that winter and the months he would be gone over the summer fire season—now at least he was here. Now I should take what he had to give and be grateful. His hand shook. His entire body beginning to vibrate, and his other hand settled into the small of my back, drew me closer to his chair, and all he really watched was my eyes.

"I love that look," he said.

"Which look?"

"All mine. For a few moments, nothing and no one else on your mind."

"It's always true."

But he broke. He smiled, and his eyes darted once, quickly,

finding a spot on my chin, returning quickly to my eyes, but his eyes now strange. Take two giant steps backward. He made love with the same intensity he used to talk himself down, and when he was done he fell back on the bed and closed his eyes.

For a moment my mind was blank: dull, sleepy, painlessly open. My eyes drifted over the ceiling and out the window. Sky. Sky with stars if you looked into the blackest places. And trees. Empty trees waiting for spring, then summer, then fall again. And what was I waiting for? Tell me that.

"Gordy?" I whispered.

"Umm?"

"You ever been to a trial? Like a murder trial?"

"No."

"I don't think I'll ever see anything the same again. It's like—I don't think anything that was said in that courtroom had anything to do with what really happened. And if it did, it was only half of what happened. Or a tenth."

"That's what they do."

"It isn't the truth."

"You shouldn't think about things like that at night. Gives you insomnia. I know."

"I can't help it. I don't really think about it. It—it floods me."

"You should try not to use 'really' so often. Try to cut it out of your speech," he said and then laid his hands across his chest and closed his eyes.

I'd been on my elbow—propped up to talk to him, and like air being let out of a balloon, I laid back down too. But I couldn't close my eyes right away. If he hadn't been there, I would have drug my rocking chair up to the window and watched the stars. But I didn't want to disturb him. He'd be gone soon enough. Long enough. How long till the next time? How long could we talk next time? I turned quietly over on my side and watched the trees, till my eyes finally grew tired and closed by themselves. But I still couldn't sleep. He was here now. As long as he was here, there was always time.

THE PHONE RANG at 3:00 a.m.

"Evelyn." It was Jaymie. "I'm down at the public phone at Super Save," she said.

"Why are you doing that? You should be in bed." I looked at the clock, and then dropped it on the floor trying to set it back down on the nightstand.

"I can't sleep."

"It would be easier to fall asleep if you went home and got in bed."

"No. That didn't work. You can read a book or drink a cup of warm milk and just nod off. I've got too much going through my head. I can't do that."

I don't know. I didn't have any patience left for her. It was time she started taking care of herself, pulling her horns in. Again. But with Gordy being right there, listening, laying on his back with his eyes open, I said, "Sorry."

"For Christ's sake, don't be sorry. I'm fed up to my eye-balls with sorry. Gordy's there, isn't he?"

I didn't say anything. She waited twenty seconds, I'm sure it felt like forever to her, but she couldn't hold it in. "I saw the truck out front. Green Jimmy with Lake County plates. I need to talk."

"You are talking."

"Over at your house. Face to face. Sitting down. In-fucking-doors. I'm freezing my ass off in this phone booth."

"Not now," I said it as softly as I could, but Gordy couldn't help but hear what was going on, probably her side of the conversation too. He got up and went into the bathroom, closing the door behind him.

"You can't come here now. After Gordy leaves, I'll come over to your place. Go home. Take your coat off, have a cup of coffee."

"You don't know what's going on."

"Have you been home tonight?"

"Home. That's . . . ." she started a sentence and trailed off. "That's really complicated," she finally said. "There's too much to tell over the phone."

Gordy came out of the bathroom and started putting his clothes on. That was definitely not what I needed.

"Look, Jaymie. Seven o'clock, I'll be at your house with bells on. I promise. I'll listen to everything you have to say."

"I've been sitting outside your house for two hours. You know I didn't want to walk right in on you. Then your lights went off finally. And I waited."

She went on and on, and in the meantime Gordy had his shirt on, buttoned it, and stuck it in his jeans. When he went out to the living room to get his coat, I put the phone down on the bed and went out to follow.

The apartment was dark except for the streetlight staring in the south windows. The weeping willows laid a tangle of shadows across the living room rug.

I stopped him. He had his coat on and whiskey bottle under one arm and was headed out the door. I grabbed his jacket sleeve and held him there.

"Please don't go."

"Sounds like your friend needs you," he said. "I'll just get out of the way. I need to make up a little time anyway."

"I need you," I said. "I haven't seen you in so long, and I wanted some time to sit over coffee this morning and just talk."

"Too much whiskey last night," he said. He gave me a short one-armed hug and then put me at arm's length. "Don't ever trust hillbilly whiskey talk," he said and closed the door behind him.

I went back to the phone. Jaymie'd already hung up.

I WOKE UP with the alarm at seven, feeling a sense of dread heavy as an impending thunderstorm. I showered. Dressed. Made myself coffee and sat down at the kitchen table. I had to find Jaymie. I'd promised and I had to find her.

April. You could wake up in April and find the newly green lawns covered with four inches of wet, heavy snow. You could wake up to sunshine and birds singing and open your windows to hear it better, and let in air warmer than your stale winter furnace air. You could wake up with someone, hold a cup of coffee with both hands, half asleep, and stare at the outside world forever. That Saturday it was raining. I allowed myself twenty minutes over two cups of coffee and started out looking for Jaymie and, as usual, found her at the last improbable place. Not home or the Tender. Not Maxwell's, J&B's or her parents' house. Seven o'clock at night I found her. At Red's Bar.

She was not alone. Oh, hardly. Trust Jaymie to attract a crowd. She was up at the bar, schmoozing with a couple of forestry students. Even I could tell that much at a distance: they all wore their jeans a little higher—like around their ankles—to make room for a pair of White logger's boots. As much a victim of fashion trends as high schoolers blowing their Christmas money on one pair of Calvin Kleins, except that the steel-toed black leather boots actually saved a few toes out in the woods. Hard to say how much good they did in a classroom or bar. But Red's attracted legions of White-booted foresters to tattoo its ugly linoleum floor.

There were two of them up at the bar with Jaymie. One in a blue plaid flannel shirt and one in red plaid. Red plaid seemed to be in the lead, touching hips with Jaymie, and his arm draped across her shoulders. I sat down on the other side of her.

"I've been looking for you since 7:00 a.m," I said.

"I've been here. I've been here since the place opened at nine o'clock. Ask Damian."

The bartender. He'd come over to take my order. A tall man with pale skin and a head of curly mahogany locks and the traditional long-sleeved white shirt, black slacks and white apron tied around the waist.

"I'd like a tap beer."

"No tap," he said. "Bud, Pabst, Miller, Rainier, Mich, Lucky Lager."

"Miller, please. In a bottle."

"No bottles. Can okay?"

I nodded. He served it without a glass.

"I'd like a glass please," I said.

"No beer glasses," he said. Then he went away again, going out from behind the bar to wipe down all five booth tables.

I wiped off the top of the beer can with my sleeve and took a small drink, looked at each of the lighted beer signs in each of the front windows and on the back wall, then turned around front again and let my eyes follow the long line of liquor bottles on the back bar. I caught Jaymie's eyes staring back at me. She didn't look away when our eyes met.

"So, what's new?" she asked my reflection.

"Would have been nice, if you wanted to see me so bad, if you'd let me know where you were going to be."

"Gordy show up, did he? What is this—about every three or four months he just parks himself at your house and demands your attention and then you just drop everything for him?" She signaled to Damian for another drink. He poured a double shot of Jack Daniels into a glass and got her another Rainier beer.

"I don't have as many dates as you do. I don't go out to the bars and wiggle my hips or bat my eyes and have guys just fall in my lap like you do." I took a long drink and started to think about the phone call again, and Gordy getting up and closing the bathroom door behind him.

"You need local talent," she said. "Someone who's around on Saturday night, can take you dancing once a week and take the edge off, Evelyn."

The two guys Jaymie had been entertaining got up and went back to the pool table and threw a quarter in the slot. They still watched us though, not wanting to give up on a half-drunk honky-tonk angel almost in their grasp, especially now that she had a friend to even things up. I ordered another beer and got another dollar out for Damian.

"I don't operate that way. If I like a guy. I don't look for dark hair or someone who'll be available. I just like him. I guess I'm just not very wise when it comes to love affairs."

"Or life," she said, drinking down the double shot of Jack.

"I would hope that my friends would understand wanting to be alone with someone I haven't seen for a long time."

"I understand. I just don't understand deserting your friends in their time of need."

"I've been pretty damn good for seven months. I needed last night—alone. Why did you do that? You walked right in and chased him off."

"You don't understand."

"No, I don't."

"It was an experiment," she said, "not drinking myself to sleep." She held her head up with two fingers pressed against her forehead. "I have ghosts, Evelyn. I thought instead of just drowning them in whiskey and passing out on the couch, last night I thought I'd just go balls out. Tell them to fuck off, leave me the fuck alone." She looked into my eyes then. Her lids were drooping but the fire in her eyes frightened me. "The assholes don't go away. They just hang around the edges till the TV signs off and the bars close and then you're sitting in the dark with nowhere to go. They start sucking at you. I went out riding around in the Bronco, but you don't leave them at home. They're in my head, Evelyn. They never leave me."

"Gene Bofay?"

"And Sherry. And Bucky. I shouldn't have left him alone with her. I know how stupid he is around her."

"It's not your fault."

"Right. Tell it to Pops. He can't even look at me."

I couldn't say anything to that. In the silence, Damian plugged in the jukebox and the bar filled with empty love songs. I started thinking about Gordy up at the jump center taking care of his new recruits.

I don't know what reminded me of the steaks Gordy had bought. They were still sitting in my fridge.

"Jaymie. I have beef steaks at my house. Big juicy steaks. I'll fix you dinner. Nice, warm meal will feel good in your stomach."

"This is my dinner," she said drinking the shot of Jack. "And my lunch and breakfast and high tea."

"That's not what you need, Jaymie."

"Tell me what I need, Evelyn. Tell me again what you did to get over your father's death. How hard it was to accept. How long you had terrible nightmares. You don't know a tenth of it, Evelyn. You didn't kill him."

"You didn't kill Bucky."

"Right. And Bucky's not dead. And the whole thing hasn't changed my entire life. And Gene Bofay isn't smiling in some nice, tidy, warm room somewhere."

"In prison."

"Ah, but still smiling, Evelyn, and doing Sunday cross-word puzzles and eating breakfast on Tuesday mornings. Bucky could have had breakfast Tuesday morning," she said.

She picked up the shot glass and slid it down the bar at Damian. "Give me another shot, God dammit. My glass is empty. What the hell is this anyway, a fern bar?"

"I thought it sounded like a lunatic asylum," Damian said.

"Oh, shut the fuck up. I don't need your free advice."

When she'd gotten her shot and drunk half of it, she turned her attention back to me. She stared at me without saying anything. "Evelyn, you are my innocence," she finally said. "Take good care of it."

"I don't know what to say to you."

"Then don't say anything at all," she said. The tears and the fire were gone. Only dull gray plates floating in a very bloodshot pair of eyes.

"I'm going to go home, if you want to go with me," I said, but she didn't answer. And she didn't come with me.

THIRTEEN

MAY FIFTEENTH, Jack took the office to Spokane for a three-day office management seminar. You know what an office management seminar is? One rich dentist stands up in front of all the other rich dentists and tells them this marvy new way he has discovered to make money faster. Usually by hiring more minimum-wage employees. Or they have a new way to make all dentists have a nice day. (Hire a minimum-wager to teach home care.) Then after two hours of droning on in an overheated room, they let you take a twenty-minute break where the dentist in charge has arranged to feed you industrial-grade glazed donuts and coffee with sugar and chemical milk. Two more hours and you get lunch, which is Crisco-fried chicken, instant mashed potatoes and more coffee with chemical milk. Two more hours and more coffee with chemical milk. They never give you a piece of fruit, let alone enough time to walk around the block for fresh air. By the end of the first day, you feel like someone's installed a trash compactor in your intestines and none of it is ever going to digest in a million years. By the third day, you look at a free buffet and wonder where you'll put it. It's a trick dentists have for making free meals less desirable.

Of course that's just what it's like for the help. The dentist, if he's Jack Paisley and can't stand sitting for more than twenty minutes, can come and go as he pleases: he can swim, play tennis and drive around and look at scenery because he can have one of his "girls" take notes so he doesn't miss anything. And he, of course, takes Maddy with him every time, since she's not one of the "real" girls. Who knows what they were doing those three days. I don't think they were in that auditorium for more than two hours over the whole three-day clinic.

Not to mention that neither one of them ever stood in the clinic's lunch buffet line. They ate out. Steaks and salad bar and real baked potatoes.

Terri said they were taking a trial honeymoon. Taking us along so they could remind themselves they were having a good time.

Sue said that was bullshit. Maddy didn't need to have us around to know she was having a good time. "All's she needs is a few dollars in her pocket and a man tall enough so's she can wear high heels. And Doc the Jock? He's only happy when he gots some poor bimbo kneeling at his feet."

"Okay, then," I said. "Then why did he take us along on this trip?"

This was Thursday night and the three of us were sitting around our one hotel room after the second full day of buffets. Sue called it the Loretta Lynn Memorial Crisco Orgy.

She had the big chair. Terri was lying flat on her bed giving her back a rest. I had the other bed with all the pillows under my aching neck.

"Look," Sue said. "The boss, he's an asshole. That's a given. The only reason I figure he brought us along is so you, Evelyn, would eat your heart out."

"Me? I don't have anything to do with Maddy or Jack."

"Except that he hasn't succeeded in lining you up yet. Seen Gordy lately?"

"As a matter of fact, I have."

"Were you fulfilled?"

I just sighed. But Terri sat up.

"You talking about Gordy *Bennett*?" she said. "I didn't know about Gordy Bennett."

"Lord, where have you been for the last year? Evelyn's been moping and pining around the place, letting Gordy come and go as he pleases. And not even trying to see anyone else," she said.

"You're going out with Gordy Bennett, Evelyn? Gordy of the Forest Service? What a hunk. He's got more muscles than anyone I've ever seen."

"Another county heard from," Sue said. "But don't listen to her, Evelyn. Terri's married. You can ogle all you want when you're married and don't have to test drive the merchandise. *You* still have a problem."

"My problem is figuring out why in hell Jack took us to Spokane," I said.

"Easy. They're a couple of exhibitionists. What good would it be to hang on each other if all they had watching was a bunch of strangers?"

"I don't know. I think something's up," I said.

Terri laid back down. "His dick is up, that's all that's up," she said.

Sue almost fell off her chair laughing. The two of them always talked like that. If you just listened to that talk, you'd have thought love didn't mean anything to either one of them. You had to know them to know it wasn't so.

Friday night, Terri's husband drove over from Missoula and picked her up in front of the hotel after the clinic was over for the day. They went off to an unnamed motel together, alone, with Terri promising faithfully to show up at 8:00 a.m., for the last half day. That left Sue and me alone for the night, and the first thing Sue said was she was tired of staring at four dingy walls in a hotel room and wanted to go out and dance. Work a little of the donuts off, she said. It'll make you feel better. And, I admit, just thinking about it made my head a little clearer. After a shower and change of clothes, we headed out for the local Holiday Inn.

That was Sue's idea, the Holiday Inn. "Attracts a higher class clientele. People who can spend $75 a night for a room, they can spend a little on a couple nice girls from out of town."

Now my memories of Holiday Inn were all tied up with graduation dinners and First Communion, and breakfast Sunday morning after Our Lady of Fatima's yearly weekend teenage retreat. The eggs were runny, but a girl could go to the bathroom without a zipgun.

These women, the barmaids and two women sitting up at the bar, looked long and hard at us as we walked in, and I'd about decided to chicken out for the night when Sue Raffin grabbed me by the elbow and pulled me inside. She sat me down in a booth off the dance floor where we could watch them back, and anyone else who walked in the bar.

"Steel nipples," Sue whispered as the barmaid walked over to us. She took our order and disappeared again. "But you don't have to talk to them."

"What kind of guys would hang around here?"

"I don't know. I don't think they're allowed to check for steel nipples at the door."

"What does that mean?"

"It means anyone can walk into a bar. We just have to wait for the right anyone—right two anyones. I don't feel like sharing tonight."

"You sound like Jaymie. She's always saying 'use your good judgment.'"

"Not bad advice. As far as it goes. Right now, I'd advise you you need another drink."

"I haven't half-finished this one."

"No. You don't have to. But you see, you have a drink you're drinking, and a drink standing behind, you let people know you don't mind a guy buying you a drink. Like dancing. You can't keep saying no all night waiting for Prince Charming t'ask you to dance. It's the frogs ask first. You don't reject them, and some shy guys'll come over and ask. No one likes to get rejected. You just get divorced, you don't want to go out Friday night and hear a bunch a women tell you no, no, no, no, no. Might as well go home and let the old lady hit you over the head again."

We ordered up a couple more drinks and sat back to listen to the music and wait for Mr. Right. It wasn't great music. What we had was a man at a piano singing Engelbert Humperdick tunes with a lot of sincerity. We had a dance floor: a polished ten-foot circle of hardwood amid a sea of conquistador-maroon carpeting, which probably needed to be shampooed, but who could tell in the dark. Sue would tell me not to worry about it, I wasn't going to eat off it. So I kept my thoughts to myself.

I checked my watch. We'd been there forty-five minutes.

"We ain't going yet. We just got here," Sue said.

"I wasn't going. I was just seeing how long we could stay."

"Drink up and relax."

"I can't relax. I'd really rather be up in the room with my feet up."

"Watching George and Gracie reruns."

"If I'm lucky."

"That's not lucky. That's lonely. You keep pining away for Gordy. Gordy ain't pining away for you. Have a drink. At least you might loosen up and feel happier."

"I can't drink. I'll look like hell in the morning and be hungover and stink like a gin mill. And Jack will know what we've been up to."

"You don't think Jack and Maddy aren't out tipping a few? One or two won't hurt you. Just don't drink more'n that." She pointed over to the bar. "See those two guys just sat down at the bar? I'm going to ask them over, and we're going to dance with them."

"I'm not sure about those two." I said. "Maybe we should wait a little longer. See if anyone else shows up."

"They're frogs, dear. But, as you noticed, we're a little tight on time if we want to be back to the room by midnight so Jack don't know we had fun on his cheap-ass trip." She got up, straightened her slacks and headed over to those guys like a kid to a swimming pool the first day of summer. In less than thirty seconds, she walked back to our table with both of them in tow and like the man with seven wives, each of these guys had two drinks in hand, one for them and one for each of us "ladies," for they had noticed we were "real ladies" the moment they walked in the room.

Sue Raffin's pick was Ralph, which left me with Jim, who immediately bought another round of drinks for the table and started to tell me his life story. As each new ex-wife and each new truckload of furniture headed down the road, I mumbled my "oh that's awful," or "oh, gee" and took another drink to keep from having to say anything else, until he finally asked me to dance. Sue and Ralph had been dancing for a half an hour by then, very close, and Sue in her stocking feet. It was then, when I stood up to dance, I realized that I couldn't stand. I thought I'd kept track of the drinks, but the barmaid had whisked away the empties so fast, I'd lost count.

"Look," I said. "I can't dance. I can't even let go of this table. I'm sorry, but I'm going to have to go back to my motel and just call it a night."

He didn't look all that disappointed. "Let me walk you to your room," he said. "It's the least I can do after getting you so drunk."

"No. I'm really turning in, all by myself. I'll just walk slowly," I said. But then I realized we only had one key to the room and with Terri gone for the night, I'd have to get up again and let Sue in when she came in. If she came in. I thought about going out on the dance floor and talking Sue into walking me back and thought better of it. "Look, big guy," I finally said. "If you would be so kind to just walk me back to my room, then walk the room key back down here to Sue, I'd appreciate it."

He readily agreed, and it was only ten minutes of lying on the bed, in the dark, with the room swimming around me, wondering if he was really going back to the bar to give Sue the key that made me realize how naive I'd been. I rolled out of bed and chained and bolted the door from the inside then went into the bathroom to barf in peace.

I slept well. Until Sue started banging and pounding at the door. Half an hour, she said, before I got up and let her in.

I unlatched the door and she stumbled to her bed. "What a night," she said. "I would've been back earlier, but those two clowns wouldn't give me the key. They kept me up all night, dangling the damned thing in front of me."

"I'm sorry," I said. I crawled back in bed, pulled the covers over my head. "I wasn't thinking very clearly when I handed what's-his-name the key."

"No kidding. Don't do that again," she said. "You know I have a reputation to uphold and a job to keep with Doc the Jock. I can't be running around till four a.m."

"Well, I'm sorry," I said again, pulling my head out of the covers.

And then Sue turned on the light on her nightstand. She had her back to me, but I could see the buttons on the front of her blouse were buttoned wrong. That looked funny enough. But then I realized when I'd left her that evening in the bar, the blouse had buttoned up the back. I started to laugh, then stifled it for fear she'd hear me. And then it was like opening a present packed in boxes of diminishing size. Starting out by realizing she'd probably had the key all night, and ending up in the tiniest of boxes, that she had probably stayed the night with both Ralph and Jim. Together. I snuggled under the covers completely to hide my smile and tried to go back to sleep.

SUNDAY NIGHT, back in Missoula, we had our own efficiency seminar on a bar stool at the Legal Tender Saloon. Took Sue fifteen seconds: nail the boss to the operating room floor. I didn't even bother to correct her. (Op-er-a-tor-y, not operating room.) Who cared? Jack sure didn't. It was just a place for him to make play money.

Once we'd dealt with Jack and his efficiency seminar, Sue looked around the dance floor. Up the other end of the bar. Maybe twenty people all told. The only twenty people in Missoula who had nothing better to do but stand around an empty bar on Sunday night.

"Never should have taken Bonanza off the air," she said as she turned to look at herself in the backbar mirror. "Tell me again what it is you like about this place? The Elbow Room is probably full of people."

"That's not fair. People who come here have jobs to get up for on Monday morning."

"Truckers. Lord, that's all I need is to marry another trucker."

"And Forest Service. I met Gordy here. Cowboys. Some cowboys."

"Who have seasonal jobs with the Forest Service to pay the bills. Worse: forty-year-old Norwegian bachelor farmers who can count the number of dates they've had since high school on one hand. On the hand that's missing two fingers. Or a teacher escaped from the Midwest for an adventure in the wilds of old Montana." She toyed with her hair in the backbar mirror. "Well what kind of boy *do* you want to meet?" she asked.

"I don't know. Hard worker. Got a little savings in the bank. One that doesn't think he's got to have a fancy car and expensive stereo to be happy."

"Maxwell's. You're looking for an accountant, girl. Insurance agent. Gotta be Maxwell's."

"Those guys are boring."

"You said you wanted a nice careful boy."

"Not boring. Gordy's careful with his money. He's not boring."

"He's also not here. Ever. That's got to be a consideration. Someone who's not afraid to call Monday for a date on Saturday night. Let you know he looks forward to being with you. Maxwell's."

"Maxwell's is suits. I don't want to go out with any suits. And none of those guys who work out in gyms. Not a pretty boy. If he's got muscles, I want it to be because he's got a job."

"Which brings us back to Gordy the Hunk."

"Look. I wouldn't mind if he came around more often. And I'd love it if I could go see him sometime. But I'm not planning to marry him."

"But, Evelyn, he's a tragic figure of a man. Some good woman has to rescue him."

"That's cutting it a little thick, don't you think?"

"No. Invite him to a potluck dinner sometime, with your friends."

"I already did. An office potluck. That one last spring, that I didn't go to. Gordy showed up at the house, too tired to go."

"Real men will eat quiche in a pinch — but they'd rather eat their cholesterol in huevos rancheros. And they don't do potluck."

"He didn't want to intrude."

"Oh, that's a good line. Makes him sound like a martyr, and he still doesn't have to get socialized." She lit up a cigarette and tossed the match in the ashtray. "I suppose he's been real supportive over this thing with Jaymie and her family?"

I didn't say anything.

"Has he even been around? Does he listen when you talk about it? Do you talk about it with him?"

I took a drink.

"Evelyn. I know what he's getting out of this so-called relationship. Getting your ashes hauled every three to four months enough for you?"

"It's more than that."

"Go call him then." She cut a quarter out of her pile of change on the bar and rolled it at me. "Here, I'll treat. Tell him you're lonely and can he drive twenty miles down here for a drink. If he says yes, I'll even clear out so, God forbid, he doesn't have to meet any of your friends."

"He won't be there."

"Call him. Get up off your ass and call him. They're like dogs. They don't know what you want till you tell them."

She pulled me up off the bar stool and walked me over to the phone. It was up by the front door, with a long cord, so on weekend nights when the band was playing, you could take the receiver outside and hear yourself talk.

She looked up the number, dialed it and asked for Gordon Bennett, then handed me the phone. "They're getting him."

"Hello," he said.

"Gordon, this is Evelyn. How are you?"

Sue rolled her eyes and made a move-it-along motion with her right hand.

"I was wondering, I'm down at the Tender, and I was wondering if you could get free for a little while tonight."

He'd been in bed. Had to get up at five for more training and resupply. "I don't know how I could do it," he finally said. "Maybe next week. I'll call."

I hung up. Sue was gone, back up at the bar, and I went and sat down beside her, looking at her face in the mirror. Not a look of surprise, or I-told-you-so. She would do that to Jack. She'd lay it thick enough to walk on with Jack. But she was different with me.

"I'm sorry," she said, and I watched her lips in the mirror move in silent echo, I'm sorry.

"He had *things*," I said.

"Just don't apologize for him, Evelyn. Just don't do that."

I was better by Monday morning, good thing too, because we had an office meeting to discuss the great truths we'd learned at the efficiency seminar. The first truth was that when the boss falls in love, he wants to keep the object of his affections close. Not only was Maddy present at the seminar, she turned up for the office meeting, and Jack took great pleasure in reintroducing the new and improved Home Care Instruction Program, the one we hadn't had for more than four years, since Vickie left. Then he introduced our new fourth employee. Maddy. For her first day of work, she wore a pair of hot pants with taupe stockings and black ballet slippers.

Jack waxed eloquent about how much nicer the practice would be. All new patients would be required to take a complete six-lesson course in home care. No more dirty mouths, he said as he marched back and forth between his private bathroom and the office, brushing his teeth with copious amounts of toothpaste, so much toothpaste that he resembled a rabid dog foaming at the mouth.

"And all old patients will be gradually brought over to the new philosophy, slowly," he said. " And if they refuse, we'll drop them from recall. Weed 'em out. It's exciting. We're going to make room for new patients who really want to keep their teeth. No more dead weight." He disappeared into the bathroom to rinse and take a final look at his pearly whites, then he returned and sat down at his desk and turned to me. "Evvy, it's your job to teach Maddy everything you know about home care."

"I've never gone through the home care course, Jack. Vickie left before we ever had enough free time for me to do it."

"Listen, kid. You've got the best teeth and best home care in the office. That's good enough for me."

"When am I going to find the time?"

"Lunch hour. You girls are always waiting around for me to show up; you got lots of time then."

"But that's when I've been filing x-rays and cleaning instruments."

"Listen, Evvy. You've got to maintain a positive attitude about this whole change. Great offices don't emerge from negative personalities. Progress. That's what we want. Cleaner mouths will be as important to you as they are to me, making our work easier."

Sue was to the side and out of his line of sight, busy rolling her eyes and making faces at the boss, waiting for her turn on the rack. All these office meetings went the same way. First, an added responsibility for the assistant, then praise for Terri the hygienist who always had great hands. Finally, would come the attack on the appointment book. He didn't fail us this time—although he was very secretive about the reason he wanted the last ten days in June wiped off the schedule.

He chose to take the offensive. "That's more than three weeks from now. I keep telling you, Susie-Q, I don't want to be appointed more than three weeks in advance. If you continue to fight me, you're gonna get burned. Great office meeting, ladies. Now let's go rip and tear. Oh, Evelyn, you should hear this. I'm taking the Porter family off recall. Bunch of deadwood there. I don't have time for charities anymore."

What could I say? Except what I did say. "It's your office, Jack."

"You bet, Evvy baby. Life is sweet, ain't it?"

And so we went to work, rejuvenated from our four-day seminar: I in my assistant's chair, Terri scraping teeth, and Maddy fixing herself a cup of coffee in the employees' lounge and touching up her nail polish until I could teach her how to floss her teeth. Sue, in the meantime, typed up Maddy's employee agreement and kept mum about the details. Always the model of professional receptionism.

FOURTEEN

I'M SORRY to say the whole thing didn't last very long—sorry, because despite my immediate dread at having Maddy with her hot pants and solid gold charm bracelet in the midst of a busy, supposedly sterile, environment, I grew to like her. Both Sue and I very quietly took her in as one of our own. Like an animal protection society.

Like I said, I had my back up at first. Jack drags a stool into our operatory, setting it right at our collective elbow, and has Maddy perch on the damn thing, so we have this perfumed face all the time hanging between us, and then he carries on this inane conversation with her, expecting me to perform immaculate four-handed dentistry like a trained seal for their own personal amusement.

Or if he actually deigned to talk directly to me, it would

be to repeat some story about their "heavy duty" sex life, as he called it, like the episode of the drowned watch. This was in the heights of passion, in the finally finished log home, in the cathedral-ceilinged upstairs bath, the second night he'd known her. It was a sign, he said. Their love was timeless. Their bodies sensed the harmony of their spirits. They would be together for all time.

"My Jewish neighbors would have called it 'dreck,'" I said.

Sue tried to tune them out from the safety of her reception desk. "I call it horseshit," she said. "But you must be grateful he's not giving you any more 'Seen Gordy lately' shit."

Which I was grateful for, don't get me wrong, 'cause it was on my mind a lot. Not seeing Gordy, not seeing anybody, you know, I started really wondering about other people, married people, how they found each other. And it was in the middle of all this reported marital bliss I picked up a cowboy at the Tender one night when I was out with Sue Raffin. We'd been making a regular thing of Thursday, Friday and Saturday nights, without me falling in love, ever. So she fixed me up with this cowboy. No big deal, except that he wouldn't leave after he was done, and I had to sit up in my living room chair till he *did* finally wake up at ten a.m., and then I had to wash my sheets because of a smashed finger — his — that I'd failed to notice the night before in Sue's expansive gesture and my gloat of Jack Daniels. Sue's response was to ask if I'd used birth control, which I couldn't remember, and then she just sighed and said, "Isn't love grand," and went on with her check writing. The perching business, along with the tales of wild abandon, did nothing to endear poor Maddy to me. So Sue started kind of padding the ledger. Like letting me know Maddy wasn't taking off early every afternoon to polish her fingernails, like Jack said, but Jack had enrolled her in tennis lessons Monday, Wednesday and Friday, and horseback-riding lessons from Whispering Sam on Tuesdays, Thursdays and Saturdays. "Oh, and Sunday afternoons he drags her around behind his ski boat trying to make her pop up like a cork."

"What for? I thought she was perfect, 'like the moon and the stars.'"

"All the better to play with her, my dear," Sue Raffin pointed out. "Since those are *his* favorite summer games, and she doesn't know shit from shinola about tack."

"Tack?"

"Horsey leathers," Sue explained. "Come winter, she'll be taking skiing lessons up top of Snow Bowl. Take her up to the top and push her off. You know what a delicate hand he has."

Of course what she meant by that was his delicate hand in my short happy fling with Gordy Bennett, and the lingering after shocks—the "have you seen Gordy latelys." So I started joining Sue and Maddy when they had lunch together. Which was fine till the end of the meal, when they drug out the makeup kits and freshened up at the table. So it stayed just lunch for a while.

Then there was the shampoo incident. Maddy told us over lunch at the Village Inn Pizza Parlor all-you-can-eat salad bar, which she said was all she could afford too since she was getting only $3.55 an hour.

"You know, it wasn't like there was anything wrong. Any fight or anything before. We're on this camping trip—it's Jack's big idea to celebrate our four-month anniversary. Anyway, Whispering Sam leads us up the mountain on this collection of one-eyed, one-eared horses that Jack thinks is just full of character and he drops us off at this mangy, mouse-infested tent in the middle of nowhere. Well, the first night it's just business as usual. Jack makes a big deal about how beautiful the stars are and he wants to sleep outside where he can see them, and even though it's cold, and I've already got on all the sweaters I brought, I sleep outside with him. So the next morning I go to wash my hair and fix my face, and none of my stuff is there. And Jack is sitting at the campfire like he's swallowed a canary.

"'Whatcha looking for Mads' he says, nice and sweet. I said, 'I'm looking for my make-up kit. I was going to wash my hair.' I'm beginning to think maybe I didn't pack it, but I can't believe that. And he says, 'You're so beautiful au nat-ur-elle,' he says. 'I sent it down with Whispering Sam when he left.' "

"Too bad you didn't kill him," Sue said. "Who could have proved murder up there all by yourselves? Push him off the nearest cliff."

"Right. Then I would have been up on top of a mountain all by myself."

"Personally that sounds a lot better than who you got stuck with."

"Now, Sue, I know you don't think he's the greatest match for me, but I love him, and when you love somebody you've got to overlook some things."

"Like your wife's make-up kit?" Sue asked.

"Hey, I've been divorced. I don't want to get divorced again. It's too hard."

When we got back to the office, Jack, as if he knew he was the topic of conversation at lunch, was full of stories from the camping trip. His side.

"You don't know how great it is, E, sleeping under the stars in a tandem sleeping bag," he said over the first afternoon patient.

"The howl of the coyote and northern lights. You miss it all being in town. You ought to get hold of that Gordy, I know he's got a tandem bag, used to go up with his wife, Bobby, before she took off with the kid and all his money. Made one big mistake, Gordy did, going to those church encounter groups. They were always asking him to list his reasons for being married. I guess he could never come up with the one Bobby liked. Not me. If something's not broken, don't mess with it, I say. Hand me an explorer will you, E?"

He went on and on about that church encounter group business every time Maddy came back into the room to observe. That seemed to be the first casualty, at least the first one Sue and I could see. After the shampoo incident, Maddy still talked a big show, but she didn't perch over us on her bar stool anymore every spare minute she had. She spent more time working recall, digging into the old files of people who never called back in, taking satisfaction at increasing the percentage of successful contacts and wearing longer skirts to the office, and blouses with high necklines.

And then a bit after that, maybe a week and half, maybe two, she came in early, seven-thirty, wearing a purple sweat suit and running shoes. Her blonde hair was unwashed and she had it tucked up into a baseball cap. I was still vacuuming, getting ready for the day, no chance Jack would be in yet.

"I left him," she said. "I left him for good and all. No sweet talk going to take me back." She collected her things from around the office, piled them on one couch in the reception area, next to the door by the bathrooms, I guess so she could lock herself in there if Jack came in on time for once, and wearing a pair of huge dark sunglasses, which I assumed meant a big black eye but I made a point of not looking at her too hard. Instead, I set about doing the dusting, vacuuming and organizing for the day.

When Sue showed up, Maddy came out of the ladies' bathroom and took off the hat and sunglasses. It was more than a black eye. Both eyes were black, but not from a punch. The whole length of her nose was blue and crimson, too.

Sue sat her down by the bathroom door. "Tell me," she said.

It came out in short, gasping sentences. "We had a fight. Dinner I think. I don't know. Something I did. I said 'I'm getting out of here' and put my coat on. He said 'You're not leaving' and followed me out the door. I got that far, Sue. I was out the door and halfway to the car, I thought I had it made, but he grabbed me and started to pull me back to the house. I told him to let me go. I hit him, I think. But then I fell down, and once I fell down, I couldn't keep my feet under me. He started dragging me first by my arm, but it hurt and I told him that. Well, then he grabbed hold of my hair and dragged me up the porch steps by my hair. You should see the bruises I got on my back and down my ribs. I look like a fucking circus clown."

"But what the hell happened to your nose, Maddy?" Sue asked.

"He's a lunatic, Sue. A fucking, raging lunatic. He dumped me inside, in the middle of the kitchen floor and told me I wasn't going anywhere he said I couldn't. I said he was full of shit and I was going anywhere the hell I wanted. I even got up and brushed the dirt off my face and hands and headed back out the door. So he says, 'No way José,' and throws me up against the wall and growls at me. He fucking growled at me, and then he bit me. I thought he was going to bite it clean off it hurt so bad. I gotta go to the doctor this morning make sure it's not broke. Listen, Sue. What I stopped in for, I need some money. Can you give me petty cash or something?"

"How much?"

"Three, four hundred. Get me a place. See if I can get my old job back. The old skinflint owes it to me for wear and tear. But I don't want him to know I took it."

"No problem." Sue went into the safe and brought out the checkbook, writing out a check for $523.43. Then stamped it with Jack's signature stamp, separated the top check from the two carbon copies beneath. On the top check she wrote Maddy's name. Then she took a blank piece of paper, lined it up with the payee line on the dupe and wrote in the name of our dental lab.

"If he notices, which he won't, I'll tell him I forgot a few crowns on last month's bill. He'll never know." Sue looked up at the clock. "And now it's too close to eight o'clock. Just in case, you better get out of here."

Maddy picked up her pile of shoes and coffee cup, sweaters and magazines, put her sunglasses back on, and left.

"I thought they were getting along," I said.

Sue gave a look. "You've been listening to the he-man too much," she said. "He'll probably come in this morning whistling and saying how much fun Maddy and him had over the weekend and how she won't be in 'Cause she just can't get out of bed.' Don't for Jesus' sake ask him how he is."

What he said was, "Seen Gordy lately, kid?" to me, which made Sue wonder if he was starting to actually relate to reality.

Then he spent the rest of the first patient's time instructing me on how I was becoming a cliché. Mostly because I lived to trap a man in marriage.

I kept silent. I got through it. Nodding my head, passing instruments and slinging mushy amalgam with infinite grace and poise, keeping my eyes as blank as possible.

"You can't imagine," Jack said as we let the first patient go finally, "the terror, the absolute terror a man feels when he realizes the little woman is brain dead. No ambition, no drive, no sense of identity. Missus Him. She looks up to him like a father. A guy doesn't want a mindless bimbo. Gordy. He's got a brain. He doesn't travel for fun, you know. It supports his ranch. He's got dreams. Adding on. Land, cattle. Maybe even registered cattle."

He followed me into operatory two, to Mrs. Reedy's crown prep, calling out to Sue to come get his cup and fill it up with hot coffee. He sat down in his chair and I lowered Mrs. Reedy, picking up the syringe to hand it over when her head was in the right position. When she was there, he took the syringe from me and laid it down on Mrs. Reedy's chart, slid his chair back and looked at the schedule for the day.

It was the first time I'd really looked at it, the late morning and afternoon at least. The thing that struck me was the one-thirty patient. Jaymie Porter. Jack waited for Sue to come in with his fresh cup of coffee.

"Sue," he said before she could run back out of the operatory. "I want you to cancel Jaymie Porter." He picked up the syringe and slid his chair back under Mrs. Reedy's headrest. Taking the yellow plastic sheath off the needle, he ran about half the carbocaine onto the floor.

Sue started to leave.

"I think," he said, "I've gotten to the point where I don't need to treat people who won't come in regularly and do what I want them to, like Mrs. Reedy here. That family's always got something bothering them. Always something that needs care right away. Wreaks havoc with my schedule."

"That appointment was made before you told us to take them off recall. I told you she was coming in last week to see Terri. You should've said something then. Besides, Terri says she hardly needs anything. Just the exam. Her "gooms" look great."

"I need some time this afternoon."

"Why?"

He squeezed a little more of the carbo onto the rug. "About an hour."

"Take it after hours, like the rest of us," Sue said. "Or give up your one-on-one today."

He looked at her then. "Get me Freddo on the phone then. I'll anesthetize Mrs. R. and take it in my office."

He left Mrs. Reedy in the chair for an hour while he talked to his lawyer on the phone, then came out and did the crown prep, gingival pack and impression in twenty-one minutes. Minus phone calls that would have made us thirty-nine minutes ahead. Perhaps we should've just scheduled the phone calls and left the dentistry for our spare time. We might've stayed on schedule.

At any rate, Jaymie stayed in the one-thirty slot and by the time she showed up, I was a nervous wreck. As Sue said, someone like Jaymie who knew Jack, knew better than to schedule on a Tuesday or Thursday at one-thirty. Might as well go to K-Mart the Saturday before school starts. "She's not here for her health, you know," Sue said.

I'd been sitting in the home care room, soon to be an employee lounge again with Maddy out of the picture, finishing up a fruit-on-the-bottom yogurt.

I said, "I really don't care. I have nothing to feel guilty about."

"Except maybe deserting a friend in her time of need."

"Hey. I sat through that whole damned trial with her, holding her hand, pretending to be the other "quiet" sister, you know the one who couldn't talk in the presence of the fiendish slayer of innocents. I mean, I did it. The rest of her family didn't do it."

"I didn't bring up the word guilt. You said guilt. I was just trying to fill in your blank."

"I don't have any blank."

"Oh certainly. There's that blank period of time you haven't called your only friend outside this office. Then there's every Thursday, Friday and Saturday night you're on my doorstep wanting to go out dancing at that bar, and all you do once you get out there and the music's playing is sit and watch the door in case she decides to prance on in. You've gotten pretty boring without her you know."

"I don't like sitting home alone."

"You're hiding."

"That's not true."

"No, I'm sorry dearie, it is true. You're hiding in a corner eating your little yogurt cup so's you don't run into her accidentally at lunch, and if she actually showed up at the Tender, you'd sneak into the bathroom so's you didn't have to say hello." She was using the door frame like a scratching post, rubbing her back up and down and sideways. "I figure yogurt is the salve for emotional crips. Like penicillin for the clap."

"Yogurt is good, wholesome food, and an easy source of protein and calcium," I said.

"I got nothing personal against yogurt. Except maybe that slime it gets when it's a little too close to its expiration date." She looked at her watch and stood up straight, adjusting her blouse over her chest, and tugging at her gray polyester slacks. "It's one o'clock. I've got to get to work." She started to leave and turned back to me. "Listen. Out of sight, out of mind about Maddy and that check this morning, eh?"

I shrugged. "What check?"

"Good girl." Sue went back to her desk.

I went back to the x-ray room and developed the morning's x-rays and put away the dry ones. Futzing, Sue called it. Hiding in the x-ray room. So I could come out at one thirty-two and find Jaymie in the reception room and say, "Oh, I didn't know you were coming today."

THERE'S TWO THINGS that always surprise me about Jaymie, and always did, as long as I can remember. I think it's because when I first met her I was so green, that all her cowboy glitter seemed too obvious. Maybe after four years I'd become used to it. I don't think so. I never really considered Missoula home or thought I was going native, though my sister Katherine continued to test me every time she called. One time she asked what a beaverslide was, which was the first and last one of her tests that I passed. And the only reason I knew was that Jaymie had taken me out for a drive one day, over Lost Trail Pass into Dillon, and showed me one.

"They use it to stack hay," I'd told Katherine. I think it bothered me more than her that I'd actually passed her test. I wondered if I really was becoming a western person—like Jaymie—and would soon start wearing fringe on my jackets.

But the next time, like all the other times after that, Katherine stumped me.

"What's a shoot rooster," Katherine had said.

"A shoot rooster?" I repeated.

"Don't you know?"

"No."

"Well you should."

"What is it?"

"It's one of those cowboys who sits on the top rail of those holding pens where they let the bucking horses out."

"Well, I haven't been to but one rodeo," I said somewhat relieved. "And that one I was too busy talking and didn't notice the cowboys, I guess."

That ride to Dillon had ended in a rodeo. And in the darkness of the x-ray room, I remembered that whole day. I was too busy looking at the back pockets of blue jeans to notice the practical activities of shoot roosters. In those days I thought anyone in blue jeans was a cowboy, so Jaymie spent the day teaching me the difference between real cowboys and rodeo boys. Rodeo boys wore Wranglers. Real cowboys wore Levis. (And the easiest way to tell was the *W* on the back pocket of Wrangler jeans.) Every sixth pair of jeans went by, she'd say, "So was that one a real cowboy?" I spent the day staring at backsides so I'd have the right answer.

It was the same thing anytime you went anywhere outside. With Jaymie, you didn't just watch the scenery float by. You had to identify. Birds and mountains had names. Like driving down from Jaymie's place to her folk's house, the two highest points—north and south—were Squaw Peak and Lolo Peak; then there was the Sapphire Range to the left going down, and the Bitterroots on the left on the way home.

What was different now, what always surprised me and surprised me again when Jaymie walked in at one-thirty, was that she was normal. Not a rodeo queen. Or a tricked-out buckarette. She dressed like everybody else. She walked in at one-thirty in cotton jeans, red leather cowboy boots and a brilliant red, long-sleeved snap-button shirt— dressed for work—and all thought of pretending flew out the window.

When she opened the office door I was standing right there at the reception desk.

"Boy you are a sight for sore eyes," she said to me.

"I miss you," I said.

"I'm gonna be right up front, Evelyn, and I don't know how much time we have to talk. To tell the truth, I'm relieved you're glad to see me. The last time I saw you I seem to remember acting like one of those mythical perfect assholes."

"You were going through a lot."

"You were, too. I had a hard time remembering that sometimes. And I want you to know that this next request comes from the old folks as much as it comes from me."

"Are they okay?"

"Tits. They're leaving for Steamboat Springs, Colorado. They bought a little retirement condo and a Winnebago and they're blowing this pop stand. Saturday. They want to see you before they leave."

"Anytime. I don't have any other plans. What about J&B? Do you have a job?"

"It's sold. But, I made a deal with the new owner, who's going to be an absentee owner most of the time, all of the time if I have anything to do with it. I run the place now. I have a contract for as long as I want to stay."

"That's great."

"It's okay. I'll miss the old man's grunting and wheezing."

"They'll visit."

"No. They don't want to step foot in Montana again. They say they'd rather live somewhere they know is fucked up than lie to themselves."

"It's Rose?"

"It's both of them."

Sue had gone into the employee lounge to make herself a cup of coffee and we just stood there, Jaymie and I, and listened to her open and close cabinets, the sound of freeze-dried coffee crystals on the side of the cup and the spoon, slowly stirring, then tapping against the sink. I looked at the clock. It was nearly two.

"I should seat you and get set up for the afternoon," I said.

"You don't mind if I take the payroll books back there with me?"

That was the other change since I'd seen Jaymie last. She now carried her books in a leather case, instead of loose like a high school kid. She picked the case up off the couch and followed me into the operatory, asking, for Wally, if the old Red Beater was still running.

Terri had been right on her diagnosis. Jaymie had no work to be done. Jack did a record short exam, sat her back up and was about to let her go without saying a word, but thought better of it. He came around my side of the chair and lifted the arm for Jaymie to get up. But then he stood there, blocking her way. Jaymie waited, with her books in her lap and a smug look on her face.

"I've started flossing," she said. "Evelyn kept at me and finally made me see the cost-effectiveness of the whole slimy mess." She tapped him gently on the knee with her car key. "Didn't think you could teach old dogs new tricks, eh?" she said.

I started washing instruments under a steady and hard stream of hot water not wanting to hear what was coming next. Instead of being pleased his patient was flossing, it only annoyed him.

"The trick I'd like you to learn, Jaymie," he said, "is to learn to come in on time for your checkups. I can't be the only one worried about keeping your teeth for a lifetime. I've got too many other, more important things on my mind. Like helping patients who do what I ask." He paused for a moment then barged along. "When you find a new dentist, I'll be glad to forward your x-rays," he said.

When he left the operatory, Jaymie shrugged her shoulders and rolled her eyes. "I'll be seeing you Friday evening? Pops is taking us all to dinner at the Hackamore Club, so dress nice."

I GOT A PHONE CALL at home, from Sue Raffin, ten o'clock that night.

"He found her," she said. "He's at her motel room."

"How did he find her? I thought she didn't want anything to do with him."

"She went out for chips and Diet Coke down at the Eastgate Buttreys. He just happened to be there and followed her back to her motel room."

"That's incredible."

"I know. Of all the gin joints. Well, it's her bad luck. I'd say she should've known better than to stay at that motel and to shop at that store. That's Jack's store. It's the only grocery store I've ever known him to actually walk into. And he never did that before his first wife divorced him. He always comes back and tells me with horror and surprise the new things they've added for the housewife's convenience."

"Well what's going to happen?"

"Who knows. My guess is she's had it up to her eyeballs, or at least the bridge of her nose, and won't let him back in. But he can be pretty persuasive, you know. I'll talk to you tomorrow kid."

When I hung up I thought that would be the end of it, but there was another phone call, much later. I'd fallen asleep with the light on and *A Tale of Two Cities* still in my hand.

I reached for the light first, then realized it was on. "Who is it?" I said into the phone.

"Evelyn? I'm sorry this is so late. This is Madelyn. Listen, honey. I've got to ask you something. Nothing against you."

There was a lot of background noise on Maddy's side. Like the TV and air conditioner and a voice, a man's voice, which she was trying to hush up, and which I recognized after a few seconds as Jack's attempts at whispering.

"Go ahead and ask," I said.

"Did you ever have an affair with Jack?" she asked. "And please tell the truth."

I thought about lying, I really did. Saying yes, when in truth the answer was no. If I told the truth, maybe she'd give him a second chance. Move back home with him. In the background, I heard Jack's hoarse and insistent whispering that it was none of my business and Evelyn had nothing to do with anything: she was just one of the girls in the office.

I surprised myself. I told her the truth. "No," I said and left it at that. I didn't mention the late night drop-in visits with a six-pack. Or the groping that went on under the dental chair the first few months. No. It was a simple word. There had been no sex. Maddy said thank you and hung up. I put my book up on the nightstand, turned off the light and sat up wondering if I should call her back and tell her to run like hell. That's what Sue Raffin would've done. I would've been doing Maddy a favor. But like Jack said, it really wasn't any of my business. I finally did go back to sleep around 3:00 a.m.

Seven thirty I was in the office vacuuming, cleaning house, washing instruments and sterilizing them. Ten to eight, Sue Raffin came in and grabbed me by the arm and drug me into the employees' lounge and sat me down.

"Why didn't you tell that poor girl the truth?"

"You mean Maddy? I did tell her the truth. Jack and I never had an affair."

"Oh you mean you never did the dirty deed. My dear you played footsie all over three operating rooms."

"We do four-handed dentistry. It looks like footsie. Nothing ever happened."

"That's not what he says."

I looked at her. "What do you mean that's not what he says?"

"He told Maddy that you were so lonely when you showed up that he took you under his wing and loved you and hugged you, and in the meantime played house—out of kindness—he's such a sensitive guy."

"Why would he say a thing like that when he was trying to convince Maddy to come back?"

"Because they weren't arguing about the divorce. They already had decided not to do that. They were arguing about firing you. Maddy said you were the hardest worker she'd ever seen. So Jack told her he'd had an affair with you. Probably figured he could kick you out on your keester for Maddy's sake. To save his marriage. Then he could've blamed you for breaking it up later, when that happens too. But then you said you didn't. And Maddy believed you. So now you're stuck working here forever, and Maddy starts again in two weeks, or whenever her black eyes clear up, and Jack's giving her a new Mercedes to make up."

"How do you find out all this stuff?"

"I called the motel room a few minutes ago, from downstairs."

"Oh shit." That was all I could say.

"Don't worry. It won't last. Jack will do something else and she'll leave him, and this time she'll have a new car out of it, and maybe she'll keep driving all the way to Nome, Alaska."

Which was of course about how it turned out, a week later, except she drove to Dallas, Texas.

But that was later. In the meantime, I had to say goodbye to Rose and Wally, Friday night over dinner.

FIFTEEN

THAT FRIDAY night was not exactly a free evening. Sue Raffin and I saved those nights for the Legal Tender Saloon: all Fridays, as well as Thursdays and Saturdays. They made a set. Like a football team running the ball the first two quarters to set up the pass. That's how Sue Raffin explained it.

Three nights. One night you could dance with the boys. One night you could talk just among yourselves. One night you could take a yahoo home. If you wanted. If someone caught your eye. If you were lonely enough for a Yahoo City Excursion.

Not just Sue and I. We started out just us two, but after a couple of weeks, the group grew, seven at most, if all showed up on the same night, which usually happened Saturday, since the rest of them had kids, and the daddies took their kids on Saturday night.

Sue and me, dental office. Then Dimpy and Carol, doctor's assistants, which is like dental assistant—minimum wage, maximum grief—except working at the Big Sky Medical Clinic, they had administrators with some authority over the doctor. Then Debbie and Roz who worked at the appointment phones at the clinic, and Rozzie's sister Hope who worked for an insurance salesman — same wage, same small office politics. She'd been divorced twice from the same guy, one kid each divorce, and not planning ahead far enough either time so she'd actually have the kid while they were still married.

So some nights, if there were four or five of us gathered around the table, a guy could come up to me or Sue or Carol and ask us to dance, and we'd get up nice and go dance, and maybe invite him back to the table, introduce him around and make a party of it. And some nights, there'd be this steady stream of truck driver toad-boys who'd go around the table asking to dance and getting turned down every time. And go away mad.

God help 'em when all seven of us showed up some night. Before the band was even halfway into the first set, we'd have three of those little bar tables pulled together and the bar chairs drawn up in a circle, like a wagon train defending against ravaging hordes of Indians. Not that we even needed that, because the talk at the table was so loud and so full of ex-husbands-this and prick-that, no male in his right mind would approach within ten yards of the perimeter.

I was the only one who'd never been married. You'da thought I wouldn't have fit in. But I had Jack. I could tell Jack stories till they threw us out of the bar. Jack dragging Maddy out of the house. Jack and his "women are never grateful" speech; or his "Evelyn you're becoming a cliché" speech. And Sue, of course, would add her own stories of Jack dropping in on her to drown *his* sorrows in *her* supply of booze, instead of bringing his own, which brought out a whole stream of cheap doctor and hoity-toity Mrs. Doctor stories. That was where Sue and I had to defer to the rest. Maddy had never put on those airs of Mrs. Doctor. Never really had the chance. Although it seemed from what the others said, that while some second wives took on the persona, it was usually the original, the one who had put him through school who seemed to think his medical degree gave her a license to pout. He worked too many hours. Didn't charge enough for his valuable services. Had too many blondes in the office and not enough Mercedes' in her driveway. Sue had barely met the first Mrs. P. and I had never even seen her, so we kept still.

But when they started dishing the dirt on the ex-husbands—beyond broken dishes, shattered windshields and occasional black eyes—I had the ultimate ex-husband story. It may not have been my own personal ex-husband the story involved, but it was the ultimate story. Gene Bofay hadn't just beat up his ex-wife. Hadn't just invaded a love nest to make a fool of himself.

When they first found out I knew all that stuff, that I'd been to the trial, heard all the testimony and not just the snippets the newspapers had published, but all of it, all of what never made it into the court records, they were full of questions. At first they wanted to know about Gene Bofay, what he'd done, and they just knee-jerked their way through all that—bad ex-husband, bad ex-husband—just like they spoke about their own evil exes. But I couldn't stop: I'd tell them about Sherry buying him booze so she could sneak out of the house once he passed out; dragging Bucky into a motel three miles from her parent's house knowing Bofay was hot on her trail. It was just too close to home. When I'd tell them it was as much her fault, they'd have none of it.

"He drove her to it," Dimpy told me.

"You don't know what went on all the years they were married before the big shee-bang," Carol said. "He'd probably been banging on her ego all those years. She just had to go out and prove to herself she was attractive to other guys and prove it in front of him."

"We're not saying she's a total innocent," Sue Raffin said. "Just that there's a lot of things on this earth you don't know horse-pucky about. That ring finger of yours is still a virgin, Evelyn. You can't figure it till you've walked a mile in her flip-flops."

"And that guy got killed? That, Bucky, you call him?" Hope said. "I've met him. Or guys like him. They got their radar out for women on a recovery cruise. He wasn't looking for a little woman with a white picket fence. Maybe if he'd kept his hands off her a couple a weeks, maybe she'd make up with her old man, no problems, no regrets. He's out for some cheap poontang—no strings attached. You pays your nickel and you takes your chances." Hope, the one who married the same guy twice and divorced him twice and was always fantasizing about the third go-round.

It seemed like the more I went down to the Tender with those guys, the more I believed in Sherry. At least to say that she didn't plan it—on purpose. And the more I began to see the whole thing through Wally's eyes.

Anyway, that only happened once in a while — with the tables, and the circle, and the marauding Indians. What we usually did was dance all night with perfect strangers and not say five words to each other. Usually Friday night. And then Saturday night we'd get the scorecards out and compare notes, but only for the first hour or so, for as Sue Raffin said, it's more fun to score the home run than read the box scores.

So having dinner with Wally and Rose Friday night, it wasn't like I had to cancel a date, but more like I'd be the new kid at school. You look like everybody else. You talk like everybody else, but you're out of it. To put it bluntly, you didn't get laid Friday night; so on the all-important Saturday night, your score was six-zip.

I went to the Tender Thursday night and danced my little heart out—that's what Sue said — trying to catch up ahead of time for Friday night. Then Friday after work, I drove out to the mall and tried on six different dresses in ten minutes, which was all I had, trying out every blue thing in every store, then settling for a white blouse, long sleeves and high collar, to wear with the old black pants I always wore for fancy occasions. Bucky's funeral. Bofay's arraignment, then the trial, wearing those black slacks every day like there weren't any skirts tucked in the back of my closet. But they were New York skirts, out of place here, and, I felt at the time, too vulnerable looking for listening to that testimony all day. I guess I just wanted to be able to sit or cross my legs without showing anything. Anything but my face that is. Then for color, which Jaymie always wanted and in honor of Rose, I bought a silk scarf—silver with brilliant splashes of red roses and green boughs, and tied it loosely around my neck. Almost casual, almost *Vogue*. Almost.

Jaymie picked me up at seven and we drove out to the Hackamore Club, way past Lolo Creek, fifty miles from town. And all the way down she kept up a running monologue of all the great features of this new condo Mom and Dad were moving to. An eighteen-hole golf course ten minutes from the front door. Swimming pool. No grass mowing. No big garden.

"Though Mom's already got "projects" for Walls to do. Like geranium boxes so she can still keep her thumb green." She lit a cigarette off the Bronco's lighter and pulled out the ashtray. "You listening?" she asked.

"Sure," I said. I just wasn't visualizing what she was talking about. They were words going in one ear and out the other.

"You could be a little more excited," she said, shifting the Bronco down into second gear to go through a school zone. "Shouldn't build schools right on the highways," she said. "Penny for your thoughts, Miss Evelyn."

"Not worth the paper to write them down," I said and went back to staring out the passenger side window. Gravel on the side of the road lay smooth one second, then jagged as new mountains, then smooth again till the next time.

Late July in the hills above the highway, people were picking huckleberries. I'd taken Jaymie's nature calendar and imprinted it on my brain. River running clear and wide, with spring runoff over, and farmers irrigation pumps not yet sucking the water down to bare rocks. I watched the river all the way down to the Hackamore Club. The river, the large sandbars, deer starting to move into the open grainfields. Wheat now tall and green with flecks of gold here and there. Two, three more weeks and it would all be gold, and each turnoff would have it's covey of pickup trucks pulled off in the dirt. Farmers standing around testing the wheat for moisture; 13 percent, Jaymie had told me, was the lucky number. Thirteen percent, and clear skies and God Help Us, no rain till all the wheat was in or you'd have rust and sprouting heads of grain, which meant cheaper bushels and standing in line for the government dole.

Montana wasn't about shoot roosters and rodeo cowboys. I'd come to realize that sometime in the last four years, maybe last summer, watching the wheat turn and the farmers worrying, sitting in their pickups off the side of the road as they watched the sky. The West was a four letter word: rain. The hired cowboy could put his hat on or his rain slicker and ride off into the sunset plus or minus a summer's wages. The farmer was rooted to the land, starving in drought or flood, just the same. And even though I understood that, I would still be discounted as a hopeless tenderfoot since my grandfather didn't stick. He was one of those fly-by-nights who couldn't make a go of it—not smart enough, not stubborn enough. What Sue always said—stupid like a fox—stupid enough to know when to give up a lost cause.

"Not like Gordy," Sue told me once. "Gordy, his father, his grandfather. His father's grandfather. They all had to work for wages on someone else's place to keep the ranch."

I'd quit wondering why my grandfather hadn't stayed. Why I couldn't call myself a third generation ranch kid. But I still fantasized sometimes, like now, seeing a log house from the highway, its windows trimmed in barn-red paint. I could've been a child here. Had dogs. Or horses. Geese walking around the yard. Ducks with their own private pond—a pond that froze over every winter for Dad and me to ice skate on. And now, this time of year, I would have memories of picking huckleberries in the early morning to bring to my mother in the kitchen to make into jam and syrup to put over ice cream instead of going to Gristedes on my roller skates and buying the eternally available can of Hershey's chocolate. Except that now I knew the truth even as I fantasized: Dad would be working somewhere else all day to support us and Grandpa still would have died of cancer at thirty-six. So what difference did the huckleberries and the log house and the ponies make?

The Hackamore was a new restaurant, without the character of the the Crossroads, but also without the familiar clientele. For above all else, Rose and Wally wanted to be left in peace. The Crossroads was closer, but there they were the tragic parents of that poor boy. Here, they were simply customers who might or might not tip. Jaymie and I had arrived first, found a table and had just told the waitress we would wait for the rest of our party when the folks appeared.

They'd worked things out, Rose and Walter, you could see that as soon as they walked into the room. There was the obvious: Rose no longer limped nor used a cane. Her step was as sure and as graceful as it had ever been. But there was more. She waited for him while he checked her coat. Watched him with eyes young and in love as he came back, put his arm around her and walked her out onto the dance floor for one dance alone before they looked for their girls.

When I was very young—my parents no older than I was now—they were more in love than Jack and Maddy could think of being. They were out for New Year's Eve in their best dress-up clothes, taking Katherine and me along in our white cotton anklets, crinolines and taffeta party dresses for the cultural experience. We went to the Roosevelt Grill for dinner and danced to Guy Lombardo and His Royal Canadians. It was a night I will never forget if only for that look in their eyes, which is what I now saw in Rose's eyes. And Walter's. I don't think the young know how to dance anymore. We're too much into doing our own thing, instead of matching steps, swinging rhythmically, a mirror of trees swaying in the wind, slow motion almost, and perfectly in unison.

Rose had healed. And the family had survived. There wasn't anything more a person could ask.

The Hackamore was a nice place. Heavy white tablecloths covered by smaller red ones on the diagonal, with white linen napkins and a handrailing from the dining room to dance floor so the old folks wouldn't fall. No smoke drifting in from the bar. No desperate twice-divorced singles lurching around the dance floor. I'd been to the old hangout, the Crossroads, once. It had had its share of smoke and lurching, and bathrooms with condom machines like Coke dispensers—but at twice the price of the Tender to discourage casual use. The Hackamore had perfume dispensers instead. Emeraude, Tabu and

Chanel N° 5, which is what Rose always wore, and was wearing that night.

Everybody ordered what they had always ordered at the Crossroads. Wally had his sixteen-ounce steak, with fries smothered in creamy ranch dressing, and Jaymie her seven-ounce New York strip. No baked, fried or mashed potato. No dressing on the salad, but heavy on the pickled beets, three bean salad and corn relish from the salad bar. Rose ate her fries and iceberg lettuce with lemon juice and one of the six deep-fried fantail shrimp. The rest she put in a a doggie bag for lunch Saturday. Just like always.

"It was a lovely dinner," Rose said, and stood up again to take Wall's hand.

As they headed out to the dance floor, Wally hesitated a moment and turned back to me. He handed me a piece of paper. A folded-up Xerox he'd had in his breast pocket. "Philbrook," he said and winked.

I stashed it in my coat pocket to read later.

"YOU WERE VERY QUIET," Jaymie said as we drove home again to Missoula. We'd left Rose and Wally to dance the night away, their last night in the valley and their old house by the river. The next day, the moving van people would box it all up like canned corn and send it into the ozone.

"I guess I have a lot to think about."

She pulled over on the shoulder. "I need one drink, Evelyn, if you wouldn't mind driving."

"Sure." I think I preferred it. Give me something to think about instead of Rose and Wally leaving Montana forever.

She climbed into the passenger seat and took a pint bottle of Jack out of the glove box, which she sipped from. Slowly. The new Jaymie. She seemed to be cured, too.

"So what did Walls give you?"

"The paper?"

She nodded.

"He said it was about Philbrook."

"The town your grandfather homesteaded at."

I nodded.

"You read it?"

"Not yet."

"Where is it?"

I dug it out of my coat pocket, and she turned on the dome—on and then off.

"Philbrook. 1881 to 1909," she said. "Eight miles east of Utica."

"That's all?"

"That's all." She folded the paper up again and got out a road map. "I think I know where Utica is. I think I was up there for a timber sale one time. Good fishing, too. But strictly a Panther Martin lure stream." She had been looking at the map while she talked and finally folded it back up. "I'll show you when we get home. It's right in the middle of the state. Little town off the Pleasant Valley Road."

We came over Lolo Pass on dry roads and were down in the narrow winding canyon when Jaymie leaned forward, staring out into the night.

"I don't know what the hell's going on up there. You better slow down," she said and tucked the bottle under the seat.

Up ahead there were taillights and what looked like searchlights scanning the tops of the trees, except they weren't moving. I slowed down to thirty-five, then twenty-five, and as we came closer, we realized the taillights stared blankly into the sky—an accident spread across the two-lane bridge ahead of us.

God only knows where we were, or where the closest phone was. I hadn't been paying any attention at all.

I pulled as far off the road as I could, then set the emergency brake and lights blinking to try to keep from being rear-ended. Jaymie drug out flares from the tool box behind the seat, setting them out behind us.

Then we walked up to the vehicle. The only lights on the road now were Jaymie's headlights: not quite close enough to shed light on the accident and the injured vehicle's damaged beams staring off into space. I saw someone waving, standing behind the overturned vehicle, and walked toward him. It was a horse trailer, or had been, and pickup truck, taking the road too fast or the driver falling asleep at the wheel, something. The trailer had tipped over across the road and the truck's front end was wrapped around the concrete bridge abutment.

It wasn't a man waving, when I came upon it, it was a horse, lying on the ground, back legs paralyzed—trying to stand up—its head and mane flailing wildly in dumb panic. No sound but the insistent hiss of the buckled radiator and that horse gasping. As my eyes adjusted to the black highway, and my ears to the ghastly silence, I saw four other horses broken and bleeding on the blacktop.

Jaymie grabbed my arm. "There's going to be traffic soon. Take these flares and set 'em up in front of us, seventy-five yards at least. Pace it off. I don't want to get killed."

"Where are you going?"

She pushed me. "Go. I have to get my first aid kit out of the rig."

It was like the road was black ice, or my shoes banana peels. I couldn't keep feet under me to walk straight. Didn't look in the cab of the truck as I walked by. I broke the flares, set them down and headed back toward Jaymie. She was climbing into the cab of the battered truck.

"Look, here's what it is," she said. "This guy in the cab, he's bleeding. And these guys back there—," she pointed behind the trailer at the horses, "they're all dead. They just don't know it yet."

I was shaking my head. I knew what she was going to say and couldn't stop her from saying it.

She handed me the white enamel first aid kit. "Here, hold this a second." Then she had the handgun out of the leather holster. She flipped open the cylinder and started loading it with bullets from her pocket.

"Watch carefully. This is how it works. This is a Colt revolver. You pull the hammer back four clicks. Spell C-O-L-T. One letter for each click. Then you pull the trigger. If you do it right, you won't have to load it again. Got it? You put it between their eyes. Right against their skin so you don't miss. One shot. And they don't feel any more pain. Don't shoot in the air. Just keep it pointed at the ground and your finger off the trigger till you're ready to use it."

"I've never shot a gun."

"I know that, Evelyn. But the number one rule of gun handling is bourbon and lead don't mix. You have to take care of the horses. I gotta take care of this guy up front. How are you doing?"

"Probably gonna throw up."

"The highway's already a mess, no one's gonna notice." She touched her index finger to her forehead an inch above her nose, like a drunk failing the test. "One shot," she said again and put the gun in my hand.

I took a breath and stood there for a second. Backlit by the flare, Jaymie grabbed the steering wheel and hung there, for just a split second. "Put 'em out of their damn misery, Evelyn, right now," she said and pulled herself into the cab.

I walked back to the end of the overturned horse trailer. There was one horse lying twisted in the bottom of the wreckage. A large bay in leather halter and saddle, his eyes staring straight out into the Bronco's headlights. I tried to close his eyes once, to make sure he wasn't dead already, but his eyes popped open as soon as my fingers left his lid. Such an enormous head when it's lying right in front of you. I placed the blued barrel as exactly between the eyes as I could figure and pulled the trigger.

I flinched but nothing happened, then realized I'd forgotten to pull the hammer back. C-O-L-T. The eyes stayed closed this time.

Five of them in all. One pinto. Two black ones. The bay and a sorrel. By then another truck had stopped and he attached his tow chain to the horses, one by one, and pulled them clear of the road. Then another car stopped and a man with a flashlight stood out in the middle of the road, directing traffic around the overturned trailer until the tow truck and the cop arrived and turned it back on its wheels. All the while, traffic inched slowly by, windows rolled down in the cool night air as people threw questions at whoever would answer and stared at the blood all over the highway.

The man in the cab had a broken arm, a gash across the bridge of his nose and internal bleeding, that was operated on that night.

"I'm sure the insurance pays for the horses," Jaymie said when I showed her the story in the paper the next day.

It was noon. I'd been up since seven, sitting at the kitchen table drinking coffee. My widow neighbor on the east side of the house had been gardening in the backyard under my window all morning, pulling weeds from her marigold beds and cutting the seed stalks from the rhubarb plants. She was young for a widow, not fifty yet, and spent hours in the backyard every day rototilling the garden, then realigning the rocks along the path from the back door to the alley gate. The garbage cans were out there, and each evening after dinner she took a quarter bag of garbage out to dump in the can. Then on the walk back, she'd tour the perimeter of her yard, reliving her day's work and making sure none of it had come undone.

She had trees. An apple tree by the street-side fence that people reached over, stealing fruit when she wasn't looking. She kept those limbs trimmed back, trying to prevent the theft, but the tree had been planted too long ago, and too close to the fence for the pruning to matter. Her little amendments couldn't make a difference.

She had many other trees. Cherry and apricot, elm and one very old fir. Right under my window, there was a delicate tree, not for shade or any ability to bear food. It was tall and spindly like a newly planted weeping willow, with a mist of purple leaves instead of green and a brace concocted of rubber tubing and cable wider around than the tree's own trunk, to keep it standing straight. I remember the windstorm that nearly killed it a year ago last March before the purple leaves had opened, and the woman had hired men to come in and stand it back up.

Each time she passed the tree, she checked the cables and the rubber truss to make sure it did more good than harm to the little tree. Mornings like this, tree care seemed much more exciting than taking a shower and getting dressed to be ready on time for Jaymie. To say good-bye to Rose.

Jaymie sat with a cup of coffee and looked into the yard below.

"What kind of tree is that?" I asked.

"What? That one with the iron lung? That's a dead tree."

"No. It's doing okay."

"It would be twice as big if it hadn't blown over. It probably has a scar or worse—a hole—running right down the middle of the maple syrup system."

She waited for me to laugh or point out, very seriously, that the tree wasn't a maple. "You guys are always just throwing stuff away and starting over. New and clean," I said.

"I take it, you're not talking about trees. Is this about horses? Or old people?"

"You know what it's about, you've lived here all your life."

"Evelyn, sometimes a tree oughta just be a tree."

It was so quiet—not even the sound of the refrigerator whirring. You could hear Jaymie waiting there for a rational answer, an explanation that I knew I didn't have. And stirring the coffee with her spoon, endlessly.

"I carry emergency supplies in my Bronco," Jaymie said. "Flares and a first aid kit, high-lift jack and a come-along, spare fuel pump, oil, oil filter, crowbar, high-power emergency flashlight, tool kit. I try to keep a sleeping bag in winter and candy bars year round, but the candy bars, especially the chocolate ones, disappear. I'm down to buying granola bars so I'm not tempted to dig into the emergency rations on bluebird days. That's just being prepared."

"You had a gun in your car."

"And damn good thing too."

"That's what I'm saying. Things happen here," I said.

"Things happen everywhere. Most places there's enough people to pay enough taxes that you got a big police force to clean up the mess. Here you live with it. Or you clean it up yourself."

"I don't think I can live here anymore."

"You live in a big city, you live your whole life thinking nothing ever happens. Nobody ever dies. Nobody gets run over. Cats don't fall out of ten-story windows. It's not my fault—that's what you all say. It's not my job. Out here, where there's no cop every twenty yards, you got to do it yourself. What would you have done if I hadn't handed you that gun? Wait for a highway patrolman? Those horses didn't deserve that. First person on the scene. You do what you fuckin' can, Evelyn."

"I'm thinking of going back to New York. This place is changing me."

"Change can be good."

"Isn't that the name of a book?"

"The one week I ever spent in New York City, there were eighty-five reported homicides. I read it in the newspaper. Every day, a little box score."

"You just need to know where not to go. And when."

"Oh, I forgot. You got cement walls around all the "bad" neighborhoods, and none of those "bad" people know how to drop a token in a subway slot or call a cab."

"I need to take a shower," I said and left her there.

But she had a new topic when I came back, hair wet, smelling of baby powder under my shorts and t-shirt. I'd started collecting t-shirts from all over Missoula. KUFM—Public Radio. Missoula's centennial celebration. This one was from the Legal Tender Saloon. A green one. I had a red and blue one, too, from the Tender, with black calligraphy and a couple in cowboy boots jitterbugging on a silver dollar. Sue said I was getting ready to leave—collecting quaint souvenirs.

"You haven't finished reading the paper," Jaymie said as I popped an English muffin into the toaster.

"What did I miss?

"More of that stuff you can't stand," she said.

It was on the legal page, with the marriage licenses, death notices, and driving citations. "Hardin Man Granted New Trial" was the headline.

"Gene Bofay," I said.

"Bingo."

New lawyer. New trial. Incompetence of the defense lawyer given as the justification. I looked over at Jaymie. She was watching my neighbor clip the dead iris blooms off the stalks.

"Will you watch the trial again?" I asked.

She didn't answer for a couple of minutes.

"I've thought about that. A month ago I would've. Two months ago. But one of those days in there, somewhere, I suddenly woke up and saw what everybody else saw already. What you saw a long time ago. These things never stop. It doesn't even matter that they can't give the death penalty, not *really* give it—give it and carry it out in what would have been the victim's natural life." She'd finished the coffee, and began turning the cup, like a propeller on a rubber band, turning it in tight little circles. "You saw it, Evelyn. You were telling me all along. This is endless. As long as there's canned spam there'll be some asshole—supposed to be locked away for the rest of his life—jerking some poor family around by the balls. Remember what Aamold said? He'll disappear off the face of the earth, he said. Bull shit. My family has disappeared off the face of the earth. Gene Bofay thrives."

"What if he asks you to sit through the trial."

"Aamold? See that tree down there, Evelyn? I ain't going out like that. I'm cutting this off at the ankles, right now. I lost everything. Bucky's dead, Rose and Walls are moving to a retirement condo, for God's sake. J&B sold to a perfect stranger. Aamold's already gotten more than a pound of flesh out of my family."

"So it will just be me?"

"I would be sorry to see that."

"Someone has to see that justice is done."

"Like a backseat driver can't fall asleep or look away, or there'll be an accident? I hear it. But justice isn't going to happen in that courtroom."

"You going to tell your parents?"

She shook her head. "They don't want to know. You shouldn't either. I can tell you from experience, it doesn't help to watch."

"It won't help to sit at home and wonder what's going on."

"What about Jack? You suppose he's gonna let you take a week off to sit and watch a second trial?"

"He owes me vacation time. He doesn't have to know how I spend it."

"That's it then?" she asked.

"That's it."

She put the coffee cups in the sink and rinsed them. "Are you ready to go wave bye-bye?"

"I'm ready."

"Then let's blow this pop stand."

W A L L Y A N D R O S E had parked the Winnebago in the farthest back corner of the backyard, as close to the cottonwood trees as they could put it for shade without getting the brand-new aluminum cruiser all scratched up.

It was very nice. Very new. Very clean. Neither one of them had taken time to add photos to the decor, which was the usual boring combination of orange, brown and bland ecru, with pom-poms and fringe reminiscent of a K-Mart blue light special.

Jaymie would have defended them saying they were simply too busy—selling the house, the business, reinvesting and hiding their capital gains from the IRS. But I would've argued it wasn't like any of this family to tread so lightly, to not leave their thumbprint somewhere in the new home. But then I'd never imagined them as transients. I think that's what I remember most of that afternoon.

That and Rose saying good-bye.

She'd spent the time since the moving van left, cleaning the house, readying it for the new owners to just open the door and move in. We found her at the kitchen sink, gathering up the cloths, sponges and cleaning liquids into a box, which she handed over to Jaymie, saying she didn't need a bunch of rags going moldy or open containers spilling on her trip down to Colorado. Then she grabbed her old gardening hat off the top of her purse—a wide-brimmed, expensive woven jute hat with the Montana State flag twisted and tied around the crown, like a hat band.

"This is for you, Evelyn," she said, with no more explanation.

I took the box and hat outside and set them in the back of the Bronco. When I came back inside, Jaymie stood at the kitchen sink by herself.

"You better go get Pops," she said softly. "He's gonna have to gentle her out of here."

And that's what he did. You live in a house for thirty years like they did, it begins to own you.

Wally found Rose leaning against the wall in Bucky's room. "The house is cold," he said to her. "I'll go fire up the Winnebago and put on some nice music. That's what retired people do isn't it, Rosey, keep warm and happy?" He slid an arm around her waist and held her gently from behind.

Rose laid her head on his shoulder. "Thirty-two years, Walter. That's a long time to live in a house. I feel like I'm deserting her."

Like an old dog you're putting to sleep, I thought. We'd done that, and my father had been the only one of us who could stay and hold her, stroking her till she was gone so she wouldn't be alone. There's always one member of the family who takes those hard jobs on. And here was Rose, stroking the walls and door frames of her home.

"This is the only place he ever lived, Walter. We can't leave here," she said and Wally put his other arm around her, holding her tighter. "Walter, I've been so good. So good. Why doesn't he come back?"

I could feel Jaymie behind me in the hall, her hand reaching for mine, and I turned to see her wipe tears from her face. She pulled me outside.

"That's too hard," she said, and we sat down on the front porch together silently and waited for the folks to come back outside and say good-bye.

Wally and Rose taught me something that bright afternoon. It hurts just as much to watch someone drive away slowly in broad daylight—watching them grow smaller and smaller— as to have them snatched suddenly right from under your nose.

SIXTEEN

THE NEW TRIAL was supposed to be a Christmas distraction in Missoula's third-floor courtroom. In the meantime they'd released him again, on bail. That took about three minutes one Wednesday morning in October, so I didn't have to take any time off work. They'd done that in a dark little courtroom on the first floor under the grand marble staircase a few weeks after Rose and Wally left. I suppose the room had been well-lit at one time, but the expansion of the county jail had left the windows ten feet from three stories of new granite wall, and the only light that entered was reflected off those walls into the tiny courtroom. It made Bofay look larger than life.

They led him in in his prison denims—two county sheriff deputies on his arms, one behind, and the prisoner between them, his hands and feet shackled with a chain, forcing him to walk slightly stooped. Bofay was still a tall man. Prison hadn't changed him.

And I was the only one who even paid any attention at his entrance. The rest of the visitors in the six-row, forty-five-person maximum-occupancy courtroom worried about their own minor misdemeanors and traffic offenses, talked with attorneys, or spouses as if nothing had happened. Bofay looked around the room, then leaned down to listen to this new attorney's instructions as they stood to the side of the judge's desk. And that's all it was really, a desk. Like one you'd see in a library or a high school science room.

I'd sat in the back, wanting to gloat, and stare at Bofay, wanting to see and not be seen by the prisoner in his brief but frustrating moment in the sun. It was to be a reclamation of rights. Bucky's rights? My rights? I didn't know. But I wanted to see punishment meted out to this man. Again.

They took Bofay first. The new attorney introduced his client to the judge, explained the awarding of a new trial and proposed a minimal bail of $5,000. He was young, this new attorney, unsuitably attired in jeans, a sports jacket and dark maroon shirt and tie.

Aamold centered himself before the judge in his navy blue, three-piece wool suit, white shirt and red tie. "Your honor," he began. "Eugene Bofay is a dangerous offender, who has no ties to the community. He is a convicted felon, already tried on this charge and found guilty, found to be a dangerous offender. We cannot allow such a small bond. The State recommends bail be set at $50,000." He'd had his hands in his pants pockets, leaning back on his heels as he spoke. When he finished, he drew his hands out of his pockets and clasped them in front of his belt, waiting patiently for the decision.

I don't think the judge even deliberated for a second. I think he'd made up his mind before he even saw the defendant.

"Mr. Aamold," he said, "This man is free of those charges as he stands before me. And I believe the honored American principle of innocent till proven guilty applies even in this case."

The judge knocked his gavel once against his little square pad. "Bail will be set at $5,000. Prisoner will be remanded to his cell until bail is arranged. Bailiff, call the next case."

I followed Aamold back to his office, trying to get his attention to ask about the new trial date, but he disappeared into a private office without paying any attention to me. A woman at the front desk asked if she could help.

"Yes," I said. "I'd like to know when the new trial for Eugene Bofay has been scheduled."

She checked a sheaf of papers on the bulletin board next to her desk. "I thought we had that scheduled. I guess it's been continued. It will be a matter of public record however, when the date is set. You can check the paper or call into this office for the date."

"I wonder if you could give me a call when the date is set," I asked.

"I'm sorry. We don't have enough employees to do that," she said. "It will be a matter of public record. You'll have no trouble finding the date."

Right. That's what she said, but that's not the way it was. When Jaymie had been in the picture, they'd left messages everywhere for her, making sure she was always present and accounted for. For me, they would answer a direct question, but I had to ask the right question at the right time. In the meantime, I missed appearances, and worse, took time off from work, and found an empty courtroom. Bofay's new attorney was very good at empty courtrooms. That happened four times over the long winter and Bofay on the street the whole time. Within an hour of setting his bail. I know. I watched from my truck, right across the street from the jail entrance, and kitty-corner from the bail bondsman's office. Lillian Yellow Bird hadn't been in the courtroom because she was waiting in the bail bondsman's office.

She was on the street waiting for her brother when he emerged from the county jail. She gave him two little pats on the middle of his back and herded him into a red Suburban after a brief little argument, probably over who would drive. She drove. They were gone before I'd even settled in.

I thought of a lot of lies I could tell Jack. Like that I was finally taking a vacation on my own time. Or my mother was coming out to see me for my birthday, 'cause that's what all those delays meant, that the trial wouldn't take place till my birthday, February ninth. In the end, I decided Jack was an adult and he could take the truth, and anyway, in case February ninth was an empty courtroom, I wouldn't be trapped into a bunch of lies when I had to change my vacation date again.

But the last thing in the world Jack wanted me to do was take an unauthorized vacation. That's what he called it anyway. His problem was he didn't have another assistant. Didn't need another assistant unless I was going to start being irresponsible, he said, and then he started giving me a hard time about wanting to see not just one trial, but two.

"It's all the same, Evvy. Like watching reruns of Gilligan's Island."

"No. There's a different lawyer. This one is actually going to defend the case. It might even be a fight. A fair fight. And more chance that Bofay will get off."

"And you want to watch that?"

"I haven't asked for many days off on my own. I've always taken off when you take off, tried to keep you working. But now, this is what I want. Five days. That's all it will take. Maybe less. It's very important to me, Jack."

This was in his private office, Monday morning, when we'd

had a cancellation and Jack had been about to call another of his office meetings. Sue guessed what was coming ten minutes beforehand and started collecting all his greasy little red pencils so he couldn't smear up her appointment book. It wasn't a good week for him anyway. Maddy had shown up in town again. Gotten an apartment. She'd even talked her old boss at the county into giving her her old job back. And Sue Raffin had had lunch with her twice that week. Jack found out right away about the lunches. It drove him mad knowing his little woman was spreading lies about him in his own office.

"It's your own fault," Sue had told him. "You shouldn't have brought your love dumpling into the workplace."

There were lots more stories about their fights. Little fights at this point, Sue said, because without her living there with him in his house, where he was paying the bills and had all the leverage, he was walking on eggs.

Jack had a pile of red pencils on his desk, and was going through his drawers looking for more while I tried to talk him into my vacation. He'd pull one drawer completely out, leave it hanging on the edge of the roller, piling papers, books and doodads into enormous leaning towers, then starting on the next drawer, leaving everything from the last one still piled and hanging by its teeth.

He mumbled as he did this, filling the spaces between thoughts so I'd be too polite to break in. I broke in anyway. This was one mess I found amusing, because it was one of his few messes I didn't have to clean up. The private office was Sue's territory. Everything north of the x-ray room.

"Look. Jaymie's not going to this trial. With the new owner, the shop is completely in her hands. The district attorney needs me to sit in the front row and be the family." That was a lie, of course. The district attorney was still acting like he didn't need anyone or anybody to help him put Gene Bofay behind bars again. He'd done it once easily enough. Twice would be a cakewalk.

"I need to be there. I need to be in the front row and make the jury think about what Bucky's family was like."

Jack set a pocket dictionary on top of the fourth pile of papers. It slid, slowly, starting the papers on a sideways shift headed for the floor. He had his face in the fifth drawer. I could've said something, warned him. Instead I let it fall down, taking all but the last quarter inch of papers with it.

Jack looked at it like it was this big goddamn surprise. "Are we done?" he said to me.

"I don't know. Do I have the vacation time I want?"

"Take what you want, Evelyn. Me and Suz'll muddle through."

"I'm sure you will. You could even hire temporary help. Dr. Dash is on vacation that week. His assistant could come help."

"Maybe you should think of moving on, Evelyn. You don't seem to have your heart in dentistry anymore."

"I'm asking for one week off in years, Jack. I've spent a lot more time sitting on my hands waiting for you."

"There's two kinds of people in the world, E. Ones who make work for themselves and those who sit on their hands."

"It would take two minutes for Sue to call Dr. Dash's office."

"Not your problem anymore, Evelyn," he said. "Go get Susie-Q for me, would you? And tell her to bring her appointment book."

What he did, Sue told me at lunch, was cancel the whole week I was supposed to be at the trial. Then she thanked me for getting Jack so mad he dumped out all his desk drawers. She was serious about that thank you. Gave her the opportunity to confiscate all his other red pencils. Pencils from what she called the earlier, less professional receptionist regimes.

"You know, we do need those to make out treatment plans?" I said laughing at her.

"Two to an operatory. There's too goddamn many of these greasy red pencils floating around. This ain't no kindy-garten class. This here's work. More work'll get done if the doctor stops coloring in my appointment book."

That night, that was another Tuesday night, I got a phone call from a long-lost "friend." Gordy Bennett. It was ten o'clock when he called.

"How's life been treating you?" he asked.

"Life's okay," I said. "Where have you been?"

"Well, the last month or so, I been at the smoke jumper headquarters doing paperwork and repairing gear. I'm about to take off for West Virginia again, work the rest of the winter with my brother, since he thinks he can get me on again, slinging cement. I just thought I'd call and see if we could get together."

"You said you'd call last spring and summer."

"Well, I didn't do that."

"No, you didn't."

"Would you like to get together tonight?"

"No, I wouldn't," I said. "In fact, I'm going to hang up." And I did. I didn't even wait to hear what his argument was. So he could talk me into letting him come over that night. But I spent the night thinking of him. Almost all of it. And wishing he'd called more than once last year. Or sent a postcard. Or anything. Simply anything would have kept me going.

Then Thursday night, Sue Raffin and I walk into the Tender, me in my buffalo hide cowgirl boots and brand-new, boot-cut jeans, and there he was at the bar. We'd come late, enjoying a few Kiltlifters at Sue's house first. Kiltlifters—drambui and scotch—little drinks that knocked you on your ass, Sue said. I'd told her about the phone call.

He hadn't changed a bit. Still tall and dark with big green eyes, clear, healthy, olive skin mottled by freckles and working in the sun all year. He had on Levis and dress cowboy boots, and the ever-present white cotton, long-sleeve snap-button shirt.

Sue grabbed me by the sleeve and steered me away from the bar where Gordy, and every other man in the place, stood facing the dance floor with one elbow on the bar and one booted foot on the brass rail.

"He ain't here, honey," Sue told me. "You kissed him off last night. Remember?"

"I remember. But he sure is pretty."

"Pretty is as pretty does. Where's he been for the last ten months? And, more to the point, who's he been boinking instead of you?"

"You're right," I said.

"Damn straight, I'm right." She sat me down at the table. Three of the other girls were there already, the insurance girl—Hope—and Dimpy and Roz from the clinic. "Gordy alert," Sue said as she planted herself in a chair and pulled out her cigarettes and lighter from her coat pocket. That's what they all did—was keep their money and valuables in their pockets instead of having to leave someone at the table to guard the purses when everyone else was dancing. Most nights it didn't make any difference, but on a hot night, when there were lots of guys, the last one up would resent having to say no just to watch a bunch of cheap K-Mart handbags with two baby pacifiers, an assortment of nose spray and Chapstick tubes and a total of $12.37 in change.

"Up at the bar, twelfth from the right," Sue said without looking that way.

And before I even turned around, not that I needed to look at him, he was at the table and asked me to dance. I got up automatically and walked out onto the dance floor with him. It was a slow dance. Kind of a quiet Patsy Cline tune you could talk to. But Gordy, he ruined it.

What he said was, "I'm glad to see you're feeling better tonight."

"As compared to what?" I said, because he caught me off guard.

"As compared to when I called last night. I'm glad to see you're feeling better."

"There was nothing wrong with me last night," I said.

"Oh," he said.

"At least nothing wrong with me that a phone call last April or a post card last August or a date last New Year's wouldn't have cured."

And that's where I left him—on the dance floor. I didn't dance with him again. I danced with everyone else though, and around midnight had settled into dancing with a Gordy-clone—another dark-haired cowboy in blue Levis, boots and white cotton shirt.

Gordy did watch, or so Sue Raffin told me, since she'd designated herself my watchdog for the night and warned the other girls at the table not to touch Mr. Bennett or there'd be a cat fight in the girl's bathroom later.

"The asshole's been watching you all night. Still watching you," she said. She told me this when my cowboy went off to the men's room. "That's why you're going to take doofus home with you," she added.

"I'm not taking that guy home," I said.

"Well, maybe not that doofus, but some doofus. Just find a healthy doofus, Evelyn. You don't want to catch nothing nasty and bring it to the office. And for Christ's sake don't take him to your apartment. Rule number one of The Recovery Cruise: Don't shit in your own nest—go to his place or a motel. Then, when you wake up and look at yourself in the mirror, you can walk away and forget it."

But he didn't have a place and he didn't have money for a motel, so we ended up going to my place, which ended up explaining Sue Raffin's rule number one to its fullest: it's an awful lot easier to kick yourself out. Otherwise, it gets messy. This one got very messy.

He wasn't so bad. We were both drunk, that's all. And it didn't help that five minutes after I deposited my "date"' in the living room, Gordy knocked at the door, wanting to know if I was really through with him, if he'd really screwed up, he said.

He pulled me outside the apartment door onto the landing. "I just want to know. I want to see it in your eyes," he said.

"I don't know what you want out of me," I said. "You never call. You never write. I don't know if you're alive from month to month. Hell, I haven't heard from you in almost a year, and you call me at ten o'clock and want to pick up where you left off."

"I know I've really screwed up here. Not just here. I've been running my whole life right into the ground."

He was shaking violently while he spoke, hardly keeping his voice in control. And while he spoke, with his hand firmly wrapped around my arm, I thought, if he lets go, he'll fall down. I covered my face, not wanting my eyes to tell him the truth and wanting him to go away before the doofus in my living room roused himself.

"I'm in love with another man," I said. "He's here all the time for me."

He just looked at me, his hand still on my arm, but now lax, and the arm sagging like an old rubber band between us.

"And I have to go," I said. "I can't keep him waiting."

"That's what you want?" he asked.

"Are you going to be around?" I asked.

"I can't promise that."

"Then, that's it. That's what I want."

He let go. He nodded. Then he walked down the stairs leaving the outside door open and driving away in his truck. I walked down the stairway and watched from the door, closing it only after all echoes of his truck had disappeared into the darkness. Upstairs, supposedly, was the love of my life.

In the quiet, I could hear my downstairs neighbor walking around in her front room, checking out the window looking for signs that she could go back to sleep in peace. I walked back upstairs and found loverboy sprawled out, with a bottle of Beam in his hand, across my reading chair.

"What was all that about?" he asked.

"My neighbor downstairs. Asking us to be quieter."

"Goddamn, we just got here," he said, in a loud voice. "What the shit does she think this is—a fuckin' cemetery? People gotta live. They gotta make a bit of shittin' noise, for Chrissake."

"Look, don't worry about it. It's three in the morning, and I'm a little more tired than I thought. Let me fix you a little breakfast before you go." Right. Thaw out Gordy's steaks and broil them up.

"We can get to breakfast in a minute sweetheart. Come on over here." He beckoned to me with his entire arm, waving like a palm tree in a hurricane.

I moved a little closer, wanting to keep my voice down, but wanting to stay out of reach of that arm.

"Listen," I said. "I'm not really in the mood to have company anymore. I was, but now I'm not, you know how it goes?"

"Oh, but honey, it hasn't gone with me. You know what I mean. I need a little loving here, Sweet Lips.

"Listen, guy. I don't know what's wrong with your hearing,

but I'm asking you nicely to go home. Now please go home."

He stood, tentatively, propped up against the couch with the back of his calves and one hand balancing the leaning tower of his body.

"This way," I said, leading him out to the door, staying enough ahead of his attempts to grab me that I kept out of his grip, until we reached the door. Then, as I opened it, he grabbed me around the waist, trying to kiss me and hold me, while he kept hold of the bottle.

"Oh Christ, knock it off," I said, and wedged my hands between us, giving him a hard push and ducking at the same time out of his arms. "The party's over. Just go home."

He lurched at me again, but now with the door open, I pushed him again, as hard as I could out the door. He grabbed for me, caught my blouse, but was headed out so fast, between my push and his own momentum, the blouse tore in his hands, and bouncing off the wall across the landing, he lost his balance completely and stumbled down the steps. For the first three steps he maintained a basically upright position, but as he reached the turn in the staircase, he careened backwards and fell head first, with a sickening sound, down the rest of the twenty-seven steps.

He lay at the bottom of the stairs unconscious. Or at least not moving. My downstairs neighbor opened her door and looked at this stranger, laid out at her feet.

"Is he alive?" I asked as I started shakily down the stairs.

"Just my thought," she said.

She felt the side of his neck for a pulse and nodded.

"Oh, thank God," I said.

"Friend of yours?"

"Uh." I thought for a second before I answered. "Yeah, I suppose."

"Well, he wasn't visiting me," she said. "What's his name?"

"I don't remember."

She nodded, then reached in his back pocket without moving him to find his wallet. "Ah, he's a local," she said. "Let's try calling his house and hope someone answers."

She led me into her apartment, which was exactly like mine except this woman had furniture everywhere, and photos on the walls, at least the walls that weren't covered with bookshelves. There was hardly an inch of space anywhere not covered with pictures. In the kitchen, where the phone was, the ironing board was a permanent piece of furniture with several neatly folded piles of clothing eighteen inches high stacked along the length of it. And the doorway was blocked by clothes—vintage dresses in various stages of repair—hanging from a shower bar.

She tried the number she'd found in the phone book, waited for many more rings than was polite and hung up. "I think it's time to call the ambulance. Go see if he's still out cold," she said.

I checked. He hadn't moved. Though he was still breathing okay. I tapped him on the forehead, right between the eyes, trying to wake him up and all he did was groan. I talked to him. "George," I said. That was the name on his driver's license. "George." No answer.

I was squatted there, still trying to rouse this George on my doorstep, when my neighbor reappeared at her door.

"I called an ambulance," she said. "They'll be here in a few minutes. Has he answered you yet?"

"No."

"Would you like to come in and sit?" she asked.

"No, I think I'll stay here and keep an eye on him till the ambulance comes."

But the ambulance didn't come alone. I thought I could maybe catch three or four hours sleep before I had to go to work, but that proved impossible. In fact, I was late for work.

They scooped George up quickly enough, after making sure he had no spinal injuries. A broken wrist was all the damage he'd done. The police were a bit slower about their work. And after a while I started wondering if they thought I'd pushed George on purpose. Trying to kill him.

One of the officers started with the neighbor. The other officer walked me upstairs to keep me company. Then the first officer came up and joined us. I'd put coffee on in the meantime.

"Your neighbor tells me that she heard an argument, two arguments within a few minutes of when the victim fell down the stairs."

I decided to simplify the scene by admitting to only one night visitor. "Yes. This man came into my house uninvited, was trying to force himself on me. Luckily he was very drunk and I was able to push him away. Unfortunately, he lost his balance and fell down the stairs."

"Have you ever met the victim before?"

"No."

"You meet him tonight?"

"I was out dancing with some friends at the Legal Tender Saloon, and this man asked me to dance. Then he followed me home. I tried to get rid of him."

"Did you call the police?"

"When he fell."

"No, I mean when you were being bothered by the man."

"No. I thought I could handle it."

"You didn't call anyone for help?"

"I didn't mean to push him down the stairs. He frightened me. He kept coming at me. I'm sure I have bruises on my arms from him grabbing me."

They asked the same questions over and over, until they finally let me go at six-thirty and I showered, dressed and turned up almost on time for work.

That day, I was the world's worst dental assistant, and if there was ever a day when I thought Jack had the absolute right to fire me, that was the day. But he was in a cheery and patient mood and was content to nurse me along. He apparently had had a night visitor, too, except his was his wife. Another night of lustful splendor and marital bliss that he regaled me with most of the day.

"You bet, Evelyn," he kept saying. "God's in heaven and all is right with the world."

SEVENTEEN

So HOW DID Jack's bubble finally burst? The last day of March, I decided I was tired of being poor, tired of being idle while Jack was off skiing or hunting—with no money of my own to do anything interesting—and I confronted him again about the difference between Sue's earnings and mine.

Jack already had me filling out the dental charts. After he was done drilling and while he was getting a cup of real coffee downstairs or talking on the phone with his lawyer or Maddy—depending on the stage of their relationship—I inked over the red decay on the tooth chart, then recorded the work completed on the back of the patient's record. Then I added up the total of fees for Sue, which she of course, double-checked with her adding machine and billed the patients.

It made me a lot more aware of the money Jack was pulling in. With my help. And I began keeping track of the daily and weekly totals.

To be fair, I kept a tally of expenses, too: lab fees, crown and bridge as well as plastic lab stuff, and then, when Sue was paying bills, I chatted her up, taking a little extra time to look at utility bills and building expenses. It soon became obvious Jack had good reason to take his accountant's advice to only work 125 days a year. Even with overhead and improper deductions, if he worked any more days than that, he was just turning it all over to the IRS.

I figured he could afford to pay me just a little more.

So after work, after a particularly hard day, with teeth crumbling under the lightest touch of the excavator and allegedly healthy walls caving in once the old amalgam was removed, I walked into Jack's private office. He was packing up his gym bag to leave for a week-long helicopter skiing trip.

I'd learned by then to avoid subtlety. "While you're gone," I said, "I want to come in a few days. There's inventorying and cleaning, deep cleaning that needs to be done. Places that haven't been properly sanitized since this place was built." I'd also learned to not give him space to interrupt. "If the dental board came in here, we'd be closed down in a minute."

I could hear it all running in his head: Evvy, when the going gets tough, the tough get going; there's two kinds of people, the ones who take chances and the ones who don't get off their butts. He broke into my thoughts.

"E, there's two kinds of people in this world," he started.

"Yes, I know Jack. There's the ones who are kind and the ones who take advantage of other people's kindness. There's the cheap and there's the poor. There's men and there's women."

He just looked at me.

"Jack, I can't afford to work full time for you if you don't pay me the equivalent of full-time wages. What are you going to do? Keep someone who knows your office and pay me what I need? Or hire some new, happy to-be-working, empty-headed lump?"

He'd been thinking while I was talking, I could tell. He'd stopped packing his bag and raised his left hand to support his chin.

"I don't know what happened to you, E. You used to be such a sweet girl. Ready to take the curve ball or whatever life threw at you. I need to think about this. I'll get back to you in a week. That okay?"

"No. I need to work a few days while you're gone next week. Or I need to find a full-time job."

"Then I guess you're looking for work, Evvy. I hope you don't take that attitude into your new job."

He stood up then and opened the door to the reception area. "Would you step in here a minute, Susie-Q?"

She came, with pencil and paper, expecting to be writing up a new employee contract.

"E's leaving us. Draw up her pay and any vacation she's got coming," he said. Then he sat down again, packing his bag. Ignoring me.

"Ah, shit," Sue said.

I think it's what I expected. Being fired. It was no shock. In fact, it hit me like the dropping of the New Year's Ball in Time's Square. Out with the old, in with the new, whatever the new was going to be it had to be better than this.

"You got an employee termination agreement form?" I asked.

They both looked up.

"No. I mean it. I want to sign an employee termination agreement. After five years, I want it in writing."

"You want a plaque, too?" Sue asked.

"The agreement will be fine. With all parties signing."

"And a check?" Sue said.

"Of course."

She left the room. Jack and I sat there. He was packing. I was gloating. If I'd known it was going to feel this good, I would have done it years ago. But then it wouldn't have felt as good years ago. I found myself grinning. Watching Jack.

Sue walked in again. "I amended the employee's agreement. It now says that you are fired. You are fired, right?"

I nodded. Jack ignored us.

"And that you didn't steal any of the tools." She offered it to me to sign.

"Instruments," I said and signed the form.

Then she put it in front of Jack and he signed it. He pretended he didn't care. And maybe he didn't.

She handed me the check. "You are now officially not a dental assistant," she said. "Congratulations."

Without looking up, Jack said, "You girls got nothing better to do than stand around? I got packing. Sue, you need to get me an expense check."

For the trip. His pocket money, which was twice what my termination pay was, which Sue had figured wrong anyway. I didn't complain. She'd given me $473.47 too much.

"And call the paper tonight, Susie-Q. Place an ad. You can interview while I'm gone. Thin the pool down to the best and brightest."

"Yes, Jack," she said. "Yes, Jack."

She ushered me out of his private office, down the hall and into operatory three.

"Like he's going to get a rocket scientist for minimum wage."

I started to interrupt, wanting to gloat some more. To celebrate a little.

She handed me a manila envelope, thick and sealed shut. "I need a big favor. Would you take this over to my mom? She's over on the north side, on Howell Street, you remember?"

"Yes. White house, red trim."

"And a big-ass fir tree in the yard."

"Yes."

"And not a word. I don't want Mom getting mugged over my vacation pay."

"Got it."

"What are you going to do tonight, Evelyn?"

"Celebrate."

"Fuckin' A."

I DID CELEBRATE that night at the Tender, like it was New Year's Eve all over again. We had a full table for Friday night and a full quota of men standing upright at the bar. I danced and flirted, and danced some more. Sue never came but around midnight, Maddy showed up. She came and sat down with us, and I introduced her around, not mentioning she was a doctor's wife. But when I was done, she did it herself, except she called herself a doctor's ex-wife.

"The doctor's having a tough day," I said. "I quit, too."

She said, no, and I pulled the Employee Termination Agreement out of my back pocket and unfolded it. That's why I got it, after all, not for me, but for everyone else who'd ever heard me say I was quitting before—so they'd believe me this time. But keeping it in the back pocket of my jeans, it was already getting pretty well pressed and starched.

"I quit, too. But I won't have my piece of paper for a while."

"I thought you were going helicopter skiing," I said.

"Oh no. Oh no, no, no, no. Not that skiing shit again. Not me. Been there. Done that. And nothing else. No more horseback riding lessons. No more water-skiing lessons. I ain't an outdoor girl, Evelyn. I love my furnace and my shower. And cars. Cars are good. You just turn a key. Don't have to get up at five in the morning and pitch them a pile of hay. Just drive up to the pump once a week or so and pay the man."

"You're really going to leave him this time?"

"Already told Sue. Can't go back now."

"Yeah, she'd really make you feel like a fool. But what I want to know is why now? After everything else."

"Evelyn, you got it eight hours a day, and I'm sympathetic, but I had it everywhere else. In the bedroom, in the shower, on the goddamn mountaintop. The man never stops talking. What's wrong with my furniture, what's wrong with my riding. My hair. My weight. For Christ's sake, Evelyn, he thinks I'm fat. I'm five four and weigh 108 pounds. I got tits, you know? I got tits weigh more than my butt and he's waiting outside the shower with a towel and tells me I'm fat. I tell him, 'Give me the goddamn towel,' and he's giving me the twice over. Shit."

She took a sip of her black Russian.

"He's been giving me shit all week, Evelyn. How I'm lazy just 'cause I won't go on his ski trip. I got a job. You know how that is, Evelyn, you have to show up five days a week or they think you're flaky. I never had a reputation with any of my bosses for being flaky. I ain't starting now."

"Jack's not paying your bills anymore?" I said. Maybe it was unfair, but maybe it wasn't. She didn't have to work as long as Jack was paying her bills. Why work at a phone if you didn't have to?

"He walks in, the asshole, without warning and tells me, 'The gravy train is over.' Gravy train, my ass. Every dime he gave me Evelyn, every goddamn thing he gave me, I paid for. He's in my face, or he's making me over into something he thinks I should be. Shit. I told him not to let the door knock him in the ass on the way out. I ain't taking that crap without compensation."

"Compensation?" I said. I had to laugh.

"You think I liked it? You think I liked getting told I'm not good enough to be A Doctor's Wife? I can't believe his ex put up with it for twenty-five years. Jesus. She deserved a medal."

"So you're slumming down here with the office girls looking for Mr. Right."

"Evelyn, I *am* an office girl. And I'm not looking for Mr. Right. I'd be very happy to find Mr. I-got-a-job, you-got-a-job, let's be nice to each other. You think there's one or two of those around?"

"Don't ask me. I thought Gordy was one."

"Oh, The Cruiser," she said, then touched my arm. "Sorry."

"It's all right. I think Sue was right, too. Now."

"So you're on a recovery cruise, too?" she said.

I looked around. "It's Saturday night. Bright lights. Happy people," I said.

"Like us."

"Better than sitting around watching old movies."

"I guess that's what Sue's doing."

"I don't know what Sue's doing. I thought she'd come down and celebrate with me tonight of all nights. Maybe tomorrow night."

But Sue didn't show up Saturday night or the next Saturday either. She was in Idaho. I found that out from the paper, that second Monday morning I had no job, hadn't even started looking, and still lying around in bed at eleven in the morning.

WOMAN ARRESTED FOR EMBEZZLEMENT

Susan Rae Raffin, missing for seven days and suspected of embezzling more than $127,000 from a local dentist, was arrested early Sunday morning in Pocatello, Idaho, by local police. She was held in lieu of $20,000 bond in the Pocatello County Jail pending return to Missoula County. If convicted, she faces ten to twenty years in prison.

My first thought was that Sue, Maddy and I had all quit him the same day. But the second thought sobered me up: somehow it seemed logical that Sue would get ten years and Gene Bofay—if he ever even had a second trial—would go scot-free. That new lawyer of Bofay's was questioning everything and delaying the trial over and over. Gene Bofay had been out on bail six months already and no trial in sight. As I made a note to myself to give Sue the name of Bofay's lawyer, I remembered the envelope she'd given me for her mother. Shit, it was still on top of the fridge.

I ran into the kitchen and grabbed the envelope. It was thick. And my stomach sank into my feet. First thing I thought when she handed me the thing, money. But then I thought, don't be silly. Standing in the kitchen now, it really felt like money. Lots of money.

I opened it. And then counted it. $7,847. Probably cashed a bunch of her doctored-up duplicate checks. Sue and her odd numbers. I guess she thought she'd only get caught if she stole whole numbers of money. But $127,000, that was a pretty whole number.

Now what? Would I be an accessory to embezzlement if I took the money over to her mother's house now? Or get picked up. Someone watching the house. Jack having all of our phones tapped. I set the money back on top of the fridge and tried to forget about it. I'd been filling the bathtub for a hot bath. I went back and checked the temperature. Thought about the money as I added a little hot to top it off. When I started brushing my teeth a second time, I went back out to the kitchen.

The money was still stacked on the table where I'd counted it out. A stack of fifties. A stack of twenties and a stack of fives. Then the two ones all by themselves. Sue would need a lawyer and I could give him the cash. Say it was from my mother—a loan. Mothers do that. Then I'd have to call my mom and tell her what I'd done in case the cops called her to check up on my story.

Or I could tell them Katherine loaned it to me.

But then I quit the same day. I could be a suspect.

Bury the money?

Burn it?

I had to do something with it—and before I went back to New York. Why not just take it to Sue's mom like she asked me to? In a box of groceries, non-perishables, I could say Sue asked me to pick up from her garage, and I forgot till today. Shit. I watched the widow out the east kitchen window, digging up her rhubarb patch, separating the roots and replanting the youngest plants. A package of money, in a zip lock bag would be easy to bury in that soft dirt. If she was done messing with the rhubarb. And if she didn't catch me planting it. She caught at least half the people who stole apples.

Shit.

Take the money to Sue's mom. Act innocent. What act? I *was* innocent.

So I took a walk. The old familiar walk down South Fourth Street west to the railroad tracks then north, maybe doing it for the last time, past J&B's backlot across the railroad trestle and over the river. Across Broadway over to the north side. No one following. On this path, no one could follow without my knowing. I left the tracks just over the overpass and turned right into the alley behind Howell Street, hoping I could recognize Sue's mom's house from behind.

It was dark, which was good. And once I got into the alley, I was out of the wind. Three blocks from the main drag, I started looking more carefully at the houses and watching behind me. No one, still. Mid-block, white house. Red trim. Big-ass fir tree. There was only one on the block, and I walked up to the backdoor. I saw Sue's mom from the back porch and knocked the shave-and-a-haircut knock Sue always used.

Mrs. Rightnour turned and stared at me.

"Evelyn," she said, looking startled. "Come in, come in. God it's cold out there tonight."

"Yes," I agreed. "It is." I hung back in the mudroom. In the safety of the coats hanging on pegs, and snow boots and a shovel.

"Come on into the kitchen. I was just making a cup of coffee. You look like you could use something hot, too."

"That would be nice," I said.

She took a cup of water out of the microwave and stirred in a teaspoon of instant coffee—the cup she'd been ready to sit down to. The money was in my coat pocket. I kept it there while I drank, still not sure this was the right thing to do. I wasn't going to return it to Jack. I just wasn't sure I wanted to hand-deliver stolen goods.

"Have you heard from Sue?" I asked.

"Last night," she said. "She asked me to call this lawyer and get bail arranged. I was half-expecting to see her at the door just now."

"I'm sorry."

"No, it's okay. I'm glad to have some company while I wait."

"Yes, I suppose that's hard. Waiting."

She nodded. I didn't know what else to say, so I sipped at my coffee. It was awful. Bitter and no milk. I could've asked for milk. But now I was wishing I hadn't accepted the coffee. Or knocked.

There was a picture of a little girl over the doorway to the dining room. A little girl in her First Communion dress. "Is that Sue?" I asked. I was pretty sure Sue had no sisters. Only a brother, killed in Vietnam when she was in her teens.

"Yes, that's her. 1959."

"My mother has the same picture of me on her breakfront," I said. Same picture, same year. I'd always thought of Sue as being much older and wiser. She was just as old as I was.

She nodded as I drank the rest of the coffee. "Another cup?" she asked.

"Oh, no thanks. I've got to be back home pretty soon." Which was a lie. I had nowhere to go, no place to be—I just didn't want to be here when Sue showed up and get any more involved than I already was. Mrs. Rightnour picked up my cup, and when she turned back to the sink I pulled the envelope out of my coat and set it on the kitchen table. More from fear of Sue, what she'd say if I ditched the money, than any moral decision.

"I've got a couple more stops before I get home, and it's pretty dark already."

She walked me to the backdoor. "Well, be careful," she said and pulled my collar up around my neck. "Helps keep the body heat in," she said and closed the door behind me.

I walked back toward the overpass and before I knew it had walked a half mile further north, the wrong way if I was going home. I kept going, knowing where I was really going all along, now, and ended up at the cemetery gates. Bucky.

The cemetery had bought more property from the old plywood plant and Bucky's row of graves wasn't the furthest north anymore. Two more twenty-foot-wide strips of neatly trimmed grass now stretched between him and the chain link fence. The fence was new, too, and shiny. Six feet high, posts perfectly spaced eight feet apart, protecting the last possession of the dead—their headstones—from vandalism.

Bucky now had one of his own. The sky was dark now, the wind colder, but the trees in the old part of the cemetery provided an effective windbreak. Besides, Mrs. Rightnour's cup of coffee was still burning at my insides. I sat down on the grass and touched Bucky's new marker. It was a stately and graceful piece of silver gray granite. Not at all like the boy who almost choked on a hot dog when he was eight. Or whacked off his toe with a lawn mower at fourteen.

But there was no question this was his home. Not just the cemetery—the whole thing. There was a clear picture in his mind—houses, trees—when he said he was going home. No confusion or hesitation. Just rodeos and fir trees. Copper mines and cattle ranches. I closed my eyes and tried to picture "home." It was all confused, with Katherine and Jaymie, Rose and my mother.

"So tell me where I fit in," I said to Bucky. "And I'll tell you where I'm going next."

Walter Henry Porter III was all he said. That was all he'd been saying for a year and a half, but I'd never been able to hear the silence quite so clearly before. It had to be the stone. I'd always kept up the dialogue before. Both sides of it. Now all I had was questions. Questions and no answers. So tell me, if it was Jack's bubble that burst, why did I feel so lost?

Walter Henry Porter III.

"Rest in peace," I said and headed back home.

I T W A S A L M O S T T E N o'clock and cold, with a needle rain coming in at a sixty degree angle as I crossed the trestle and stood above the J&B backlot. I'd sat out here many afternoons the last two weeks instead of looking for a job. Waiting to get the guts to drop in on Jaymie. Never had the nerve to tell her what I was thinking of doing. Instead of finding another job, or looking for Mr. Not-Quite-Right-But-Here. That night, everything was unconscious. I was down the embankment before I'd even checked to see if the Bronco was parked out front. It was. Well, hell, I thought. Get it over with. Hell, maybe Jaymie knew.

"I'm going back to New York," I said as I walked into her office.

She never locked the place. All alone counting money, and the door was unlocked. Kept Wally's .41 Mag in the top drawer.

She looked up. "What, are you kidding?"

"No. You got any boxes?"

"You're kidding, right?"

"You got boxes, I can start packing tomorrow. I figure I can take eight or ten boxes in the truck and maybe a suitcase or two. But I've collected a lot of junk in five years, even if I leave the furniture."

"Oh sure, hire a moving truck for the Salvation Army re-runs. You're kidding. Aren't you?"

"I figure that's why I haven't started looking for a job. I went down to the unemployment office and they told me I couldn't turn down a job as dental assistant. There's jobs everywhere assisting. They're never going to offer me anything else. And what else is keeping me here? I could be living in Calcutta."

She smiled. "You need a job, I can get you a job."

"Maybe it's time to go back to school."

"There's a school in Missoula. University of Montana's in Missoula. Fine school: forestry, pharmacy, finance. And that's just the Fs."

I sat down in the client's chair across the desk from Jaymie. "You were right about the trial. I'm not going. I've waited and waited and waited for the trial, but it's never going to happen. I'm tired of putting my life on hold. I'm going to be like you— cut this thing off at the ankles and start all over again."

"Evelyn. Please don't go. I don't want you to go."

"It's not home, Jaymie. This isn't home. I can't spend the rest of my life wandering around."

"Wandering? Where have you been wandering? You go to Butte? To Sacred Heart Church? You been to Philbrook? You have a history here, too."

"Two generations, twenty minutes apiece. Besides, Philbrook doesn't exist. Philbrook is a footnote in some dog-eared book of defunct towns. Towns that never made it. There's thousands of them. I called and asked."

She shrugged. "Hundreds, I'll give you. Thousands, you're exaggerating. I've told you a thousand times, don't exaggerate." She waited for me to smile, but I couldn't.

"You got boxes out back? Can I pick through them?"

She nodded. "I can't help. I'll be here till midnight closing the books as it is. Besides. I won't help you leave. I think you're wrong. I don't think you can leave here and never look back. Not now. I think it's in your blood now."

"I'm not a fifth generation ranch daughter, Jaymie. I'm not even the daughter of a half-breed Blackfoot Indian. Irish. It skipped a generation, but I have my grandfather's wanderlust. It's time to buck the trend and set down roots."

"So. You going back to The Old Sod."

"Just New York."

"There should be a bunch of boxes out back. The guys haven't burned them in a couple of days."

But before I got up from the chair, she dialed a number on the phone and handed me the receiver. "You tell Rosey," she said. "You tell Rosey what you're up to and then you can have the boxes."

"No."

"Take the phone. You tell her. I'm not telling her," she said and then looked at the receiver. Rose's voice, I could hear it ten feet away. Jaymie put the phone to her ear. "Hi Mom. Evelyn's leaving. No, really. She's packing up tonight and going back to New York City."

She watched me as she talked.

"Mumsy wants to talk to you," she said.

I shook my head, but she just kept the phone out at arm's length. I took it. Rose was already talking.

It was too soon, she said. I hadn't given Montana a chance. It was too late. It was in my blood. Jaymie needed me. We needed each other. New York City was too dangerous. Too crowded. Colorado was bad enough, but New York City? There were schools, jobs, lots of jobs better than Jack P. Wally could make a couple of phone calls.

"He should've done it a long time ago. About the first time Jack had one of those office meetings. It's in your blood, Evelyn. You won't know until you cross the border and you'll turn around and look back at the mountains and wonder what the hell you were thinking about. You'll get as far as Glendive. Maybe even, if you're stubborn enough, stubborn like Jaymie and Walls, you'll get to Nebraska before you wake up. Before you admit you've made a mistake. Don't be silly. And call me tomorrow when you're feeling more yourself."

I hung up, looked at Jaymie who was pretending to count money. But she was counting the same pile for the third time.

"Probably the same lecture she gave Bucky before he went to graduate school," she said.

"So why did *they* leave? Why is it okay for *them* to leave?"

"It wasn't their dream anymore, Evelyn. I don't know. If you want the boxes still, they're out back. But I've never known Rose to be wrong."

"Right," I said.

"Not about something important. Not about people she loves."

"I have people who love me in New York, too."

"It's not the *place* you love. People you can put on an airplane. Or talk to on the phone. When did you ever see someone move a mountain? I mean really move a mountain. I've seen a gold mine take a mountain apart, but Evelyn, it's just gone then. They can't reassemble it in Franklin Square. You dreamt all your life of being here—and now you're going to let the assholes have it to themselves?"

"I'm taking four boxes tonight. That's all I can carry," I said. " I'll come back with the truck for the rest."

I walked back home along the railroad tracks. Nothing to keep me here. No job. No money. Just pack what I wanted to take and give the rest to the dumpster. Which took all night. Seven trips to the dumpster, mostly the stuff I'd brought with me. All the rest fit into the four boxes: books, trinkets, my photos, and souvenir t-shirts and hats. I left my jeans and boots and Rose's straw hat out for traveling clothes.

Then I slept three hours, woke up at five and drove out of Missoula before the sun could come up.

EIGHTEEN

I GOT AS FAR as Scottsbluff, Nebraska, the first day. Eight hundred and thirty miles, with gas stops and fast food. I figured Mom's driveway was 2,346 miles away. The plan was: if I drove just over eight hundred miles a day, I could make it in three days.

Fine.

So I got up at six the second morning and drove on to Chimney Rock, Nebraska. Twenty-six miles further east along the North Platte River. And then I just sat there in the parking lot of the Chimney Rock National Historic Site. In the truck at first, watching the sun come up in the east and the great orange spire glow in the sun. Then walking around. Walking and looking at the horizon 360 degrees around it, all flat like the parking lot at K-Mart. Not a tree in sight or anything taller than my old red beater's hood, which I was sitting on by then with my boot heels stuck in the grill, and wondering what the hell I was going to do next. Maybe Rose was right: I was at least as stubborn as Wally.

It had seemed easy leaving Missoula. In five years, I'd gotten a job, and lost it. Gotten a family and lost it. Like a piece of sagebrush tumbling along without even a length of barbwire to catch onto.

And then Jack going crazy on me. Or maybe me going crazy. And being glad, watching him lose it all—Maddy, Sue and me in one day. Watching his little bubble burst all over him.

So if it was so goddamn easy, why was I sitting in a parking lot?

Sue said I was running away. She'd called that last night in Missoula in between trips to the dumpster. Out on bond, hired a lawyer. Everything under control, she told me.

"So what's happening with you?" she asked.

"Going back to New York," I said.

"WHAT?"

"You heard me."

"You're giving up?"

"Oh, come on. I think I've given it the old college try. I'm not running away from anything. Except something I should run away from. I don't fit in here. It took me five years to figure that out. But I don't belong. Just give me the sane old city."

"Oh, you mean where people triple-lock and bar their doors. And walk behind their poodles with a little shovel and a ice cream bag?

"Don't start."

She was down at the Office Bar, and tried to get me to come down there so she could talk me out of leaving.

"I'm getting an early start in the morning. I've got to get some sleep."

"The Tender. I'll give you that much. I'll meet you at the Tender in half an hour."

One last time. One last drink. It seemed okay till I got out there, and then I couldn't go in. I parked next to Sue's big, shiny truck for half an hour. Sitting there watching the lights on the Legal Tender Saloon sign blink around the lettering, and the neon girl and boy dancing on the silver dollar, and people walking in and out of the door, fighting, kissing, yelling—mad and happy at each other, and one boy falling down the three-step porch. I almost got out to help him up. Then I started up the truck and went home to finish packing.

I looked up at the chimney rock. What would anyone use this dirt skyscraper to find? There wasn't anything green as far as the eye could see. Why would people try to farm this sorry piece of land? I'd learned a few things about Philbrook since Wally handed me that note. It didn't die for the usual reasons. That was a lot more fertile land than this, and eight miles down the road, there was another town still surviving from those days. The one with the railroad depot. A rancher decided he wanted the station near his house instead of where town already was. He had the money and the power to make it happen, so the merchants and the businesses moved to his property. He got the station and Philbrook died.

So maybe my grandfather was a smart man, moving back east. Maybe he was no dreamer like his granddaughter. I would have believed this chimney rock was the gateway to Eden. I had, in fact, believed Montana was some kind of Eden.

The sun was up—the wind picking up and tourists starting to take over the parking lot. Winnebagos and trailers. Vans full of kids and camping stuff. They all stopped and emptied their garbage, read the historical marker for the great chimney rock, and then decided it was too far and too windy to walk out to the actual thing. Maryland. Vermont. New York. Pennsylvania. License plates from all the places they were escaping from. I looked into the eastern sky, a regular daytime blue by now, and felt suddenly that I wasn't as smart as I thought. Going east. It was going to get more and more crowded; there'd be more cars, more asphalt and more people the further I ran. Standing there in my jeans and boots, and Rose's straw gardening hat. Just being stubborn?

Shit. So what was I going to be in New York? A Midnight Cowgirl working at a travel agency? I'd changed. Looking at the tourists, and them looking at me, I realized I had changed. Something maybe that didn't happen to my grandfather. He went broke too soon. Or he was already sick and barely had time to sightsee.

I got back in the truck and drove east some more, still thinking, barely making the speed limit, and this time got as far as the first town, Dalton, Nebraska, before I pulled off the interstate looking for a phone.

It was noon and the sun beat down on all four glass sides of the public phone booth. I dialed J&B, hoping Jaymie hadn't gone anywhere for lunch. She was at her desk, eating a peanut butter and jelly sandwich.

"Tell Rose I got to Chimney Rock National Historic Site before I slowed down."

"What?"

"She said I'd make it to Nebraska only if I was as stubborn as you and Walls."

"Chimney Rock?"

"I sat at that monument all morning. And it suddenly dawned on me, I was fighting my way upstream. I was going the wrong way."

"So you're in Chimney Rock and you're coming home."

"I'm in Dalton. There's no phone at Chimney Rock. It's what you call a 'primitive' site. I'm in front of the farm implement store in Dalton, and as soon as I'm done talking to you, I'm calling my mom. I don't know how I'll explain it. But I don't think she really expected me to come back again in the first place. Then I'm taking the long way home. There's a Pony Express Station Museum somewhere around here, then I'm stopping at the Mitchell Corn Palace and Wall Drug. Then Mount Rushmore. I didn't do that the first time out. Didn't think I had the time."

"And Philbrook. And don't take the damned interstate unless you have to."

"No, I won't."

I hung up and called my mother, to let her know I wasn't coming.

The wind was still blowing and the sun was still shining. Tomorrow I'd be back in the mountains and trees. Logging trucks, J&B's backlot piled twenty-acres deep in new growth logs. The trestle on a hot summer evening. There was time to catch a fish—on horseback—behind Jaymie's house: my own Miles City postcard.

The old Ford started up on the first try.

EILEEN CLARKE lives in southwestern Montana with her husband, the writer John Barsness, and two amazing Labrador retrievers.

She also writes non-fiction, primarily about natural history and the outdoors, and is the author of a critically acclaimed series of game and fish cookbooks. Her natural history and outdoor writing has appeared in numerous national publications, including *Gray's Sporting Journal* and *Montana Outdoors.*

She is currently at work on a book of classic fish recipes.

OTHER BOOKS BY EILEEN CLARKE

The Freshwater Fish Cookbook

The Venison Cookbook

The Wild Barbecue Cookbook

The Art of Wild Game Cooking
(with Sil Strung)

THIS BOOK was typeset in Stempel Garamond by
Kitty Herrin of Arrow Graphics, Missoula, Montana.

PRINTED BY Thomson-Shore, Inc., Dexter, Michigan.